COURAGE

COURAGE

BARBARA BINNS

HARPER

An Imprint of HarperCollinsPublishers

Library of Congress Control Number: 2018933336
ISBN 978-0-06-256165-7 (trade bdg.)

Typography by Torborg Davern
18 19 20 21 22   CG/LSCH   10 9 8 7 6 5 4 3 2 1
❖
First Edition

This book is dedicated to Katherine Lydia, my beloved daughter, and the real diver in our family. Also to the Chicago Park District, which believes that every child should learn to swim.

COURAGE

CHAPTER
ONE

CHLORINE FILLS THE AIR, THE stinging odor so
strong it bites all the way down my throat. I am in the
pool area of the Sports and Wellness Center at Windy
City Community College, the place people who live on
Chicago's South Side call W3C. Many of the high school
graduates from this part of the city attend this college
after graduation. The school sign declares they are dedicated to providing higher education for people from
diverse backgrounds through teaching, research, service, and community development. Once a month, on
Saturday afternoons, the college holds Family Day for
Windy City students, employees, staff, faculty, and their
families. No one else is allowed inside at this time.

I'm here with my neighbor and best bud, Dontae Morrow. He adjusts his swim trunks and puffs out a chest with skin a few shades darker than mine. Since his parents want him to stay in the warm water pool, I mostly hang there too. The older people who laze around there don't mind when I swim a few laps for practice. Right now, Dontae and I are heading for the concession stand.

"You were eating up that water, T'Shawn," Dontae's mother says, handing me a lemon snow cone, my favorite. Mrs. Morrow has the same hook to her nose as Dontae does and big dimples in her cheeks that widen when she smiles. She works in W3C's Food Service Department, one of her two jobs, which means I get to come as part of her "family." Since she's running the concession stand right now, it also means I get a free snow cone, and Dontae gets handed a bag of apple slices. "Who taught you to swim like that?"

"My brother," I say, before I remember that he who should not be named shouldn't even be mentioned. My father's twin brother drowned when they were kids. Dad taught my older brother to swim so he wouldn't die the same way. My brother taught me for the same reason. Someday I'll teach my little sister, Rochelle.

Dontae and I move to a table where we can eat and

watch the water action in the main pool filled with cold water. He grimaces as he eats the apple slices. "You never told me you had a brother." Dontae shouts directly in my ear. It's the only way to be heard over the shrieks echoing around the crowded pool. "I wish I had a brother or sister. I hate being an only."

I shrug. "I haven't talked about him since I lost him." I pick my words carefully. I know he's going to think my brother is dead. That works just fine for me.

I know I'm not the only kid with a family member in prison. Doesn't mean I go around boasting about it. Heck, there are days when I forget I ever had a brother.

Not many days, but I'm working on it.

"Did you ever think about having your birthday party here?" Dontae says between bites. He changed the subject to something happy, just as I expected.

"No way. My mom could never afford renting a place like this." Three pools: a ten-lane, fifty-yard pool; a separate diving well; plus the smaller warm-water pool. No way. "I am thinking a superheroes theme, with me going as Black Panther."

He almost chokes while laughing. "From super geek to superhero in one year?"

"The power of thirteen. Black Panther is pretty geeky too, the smartest superhero ever," I remind my friend.

This year Mom promised I could pick the party theme. For my twelfth birthday, she did the science lab thing. I lost a lot of friends over that one, and lots of people still call me Nerd. Science is awesome but not for a birthday. I want to play the part of a king, genius, and superhero all in one. And the costume will cover my too-thin shoulders. But it won't be here. I can't even count the number of times I've sat through Mom's we're-not-made-out-of-money speech, usually when she's paying off another bill from the mountain of medical debt. She says she hopes to have something special for me this year. Our pastor, Dontae's father, says prayer can work wonders. I don't want her getting the idea I would think a birthday here was something special.

"I can't imagine having a birthday on Friday the thirteenth," Dontae says. "You should think about skipping this year and spending the day safe in bed under the covers."

"You're just jealous because you have to wait three whole months before you get to be thirteen. I only have a few weeks."

"On Friday the thirteenth, the unluckiest day in the whole world." His hoarse laugh makes people nearby turn and stare.

"I don't believe in unlucky. I will officially be a real

teenager. There's no way that can be anything but good."

Dontae sticks the last apple slice in his mouth. He almost has muscles, and he's taller than me too. Sometimes people mistake him for an eighth grader. How does he manage that when he's the one in the modified gym program? Because he has sickle cell, his parents want him to keep relaxed and hydrated all the time and to keep out of the cold-water pool. Sometimes I think he only comes for the free snacks.

I come for the snacks too. And to swim, the only sport I don't hate.

And for the girls in swimsuits.

Well, for one girl, at least.

Carmela Rhodes.

She's the brown-skinned mermaid in a shining blue-and-black swimsuit with a white swim cap. She's already thirteen and is the prettiest girl in my seventh-grade class. (If there is any question on that, you can ask her or one of her satellite besties—Marianne Smith, Fantasia Grey, or Linda Murhasselt.) Linda is at the pool with her today, only she sits in the bleachers. Carmela stands beside one of the diving boards. I have one goal that I'm aiming for—a birthday kiss from Carmela Rhodes. My first real kiss ever.

A line of kids snakes up to the diving board. Carmela

is talking to some older guy standing near the front of the line. I bet he's in high school.

"Earth to T." Dontae waves his hand in front of my eyes. "Stop the puppy panting."

"I'm not a dog."

"Woof, woof!"

I playfully push him aside. "Get lost."

"You need to get real," he says. "Carmela's not the only girl in school."

She's the only one that counts. "I wish she'd look at me sometimes," I mumble.

"It's like that with girls." Dontae sounds like he's some kind of expert. He claims he had a ton of girlfriends back when he lived in Florida. His family moved to Chicago a year ago. I might believe him if he didn't have a face full of pimples. "When girls really, really like you, they get snotty and try to act like they don't care."

"But what if she really doesn't?"

"Then get over her."

"You just say that because you don't care about girls."

Dontae shrugs. "Friends and family are important. Girls are just girls." He stares at my snow cone, raised eyes silently asking me for a lick. He's not supposed to, but his life is unfair. Besides, a little can't hurt him. I hand him what's left and move a little to shield him in case his mother looks this way. He grins and finishes it off in two bites. He licks his fingers, gets up, and runs toward the warm-water pool.

"No running, Dontae!" his mother shouts from behind the concessions counter.

He slows to a fast walk. He has to stay where his mother can keep an eye on him. He jokes that he's only allowed in the pool because his mom is around to make sure he doesn't get to do anything fun.

I think about following Dontae but instead head for the diving well. Carmela is still there, standing next to her guy friend. It's weird. Like most of the guys, I barely noticed girls last year, and when I did I just made jokes. This year there's something different. I move in behind Carmela. I want to say something cool, but nothing pops in my head, so I just stay close, moving forward when they do.

The guy reaches the ladder. He climbs up and stands on the board. Carmela steps to the side, watching the way I do. He moves exactly like the divers on sports shows. Running down the board, bouncing at the end, he flies high in the air, twists, and somehow goes into the water hands first with barely a splash. Then the show-off swims to the side and pulls himself out of the pool without even touching the ladder.

Carmela laughs and claps like he won a trophy. She turns to me in a move so sudden I step back and bump into someone. I start to turn and apologize, but Carmela speaks first.

"Do you dive, T?"

I don't say anything for a minute, surprised Carmela is actually talking to me. "Uh, yeah, it's my favorite thing in the world," I say, trying my best to sound cool.

"Are you a good diver?"

"I'm better than good." What else can I say, except that I've never even been on a diving board? I've jumped in, dived, and cannonballed off the side of the pool. How different could it be on a board only a few feet higher?

"Move it!" Someone shoves me in the back.

I stumble and turn. An Asian kid with neon-green trunks is glaring up at me. Long, black hair falls onto his forehead all the way down to his eyebrows. He's short, with a thin face, but muscled and with a deep voice. I can't tell if he is older or younger than I am.

"I'm sorry," I begin.

Carmela steps closer to the kid, her lips tight. "Calm down, Sammy. Wait your turn."

"He needs to hurry up and do his dive. I hate waiting," Sammy insists.

My dive? I look around and see several people lined up behind this boy, Sammy. He thinks I'm at the head of the line and about to dive.

"Go on, T. You're next," Carmela says, looking at me with expectation. "Show me what you can do."

"But I . . . I'm not . . ." I clutch the ends of my towel. "Sorry, I . . ."

"Come on! I can't wait forever." Sammy's lips twist into a tight scowl. "Dive already."

People all around stare at me. I know what they are thinking, that I'm a gutless fake. It's one thing to play around in water. To submerge my head and stroke and kick and make it to the other side . . . This is different. I should step aside and let him go up the ladder. But I can't back down, not in front of all these people. And definitely not in front of Carmela. I'm trapped, like a prisoner on the pirate's plank. I can be brave and walk off the end of the board myself or act like a coward who needs to be poked in the butt with a sword and forced off the end. A quick death or an embarrassing one.

I step forward and grab the bars on each side of the metal steps. They are smooth and so cold my hands slip. One step, two, three, then I'm up on the board. It bounces so much I almost fall right away. The board's rough surface scratches the bottoms of my feet. I take a deep breath and look over the side. Major mistake.

The water looks like a solid blue wall waiting for my fall. My stomach punches up and bounces around in my throat. I look across the pool to the warm water where Dontae is splashing around. Inside my head, I yell for him to do something. Call me, say you need me. He never even looks this way.

"You're not going in with your towel, are you?" Sammy snickers.

Maybe. How big do parachutes have to be?

"Be quiet, Sammy. T knows what he's doing," Carmela says. She reaches up and takes the towel from me and then smiles as if my skinny arms don't matter.

"Are you going to do something like a dumb cannonball, silly baby?" Sammy hisses from behind me.

That kills my great idea.

I close my eyes and try to remember every move I saw the other diver make. He ran down the board, jumped twice at the end, flipped in midair, and stretched his hands toward the water.

I can do that.

Or I can bust open my skull.

Maybe Carmela will visit me in the hospital.

"Go already!" Sammy yells.

I take a deep breath and start running as hard as I can. I manage one bounce at the edge of the board, and then I'm high in the air, over the water, legs pumping like there are stairs to climb, but there's only air. Things happen so fast I can barely breathe. My arms circle, flailing for something to grab. The world swirls around me, fast, faster, superspeed. It's like being on a roller coaster at Six Flags Great America just as the car tops the crest of the first hill. Only there's just me and the air.

Goodbye, Mom. I love you.

Love you too, Sis.

And . . .

Nope, not my brother.

I have time to see Carmela with her mouth open. Time to see water, walls, water, people, more water . . .

And then the pool swallows me.

My throat fills with water. I choke and kick and flail and struggle to the surface.

Alive.

I swim to the side of the pool and hang on the ladder, shaking and coughing. My chest hurts. I had no control during that flight. It was unbelievable and scary and . . .

"That was awesome," Carmela says. "You can

somersault and twist and . . ."

I climb out, race past her, and get in line. I don't have time to talk. That was like flying. I can't believe I never did that before.

I've got to do it again!

CHAPTER TWO

SAMMY TURNS OUT TO BE a hotshot diver. For the next half hour, he does all kinds of stunts on the board, including a backflip. I watch in awe.

"That was a one and a half," he says when he comes out of the water. "My coach says it's time for me to work on more rotations."

I did a backflip in gym once; the teacher called me super flexible. It's almost closing time when I decide my last dive will be my own backflip off the end of the board. Major mistake.

At least my life doesn't flash before my eyes. But the water was a hammer, turning my back into splintered glass when I hit. The buzzer ending Family Time sounds as I gingerly climb out of the water. Lifeguards wave everyone to the locker rooms.

"From now on I'll call you Spider-Man," Dontae says. He takes a picture of my bruise and threatens to post it online. I'm seriously glad Mom doesn't use Instagram. One of the pictures features the giant reddish-purple mark spread over the brown skin of my back. The bruise hurts worse than a hundred spider bites, but I don't flinch as I pull on my black, long-sleeved hoodie.

"Hey. You're not much of a diver." Sammy appears and leans against a nearby locker while I pull on my jeans. "You can't think of the pool as an enemy. I try to make the water my friend when I dive."

"Could you teach me?" I ask.

"I'm not a coach," he admits. "But Coach Mung could teach you. If he decides he likes you."

"Where is he?" I ask, looking around at the people in the locker room.

Sammy laughs like I made the biggest joke ever. "Coach doesn't do the family-swim thing. Besides, he doesn't work here. The Racing Rays rent space in the pool and gym from the college."

"What are those?" Dontae asks.

"The Rays are the very best swimming and diving

club in the whole entire city," he answers, spreading his arms wide as he speaks. Definitely younger than me, I decide. "You're looking at the number one diver on the whole team. But we could always use more divers. How old are you?"

"Thirteen. Almost," I admit.

"We'd be in the same age group. I'm twelve. Almost."

For real? His voice is a little deep and doesn't crack like mine sometimes does, always at a bad time. And he has actual muscles in his chest and arms although he's a year younger than I am.

"Life isn't always fair, son." I hear Dad's voice inside my head. I know that, but my dad had enough bad luck to cover me for the rest of my life.

Dontae and I finish dressing, and he, Sammy, and I leave the locker room together. The sun shines bright through the windows lining the aquatic center hall. Sammy leads us over to a wall filled with papers, announcements about activities in the facility. Most are only for the college students. But there is a shelf lined with flyers about the Racing Rays Swim Club.

Sammy grabs a bunch from the display and pushes them at me. "Take these to your parents and have them sign you up. We practice here in the afternoons three times a week and on Saturday mornings."

"Did you practice today?" I ask.

He nods. "Then I just stayed here late since my mother had to work today. She teaches all about finance—you know, money management and stuff. She's a big deal with math."

Before I can ask a question, Dontae breaks in. "Wait a minute." His brows scrunch together; his expression turns doubtful. "That's like all the times when me and T get together. What about us?"

"You should join too," I tell him.

"You know I can't," he mumbles, his voice sounding bitter.

Sometimes I forget he isn't allowed to do everything I can.

"Your parents will like it when you bring home medals," Sammy tells him.

"Yeah, but his parents hate it when he ends up in the hospital with a sickle cell crisis."

He hates being the "sick" boy. There's nothing on the outside that reveals his invisible disease until he has an attack. But with SCD, sickle cell disease, his blood tries to kill him. At least, that's how he describes it. He told me that when he has an attack, his normally round blood cells form into sickle shapes that clump in his arteries. Every joint aches, and it's like being stabbed with a butcher knife, over and over. He's on special medicines to stop the sickling process, keep attacks from happening, and help him make new blood cells.

"Hey, T." Carmela steps up and points at the brochure in my hand. "Are you joining the Rays? That's awesome."

"Are you in the club?" I ask.

"I'm one of the top swimmers in the twelve to four-teen age group. Wait until I tell Coach Mung I discovered you."

"You didn't discover anyone," Sammy says.

She ignores him and pushes another brochure into my hands. "You need this too. You have to pay the USA Diving Association fee to compete in meets. Get your mom to sign the papers and pay the fee right away so you can start practicing with us on Monday."

Fee?

I look through the stack of papers and automatically begin counting. Enrollment fee; team swim trunks, jacket, and swim bag; monthly fee.

Why does everything have to cost money? Mom and her friends compare their skills at pinching pennies and clipping coupons and making do while telling me there's no reason to worry. No reason? I see the truth in her face. I learned addition from the medical bills Mom still has to make payments on four years after Dad's losing cancer fight plus the expenses for Rochelle's birth. Subtraction came when I counted how little money we had left after those bills and after my brother did something stupid and got locked up. Division came from watching her figure out how to support me and my baby sister on what was left. Multiplication from . . .

I don't want to add more bills to Mom's pile. I pull out the swim-team papers and take another look at the fees and the big total my mind calculated. Most sports are expensive. That's why a lot of guys around here play basketball. All you need is a hoop, a ball, and a good pair of kicks, and you can play all day. Almost everything else means equipment and money, usually lots of money.

I can't get a real job, but I earn a little money in the winter shoveling snow out of parking spots and clearing out the alley in front of garage doors around my block. Not much, but it helps me help Mom and my little sister. That makes me feel like the man of the family. But it's almost March, and that means spring, so that money source is drying up. There may still be snow; here in Chicago we sometimes get snow in April. But it won't be enough to mean real money.

I look back at the board and see a few Help Wanted signs posted. Everything but the part-time custodian position wants at least high school graduates. Even if I could lie and get a job, it means I could end up like the guy over in a corner right now, mopping up a wet mess on the floor. I sort of like the school custodians. A lot of us are friends with the custodians, talk to them about things we usually don't tell other adults. They smile and listen and don't judge like some teachers and even counselors. They all spend a lot of time struggling to remove graffiti ghosts from the walls and fronts of lockers or dealing with a stopped-up toilet or the smelly locker rooms

"You have chores, T," Dontae says quietly, reading my thoughts. "Even if you found someone to hire you, how would you get your schoolwork done and practice? How long would your mom let you do this if your grades fall?"

He's right. I'm almost always number one in my class, and Mom expects that. She'd never let that change. If working ends up meaning I can't find time to practice, why bother joining? I fold the papers and sigh.

"Club membership doesn't cost that much," Sammy says. "Mom says it's a bargain considering the quality of the coaches, and she knows. She used to be a champion diver."

Sammy's clothes and shoes look pretty expensive. So does the gym bag slung over his shoulder. Carmela's not rich either, but her family isn't paying off old medical bills or new day-care payments. Or sending care packages to a son in prison.

"Samuel Baker, hurry up," a voice calls from down the hall. A woman about my mother's age stands there waving one arm. Tall and white, with long brown hair that hangs around her shoulders. Standing in tall heels and a pink fur coat, she looks a little like the Snow Queen from fairy tales.

"Oops, there's my mother," Sammy says.

"She's pretty," I say. "And really tall."

"I know. I don't think I'll ever be that tall," he says with a tiny frown. "My dad always asks why she wears those heels. They make her taller than him. Maybe that's why."

"Are you rich or something?" Dontae asks.

"No way. My parents give me anything I ask for because they think they have to make something up to me because they adopted me." He grins.

Dontae and I look at each other.

"Sammy, now. I don't have all day." The woman frowns. She's just as impatient as Sammy was when I first climbed on the board.

His lips tighten for a second. "Gotta go, but, hey, I hope you'll join." He throws one last look at me before running to his mother. His gym bag bounces against his back as he runs, and they both leave, her heels clacking on the floor. His legs move fast to keep up with her.

A few minutes later, Dontae's mom pulls up in a car that's older than I am. It's pink and square shaped but clean, with no rust spots. I'm happy to climb into the back seat and let her drive us home. That gives me time to plan how to get Mom to agree to let me join the Rays.

I know how to get around the city on CTA buses or by renting a Divvy bike. Divvy provides a fleet of bicycles for sharing around Chicago. The big blue bikes are situated at docking stations all over the city and can be rented for thirty-minute trips. Mom has an annual membership so she can bike from our apartment to the CTA train station in the morning and then back home in the evening. You're supposed to be sixteen to ride a Divvy, but I sometimes use her personal key to grab a bike for a short ride. But the afternoon is chilly, I'm damp, and I don't want to ride the bus or a bike if I don't have to.

Besides, it's good to have more time with Dontae.

Dontae and I joke together as we begin the ride home, traveling east toward the lake. The University of Chicago is to the north of my home, and Windy City Community College is to the west. Maybe, with a scholarship, I might be able to attend one of them someday. Another option is being a star at sports or a perfect student or both. Both bring a real chance. Dad always said he hoped his sons would go to college. I don't plan to fail him the way Lamont did.

I look out the window as we drive, trying not to move so the bruise on my back doesn't start throbbing again. My city is big, endless. The weather is still chilly, but in a few months, the outdoor festival season will begin. Every year we attend the gospel and blues fests in the downtown parks, because music moves me. My mom sets up a blanket, and we sit on the grass and let the wind blow waves of music and cool air over us. Here on the South Side we have the lakeshore, baseball (Dad taught me to love the Sox; I don't care about the Cubs), and every kind of food. Chicago dogs, Maxwell Street Polish laced with greasy mustard and fried onions, super sweet churros, and spicy Jamaican-style beef patties or Jamaican curry chicken. Those are all my favorites, and at the end of summer, I can find them all at the annual African Festival of the Arts.

Dontae's mom crosses over the Dan Ryan Expressway, with its daily load of cars lined up bumper to bumper in both the north and south lanes. From the road above, the multicolored car tops look like scales waving on the back of a giant snake. The train tracks of the Red Line serve as the Ryan's backbone.

I glance at Dontae. Sweat keeps popping up on his face.

"You should drink some water," I whisper.

"You're not my mother," he snarls.

"Drink your water, Dontae," Mrs. Morrow says from the front seat. His family is always watching his health closely. Luckily for him, his father is our minister, and he spreads prayers the way gardeners spread seeds in the community garden near our school. Dontae jokes that God is on his side.

We pass houses and our church, along with a few abandoned buildings and vacant lots. My neighborhood isn't the kind of place where rich people live. We are all ordinary, with rent to pay and day care and bills. There are always bills.

I pull my bag onto my lap and hear the brochures rustle inside. Maybe I can talk Mom into letting me be a member for my birthday present. She said she wanted to get me something special. Nothing would be more special than this. I'll tell her I don't need a party or anything else, just this.

"Why do you want to dive?" Dontae asks for the fourth time since we left the pool.

"I told you, I don't know," I say, thinking back to that

feeling of freedom as I was sailing through the air. I never know why awesome ideas simply pop into my brain. In spite of the pain in my back, I had *fun* diving. And maybe I want to learn because Lamont taught me to swim years ago when things were good. I loved him.

Once.

"Mom wants me to have friends." I'm talking mostly to myself, but Dontae overhears.

"Hey, you've got me." He points at his chest and looks upset. No, make that indignant, that was one of our vocabulary words last week, a combination of unhappy and angry. "Why bother with those guys? Mom says people from the swim club are stuck up. They never talk to her or any of the other staff members."

"Carmela is a member."

He snorts. "Like I said, stuck up."

"Sammy talked to us."

"Talked to *you*. He lost interest in me once I refused to care about the Rays."

"You know you're my number one," I remind him, and punch his shoulder. That's enough to make him relax. We have been best friends since the day he walked into my class last year and my sixth-grade teacher asked me to be his first-day buddy. I think she forgot I had only been there a few months myself. We got together and never separated. Even his parents and my mom became friends.

The car stops suddenly, throwing me against the seat belt. It digs painfully into my stomach before pushing me back against the seat cushion.

"Mom!" Dontae shouts. Mrs. Morrow mutters a curse. As the screech from the tires dies down, I turn to look at the other side of the street. There is a string of stores, including the barbershop where I get my hair cut and listen to men reminisce about what life was like when they were my age. Carmela's mother works in the beauty shop next door as a stylist. There's also a Laundromat and a drugstore—all small businesses where people work hard.

As our car crawls by, lights flash from two nearby police cars. A man stands in front of the drugstore, hands raised, brown skin gleaming above a dirty white shirt. I recognize him; so does Dontae. It's Edward Owens, one of our neighbors.

He must be out on one of his jogs. At least, he was. A bandanna covers his hair. He's wearing gym shoes and sweat pants. He's short and thin, and he loves to run, weaving through walkers on the sidewalk with a laugh and a wave. He's friends with Sergeant Rhodes, Carmela's father.

"Drop your weapon!" the cops yell at him.

I look at Dontae and whisper, "That's whack. Mr. Owens doesn't even own a weapon."

Dontae shrugs. Mr. Owens and Mom are members of the Take Back the Streets group. TBTS is our neighborhood organization that works to help clean up our area, stop violence, and help residents with any problems they are having. We look out for one another around here.

"Dontae." Mrs. Morrow's voice is hushed, shaky. "Get out your phone and record this." My phone lies buried deep in the bottom of my bag. Dontae has his in his pocket. I can tell his mother wants to blow her horn; her hand hovers over the wheel. The sound might make the officers realize they are being watched and stop. Or startle one and make him fire. Traffic has stopped in both directions. A few drivers make a U-turn and head off. Others sit on the side, staring, seeming to be fascinated but unsure what to do.

One cop hits Mr. Owens with a club. My stomach churns like a washing machine at the sight. The other officer tackles him, throwing him to the ground. "Stop resisting!" they shout, like a well-rehearsed chorus as they twist the old man's left arm above his shoulder, trying to turn it in a way shoulders don't go. A pain-filled scream rips through the air.

I can't just sit and watch my neighbor being tortured

in front of me. I can't think of anything to do.

Except jump from the car and run through traffic to get closer.

I barely remember opening the car door and spilling from my seat, racing toward the cops hurting my friend. Behind me, I hear Mrs. Morrow scream my name. I know what I've been told to do in situations like this. I had the talk from Dad before he died, and Mom repeats that lesson over and over. I know to keep my head down and stay silent. Hands in the air to show they are empty and no sudden moves. But sometimes, when I'm scared, my brain stops thinking, and my body acts on its own.

Swirling winds strike my face. I advance toward the figures, but even with his cheek pressed into the pavement, Mr. Owens stares at me and shakes his head to tell me to stay back. A cop responds by kneeling on his back until he stops moving. I freeze, not knowing what to do.

"Don't hurt him!" I yell. One cop leaps to his feet, weapon in hand. For the second time in my life, I see a gun pointed at me.

The first time, it was my older brother who held the weapon.

I stand still, frozen except for tremors that rack my body. Hands, legs . . . I can't stop shaking. I stare at the gun he extends with both hands, pointed at my chest, and wait for it to fire.

"Get over here, Jenkins." The voice belongs to the cop kneeling on Mr. Owens.

"Get back," Jenkins bellows to me. He is wild-eyed, flushed, and furious.

"He's my friend," I cry.

"Doesn't matter if he's your Siamese twin, go or end up on the ground beside him."

Another police car pulls up, and two more officers leap out, guns drawn and pointed at the man on the ground. Jenkins continues staring at me for several seconds. Then he slowly backs up to join the group. Mr. Owens continues moaning, but the sound is softer now, and his breath hitches as they join together to drag him to his feet.

"T'Shawn." Mrs. Morrow hisses as she comes up behind me, grabs my shoulders, and pulls me away. "Get back to the car before he changes his mind." She pulls me across the street. "I feared I'd have to tell your mother I got you killed."

I get back in the car and close the door. Dontae continues filming, doing more good than I did. Mrs. Morrow shakes her head. "Four cops waste time arresting a nice man who would never hurt anyone. Protect and serve who? Not us."

I cringe as Mr. Owens is thrown into a police vehicle. Mrs. Morrow puts her car in gear and drives away. I keep staring at the scene out the back window until we turn a corner.

"What they did was wrong," Dontae says, breathing heavily. "We should file a complaint."

"I forgot, you're still new to Chicago and the Chicago police," I say. "I don't know what Florida is like, but if you file a complaint here, the cops will have your name and address. And it will keep happening anyway, so there's no point."

"I'm still posting the video online," he insists.

I nod. If I had managed to film what happened, I would be doing the same.

We drive in silence for ten more minutes until Mrs. Morrow pulls up one block from our courtyard apartment buildings, where she finds a parking spot. A lot of people here don't have their own cars, but so many people live around here that both sides of the narrow street are lined with parked cars.

"Do not tell your mother what happened," Mrs. Morrow reminds me as we climb from the car. "She doesn't need to know how close you came to— She doesn't need to know."

"I won't add anything for her to worry about."

Especially since my heart is still jumping around painfully inside my chest.

"Don't forget your stuff." Dontae grabs the diving-team information I left in the car and holds it out to me.

"I don't care about that anymore." How is anything supposed to matter when I can't unsee what I saw, can't unknow what happened to a poor old man who is my friend?

Mrs. Morrow takes the papers and forces them into my hands. "You have to care about your future, T'Shawn. About life. Understand? You need something to knock that memory from your head. Go after what you want. Don't let one tragedy destroy your dreams."

I nod and take the papers. Between the car to the building, we pass an old man walking slowly, with a small panting dog on a leash at his side. His face is as rough as brown shoe leather. Bet he wishes his dog would hurry up and finish its business so he can get inside out of the cold. The old man nods and cracks a smile while his dog sniffs at my leg.

Dontae's mother unlocks the gate in front of the group of courtyard apartment buildings where we live. Five brownstone apartment buildings arranged in a U shape with a gate in front of the long, narrow court of grass and low bushes. Each building has six apartments above ground, two on each floor, plus two garden apartments belowground with only the windows visible from the outside. My family lives on the second floor of building number two. A big hulking, green ash tree stands alone in the center of the courtyard. The treetop is taller than my window, arms extending upward from the gnarled trunk. The branches are filled with buds now, but soon there will be big leaves.

Dontae and his mom watch me until I safely enter my building before they cross the courtyard to number five, the building where they live. I enter the outer door, grab our mail, and use my key to unlock the inner security door. I'm supposed to feel safe in the building's inner lobby, a small tile-floored alcove leading to a staircase. Usually I do and quickly spring up the stairs to our second-floor apartment. Today my skin feels cold, and the memory of Mr. Owens's cries fills my ears.

CHAPTER
THREE

I SMELL THE SUGARY AROMA of peach cobbler before I open our apartment door. Mom is the best cook in the world. She used to practically take over the communal kitchen back when we lived in the homeless shelter. That happened after Dad died of cancer and we lost our home. Back then, Malik Kaplan volunteered to be my temporary "big brother." He helped save me from Lamont and his gang-member friends. Malik is a college sophomore now, playing basketball at the University of Illinois in Champaign. Dontae may be my best Chicago friend, but Malik is my best friend in the whole world. Sometimes, I pretend Malik is my for-real brother. His father is Dwayne Kaplan, owner of Kaplan Auto Body Shops and Mom's boss. She works at the headquarters downtown.

"Hey, Mom . . . ," I begin as I enter the kitchen. Then I stop and worry that Mrs. Morrow was right: it's not a day to hit my mother with bad news. Mom bakes desserts when she's upset. That peach cobbler tells me something is wrong.

"Wash your hands," she says, looking up from a mixing bowl.

"But, Mom . . ." I sound like I'm whining, but I can't help that right now.

"Hands, young man."

"Hands," my four-year-old sister, Rochelle, echoes. Yellow-and-pink barrettes on her black braids jingle as she looks up from the table, where she is drawing a picture.

I can't argue with either of them. I run to the bathroom and wash my hands. I also wipe my face before I go back to the kitchen, so Mom can't send me back again. I even take a minute to look in the mirror and practice my hopeful look.

I return to the kitchen and check the bowl she is stirring. One deep breath, and I know she is making oatmeal raisin cookies. Today is a twofer—homemade cookies plus cobbler equal double trouble.

"How was your afternoon?" she asks. "Did you have a good time, T?"

"The best," I say with enthusiasm, hoping she won't ask more questions.

"What's wrong?" She wipes her hands on her apron and approaches me.

"Nothing's wrong."

"I know that look. There's something."

I will never make it as an actor. Not when I cave every time the all-seeing Mom eye is turned on me. "It's nothing. I just have these." I hand her the papers. That's easier than describing how my blood congealed and my brain blanked when the cop pointed his gun at me. The pages are a little damp; some stick together as she examines them.

"Swim club, huh?" She relaxes, even chuckles. "I remember how you used to hate the water. We'd take you to the lakefront, but no matter what bribe your father or I offered, you'd never do more than stick in a toe. Then your brother took you in the lake with him." She smiles and goes silent. She's remembering the days before, the same way I am. Maybe that's the reason for the baking.

She must have heard something that made her think of him again.

Mom takes a seat at the kitchen table and begins pulling the wet sheets apart and reading them. I grab plates from the cabinet and begin setting the table to remind her how helpful I am. I do all my chores, most of the time, anyway. Plus, I'm her number one babysitter, and I always get high grades. She knows I would never go near a gang, certainly not join and fight to become a leader the way Lamont did. I deserve a little something good.

"Uh, don't worry about that concussion-release-form thingy—it's totally bogus." I knew she'd have a problem with all the warning messages. Moms are like that, always saying don't do this or be careful of that. Sometimes a little danger helps make things more fun. "People don't get hurt swimming. Water is good for you."

"I'm not worried about that," she says.

Then the problem must be the costs. "I know it looks like a lot of money."

"It does."

"But me and the diving board—"

"The diving board and I," she corrects absently, still looking at the papers.

"The diving board and I were awesome together. I mean, I loved being up there. I made eight dives today and even managed a backflip." Sort of. She doesn't need to know about the ache in my back. "The Racing Rays is a swimming club, but they train divers too. I want to take diving lessons," I say, like it's the most important thing in the world.

Maybe it is right now.

My voice speeds up, words tumbling from my lips. "Think about it, Mom. If I can do this, you wouldn't have to give me anything else. I wouldn't need any other birthday present and not even a Christmas present. I'll do extra chores and stuff without complaining. I could go to the Olympics, become famous. I mean, this kid I met is a super diver, and he even said I was a natural! Schools give scholarships for diving too, so I could get to college someday. Please, please, please!"

By this time next year, I could be famous, the diving champion from Chicago's South Side. I could win medals for the USA at the Olympics. The city might even throw a party for me with a parade down King Drive. I can barely breathe while I think about sitting on a float and waving at the kids from my school and my teachers. I'll let Dontae sit beside me. Carmela too, of course.

"T'Shawn." Mom bites her bottom lip, looking from the papers to me and then out the window into the growing darkness. "We are not giving up on your special day. Besides, we have something great to celebrate this year. What if I told you this would be your best birthday ever?"

"Best?"

The silence goes on and on. Her tablet is open on the kitchen table. I look at the screen. I don't know what I expect, maybe a recipe or something. But definitely not a listing for bedroom furniture. Are we moving, or is she planning to get me a new bed for my birthday? There's nothing special about that.

"A lot is happening," she finally says. "We have some big changes to prepare for."

"Did Mr. Kaplan fire you?" My stomach twists into a giant knot. Her boss promoted her to be his executive assistant a few weeks ago. How could he fire her now?

"No, my job is fine, sweetie." Mom puts the papers on a shelf and pats my hands.

Sweetie? That's what she called me while Dad was dying in hospice.

"Are you sick?" I ask.

"No, I'm fine."

"Is something wrong with Rochelle?"

"Sweetie, your sister is fine too. No one is sick, I promise."

"Then what's wrong? Tell me, Mom. I can take it." Because something is definitely not fine, I can tell.

"Actually, it's wonderful news. Lamont is coming home."

CHAPTER
FOUR

I WAIT TO HEAR MOM yell, "Just kidding!" and burst into laughter. This has to be one of those colossal jokes that couldn't wait for April Fools' Day.

But Mom isn't laughing, so I can't either.

Ten years. My brother and his friends tried to rob a restaurant. He pled guilty to a Class 1 felony and was sentenced to ten years in prison. That was only two years ago. I'm supposed to be all grown up before he can come back to mess up my life again.

The world wavers. I sit down, grabbing the edge of the table because I need support. My left foot starts tapping on the green-and-blue mosaic tile floor.

"Lamont is coming here?" I ask. "How? Why?"

"He's being paroled early," Mom continues. "He'll be released in two weeks, only a few days after your birthday. Kind of like a belated present for you."

She beams, as if my scary brother really is a present.

I was ten the last time I saw Lamont. I stare down at my feet and feel myself shake as my mind returns to the past.

I loved my brother. I trusted him. After Dad died, he was there for me. We sat in a dark closet together after the funeral, and my brother held me and let me cry and never once called me a baby. I thought he was perfect. When he defied rules, I was proud of him. I totally agreed with him when he said, "What's the point of following rules when we're all going to die?" He was the man in our family, and what he said was magic. "Lamont said" were my two favorite words.

Lamont said he was happy when the director of the homeless shelter banned him for breaking curfew every night. When he came to me and said, "I'm going places. I want you with me—we belong together," I was happy to run away with him.

I left school, left Mom and the homeless shelter, and joined him in the abandoned building he and other members of his gang called home. The guys drank and smoked and made plans to strike out at enemies. Lamont talked of leaving Chicago and heading down to Memphis, where he "knew people." My great-great-grandfather, a former slave, settled near Memphis following the Civil War. My grandfather moved to Chicago after World War I, leaving many relatives behind. But I knew Lamont wasn't talking about those distant relatives. He meant gang members around the city.

I was glad to be with my big brother . . . for a few hours.

By the evening, the laughter and boasts and smack talk couldn't make me forget how cold I was and how lost I felt. The place had broken windows and no heat, and it was winter. The longer I stayed in the apartment, the more I coughed and shivered. Puffs of white smoke emerged from my mouth when I breathed. The room was dirty, with only a mattress and a few rugs scattered around the floor. And guns. Every guy in the house had either a gun or knife on them. Always. And after a few hours, I didn't feel safe. All I wanted was my mother and sister, not the string of unknown faces circling me.

Lamont began playing with one of the guns. I had no idea what type. It was just big and black and ugly and seemed to fill his hands. He pushed it across the floor to me, saying, "Take it, Short Stack. It's time to man up." His voice sounded as cold as the January wind blowing through one of the broken windows.

I reached out a finger and touched the barrel of the cold, black, deadly gun. It was just as hard as it looked. I snatched my hand back. "I don't want a gun. I want to go home."

"This is your home now. We're your family, all of us." He waved at Toxic and Darnell and all the other guys lounging around, laughing.

My teeth chattered. "I want Mommy."

Darnell stared at me the way a cat eyes a mouse. "Baby wants a bottle," he sneered, and handed me a beer bottle.

I pushed it away and turned to my brother. "Please, Lamont. Let's just go home."

"That shelter ain't home, T." Lamont stared at me through narrow, scary eyes. "Life is hard. It's time for you to man up unless you intend to end up like Dad. Tossed aside when you get too sick to be useful. Dying and leaving behind nothing but people who—"

"You'll die too," I said.

"At least when I go, I'll be remembered as a real man."

His tense voice made me shiver. I was only ten. I didn't want to be a man.

"Are you sure this is really your brother?" Darnell asked. He was an older guy, bigger than Lamont. I could see he didn't like taking orders from my brother. He reached for the gun Lamont left in front of me, but my brother was quicker. He picked it up and pointed it at me! My mouth went dry. I felt like a mouse caught in one of those sticky glue traps, still alive but unable to move or even cry out. All I could do was sit and shiver and pray.

"I decide what happens to my brother," Lamont said in the coldest voice I had ever heard.

Darnell never smiled. Hatred filled his eyes and tightened his lips as he confronted my brother. He was not going to be controlled much longer.

Then Malik showed up. He never told me how he found us, but he was smart enough not to come alone. He refused to leave without me.

My nerves tingle every time I think about guns. I am afraid. I'm scared to be in the same room, the same apartment, even the same world as my own brother.

I wish I could tell someone.

"You're noisy." Rochelle has come to stand beside me. I hit my knee to stop the tap dance I haven't done since the days before Lamont's arrest. A doctor called my leg movements a nervous tic and smiled as he said it was harmless. Then he sent my mom another bill.

I grab my little sister and pull her onto my lap. Her weight means my leg can't start tapping again. Rochelle won't even remember she used to have two brothers. She had barely started to talk when Lamont left us. She doesn't have anything to forget. I envy her.

"I thought, hoped maybe, you'd be willing to postpone your party a little bit," Mom continues. "Then we could have a combined event. You know, a birthday and welcome-home bash."

"I told you I don't want any old party!" I shout. "I don't want Lamont either." Rochelle throws her hands over her ears. I rub her forearm gently until she relaxes.

"He's still your brother, T'Shawn," Mom says in a whisper, her lips pursing like she's sucking on a Lemonhead.

At least she dropped the "sweetie."

"How is he getting out so soon? The judge said ten years." Even with time off for good behavior—as if—he should be in prison at least three more years.

"Apparently a judge adjusted his sentence. It all came up so sudden, I'm not sure of the details. Lamont is excited about coming home and promises things will be different. Your brother made a mistake; he got caught up in gang life, but that's over now." She stops for a moment, takes a deep breath, and wipes below one eye. "He thought money from selling drugs and stealing would help. But he accepts his mistakes now, and he's done with all that."

"Is that what he tells you?" I don't remember my brother ever admitting to a mistake about anything. I just remember him running around calling himself the King of the World and claiming he could save us all. I believed him. I got mad at Mom for refusing to take the rolls of money he collected.

But I was ten in those days. I'm older and way smarter now.

"I wish you had come with me to talk to him yourself, at least once," Mom says.

Once a month, Mom makes a trip to the prison to visit Lamont. She comes back wearing the same expression she had during Dad's funeral. My brother did me one favor: prisoners have to give permission before people can visit. He never put my name on his list. He knew I'd never want to see him again. I wish he hadn't put Mom on either. She could have forgotten him by now.

"Does he have to come here?" I ask. I know I sound bitter and almost as young as Rochelle. But I don't care. I want her to know how I feel.

"He's still my son, just like you. Wherever I am, my home will always be his home. No matter what happened in the past, we don't stop loving family." She lifts Rochelle away from me and sets her on the floor.

"Where is he going to stay?" I ask meekly.

"I was thinking about getting bunk beds," Mom continues, confirming my fear. "You two can share a room, get to know each other again." She clasps her hands and smiles. "Both my boys, together again. You two were always so close. I know you'll want to be with him."

My mother couldn't be more wrong.

After a dinner I can't even eat, I go to my room. I open my closet and climb on a chair and reach up to the top shelf. I push back the cardboard box holding the rock collection I began but never did anything with. But it makes good camouflage. I strain on tiptoe to reach the wooden box pressed behind it against the wall. I pull it down and sit on the edge of my bed, opening the box filled with memories that I keep hidden so Mom won't find them and cry. Things I managed to salvage after our eviction and kept close through all our travels. There's not much. A few toy soldiers that Dad and I used to play with. A picture of Dad with some of his Iraq War buddies. He's wearing the heavy silver ring passed down from his great-great-grandfather. A DVD of *Dr. Jekyll and Mr. Hyde*. We used to watch the old black-and-white horror movie every Halloween, with Mom fixing fresh buttered popcorn and worrying about the nightmares I never got.

I remember squeezing in between my dad and my brother to feel safe. I would bury my head in Dad's shoulder and inhale his aftershave every time Dr. Jekyll transformed. Dad knew the doctor's part by heart, and Lamont knew most of Mr. Hyde. "Does Jekyll tell Hyde?" Dad would ask minutes before the movie started, and then they'd recite every line those characters spoke together.

Then Dad died, and my brother became the crazed and lawless Mr. Hyde.

"Read about Aunt Nancy," Rochelle says, breaking me free from the past. She walks into my room with a book in her hands.

"You mean Ananse," I say, wiping my cheeks and sitting up.

"That's what I said: Aunt Nancy, the magic spider," she says, her eyes wide and happy.

I love Rochelle and always try hard to be a good brother. That's why, instead of correcting her again, I playfully tug one of her braids before taking the book and pulling her onto my lap. She is soft but solid, real and mine. I know by heart this book about the legendary trickster African spider and his many adventures because she makes me read from one of the stories inside every day.

How will I protect Rochelle from our brother? I ask myself. She thinks of me the way her friends talk about their fathers. That makes me feel good because I love her, and bad because it means she thinks I'm the same as a grown-up. Only I'm not.

I flash back again to when Lamont and I sat in our closet, the day our father died, and he let me cry into his shoulder while I prayed for the miracle that never came. Lamont was my hero—Superman and Batman and Iron Man all rolled into one.

Now after everything that happened, my brother is the biggest villain I know.

CHAPTER
FIVE

BEFORE HISTORY CLASS ON MONDAY, a few of us gather inside our classroom and watch the video on Dontae's phone of Mr. Owens's arrest. Our teacher hasn't arrived yet. The video went viral over the weekend. There are thousands of likes and shares and almost as many comments from all over the country. Most of the time it's a big deal to have something you upload go all over the country and even the world. This time it's also sad, because of what's in the story and what was left out. Mr. Owens wasn't important enough for anyone in the major media to pick up the story. What happened to that old man wasn't anything new. A lot of kids in the class have friends or relatives who have been struck by violence. But it was the first time I'd seen that kind of cruelty happen right in front of me.

In the end, the only charge made against Mr. Owens was resisting arrest, and the police dropped that charge shortly after Dontae's video went viral. I can guess what would have happened to the poor old man without those images. But there's not even an apology from the police. The rest of the world moves on, barely noticing. But I live here. I can't not see what happens around me. I can't stop hurting when my friends get hurt.

Almost everyone in class has something to say about the video on Dontae's screen.

"Why'd they even stop him? What did he do?" a boy asks.

"He musta 'fit the description,'" another boy says, and laughs into his hand.

"It's not funny," a crying girl says.

"I heard the cops were looking for some thirty-year-old dude in dreds. I guess a skinny old guy with an Afro looked close enough."

"Let some cop try that with me and he'll be sorry," a guy next to me says, puffing up his chest.

Carmela raises her eyes and gives an exaggerated neck roll to show her disgust. Dontae and I roll our eyes. Does that kid really think he's different? Or is he just praying he'll never really have to face the bad parts of the real world?

Kids thump Dontae on the back and call him a hero for uploading the video. I come off as a did-nothing wimp.

"'He's my friend.' Is that all you could say?" Carmela asks, laughing at me. I can't believe I even like this girl.

I can think of a thousand things I could have, should have said and done. Why do those great ideas always come to me after it's too late?

"I just know I would never, ever, *ever* call the police, not for anything," one kid says. A lot of others nod agreement.

"Why wouldn't you call the police?" an adult voice asks. We all turn to see Mr. Hundle entering the classroom. He's one of the three teachers in charge of our class. In our school, seventh and eighth grades are taught by a team of teachers who work and plan assignments together. The other members in our team are Mrs. Niobe, a black woman who teaches math and science, and Miss Ruiz, a small Hispanic woman who teaches us Spanish, music, and art.

We call Mr. Hundle the Hun. It's a perfect name for a teacher who lives and breathes and teaches history. He also teaches language arts. He's a tall white man, with broad shoulders and long arms. He's like a bear who is all growl with no bite. Well, almost none. He can be brutal about homework and pop quizzes.

"Calling the police could be dangerous," I say to answer the Hun's question since everyone else has gone silent. "You can't trust them not to hurt people, even people who never did anything."

"I heard about what happened to Mr. Owens over the weekend," he answers slowly, picking his words carefully, just like when he's giving us a lecture. "I believe some of you know him personally. But the police are here to help us all. Don't distrust everyone on the force because one officer makes a mistake."

"It wasn't just one officer," I say.

"Or one mistake," Dontae adds.

"It's not helpful to try blaming the police," the Hun says, his smile slowly growing tighter. He likes to tell us our class is a safe place and we can say what we feel. But it doesn't always feel safe. Like now, when lines cut across his forehead and his fingers drum on the top of the desk. I wonder if he notices how that sound silences us.

"The police work hard, right, Carmela?" The Hun turns to her because her father is a cop, a newly promoted police sergeant.

"What happened to Mr. Owens was wrong, but you

can't blame all police because a few go too far," she says, always eager to defend her father. "My father only wants to help people."

She's proud of her dad. Sometimes she acts like he wears a halo in addition to his gun. I understand—we all love our parents. I wish he worked in our neighborhood. He's been assigned to work in the Kenwood neighborhood, north of us. We have strangers, mostly white officers. They all seem jumpy and unhappy to be working around here.

"You come to our neighborhood every day. Do you fear for your life?" I ask Mr. Hundle.

"Of course not," he answers, holding his smile steady. "I know you, all of you. You are all important to me."

We're studying the American Revolution in class, so I say, "Well, some cops around here are like the British soldiers who didn't believe colonists were real British citizens. Loyalists might call the redcoats for help. The patriots knew better. So do we."

He gives me a long, silent stare before nodding. "Well, T, no one will ever call you a fence-sitter."

"I wouldn't want to be." Fence-sitters weren't loyalists or patriots. They refused to pick a side. That's not me. I side with my friends.

Mr. Hundle looks around and says, "All right, class,

we need to get back to our regular lesson." When some kids groan, he adds, "I don't enjoy making you memorize material, but these tests help determine your future. It is vital that all Americans know how our country was founded."

"It's not *our* history," I mutter a little too loud. The Hun turns slowly, panning the class. He stops and stares right at me. His brows pinch together. His expression demands that I say more. "No offense, Mr. Hundle, but you wouldn't understand. You finish your work here and go home to your fancy North Side digs and forget all about us."

The Hun sits on the edge of his desk, facing us. I wonder if I've gone too far, if this *safe place* is about to become real unsafe. I know I'm supposed to care about his lesson. I'm supposed to pretend to forget that American colonists moaned and complained, but England never treated them as bad as they treated slaves. My leg starts to tap on the floor. I cross my feet at the ankles before the sound betrays me and makes things worse.

"I don't know how to walk in your footsteps. I can't," he admits. "I grew up in Ogle County, near the Wisconsin border. We all thought it was the best place on earth, but it doesn't get more white-bread than that. I learned a lot, changed immeasurably after I left for college. But I accept there's a ton I don't know about your lives here."

Uncomfortable laughter skitters across the room. I try to escape the thoughts swirling inside my head and listen to what he really means.

"What I do know is the past," he continues, "and that includes why American history is also your history. Have any of you heard about the Ethiopian Regiment or the Black Brigade?"

Linda's hand goes up. "Weren't they like the Harlem Hellfighters?" she asks, her voice soft and tentative. The Hellfighters were a black regiment that was one of the most decorated American regiments of World War I. I heard about them from my parents. But they never mentioned any Black Brigade. I lean close, waiting to hear more.

The Hun nods. "Consider them the Hellfighters of the Revolution, or, as the British call it, the American War of Independence, since they fought for the Loyalists."

Black heroes we never get to hear about.

"Our people were on the wrong side?" Dontae asks.

"I'd fight on any side that promised me freedom," the Hun says. "That was what the British offered to escaped slaves who assisted them in putting down the revolt. Some of the British soldiers were willing to fight right beside black soldiers."

"But the British lost, so we got shafted again," Dontae says.

The bell rings, making me jump in my seat. None of us move, we don't want to leave.

"What should we do?" Dontae asks. "Kneel before the all-powerful cops and beg, 'Please, please don't hurt us'? It didn't work for the colonists." We learned that from studying about the Olive Branch Petition the American Loyalists sent to the King of England. They begged and pleaded and received nothing but a laugh. Nothing changed until after the Revolutionary War. Why should we expect begging to work for us here and now?

"Things only change when people act," Linda says, almost as if she is thinking my thoughts. Carmela looks at her and slowly nods.

The Hun stands. "Get to lunch. You deserve it. But you also deserve one more thing. Extra homework. Don't groan," he says as our voices drown out the sound of kids passing through the hall outside our door. "I want you to look up the *Book of Negroes*. Tell me what was in that book, and why it's important to all of you."

At dinner that evening, Mom waits until I reach for a second piece of fish before saying, "T, I'd like you to come to this month's Take Back the Streets meeting on

Wednesday. You're a teenager now. It's time you participated in the community more, Sweetie." This is what being an official teenager gets me. She's been wanting me to attend for a long time, but that's all grown-up stuff. Mom uses her *don't argue with me young man* voice while throwing in the *Sweetie!* I'd prefer Short Stack. She sometimes acts like I'm younger than Rochelle, at least until she needs me for something. Then she's all, "Act mature young man."

I don't want to be mature. I want to be with my friends. Adult meetings are always boring. I bet this one will be dry as dust. My brain frantically searches for words to turn defeat into victory and make Mom let me alone. "It's just a bunch of old people sitting around talking."

"Adults of all ages," Mom corrects me. "Including students. We're a group of people who care about our neighborhood, the kids and their future. I want you to feel a part of things."

My brother used to talk about taking back the streets, but he meant something different. The gang was never about protecting families. He used to say the gang claimed our city streets for themselves to hold against the powers that be, namely the police and other gangs. No wonder gang leaders are sometimes called street politicians. I bet he would consider TBTS his enemy. Maybe, deep down, he thinks Mom and I are enemies too.

Gangs and cops, sometimes I wonder if there is any real difference. Both act like turf is more important than people. It's like a war, with both sides going after some hill they consider theirs without caring about the people who live there. If not for Sergeant Rhodes, I'm not sure I would ever be able to believe any cop cared about people like me.

Mom continues, "Also, what happened to Mr. Owens is on the agenda."

Right then I decide I will attend the meeting. No more complaints. What happened to the old man wasn't anything new. I've seen videos, heard stories of other takedowns. This was the first time I saw anything like that happen right in front of me.

Two days later, I come straight home and do my homework, then Mom and I head for the church. Rochelle is staying with her babysitter. Our church is a very busy building and not just on Sundays. The building is three blocks north of our apartment building, and forms the center of our community. There is something going on inside the building almost every day, from the quilting circle on Monday evenings to Miss Ruiz, my music teacher at school, leading choir practice on Tuesday nights. My mother and Dontae's mother are both choir members.

Miss Ruiz also teaches piano lessons using the church piano on Thursdays after school to neighborhood kids. The Boy Scouts meet there too, and the pastor opens the door to weekly Alcoholics Anonymous and Al-Anon meetings. There are also prayer meetings and bible study groups.

Take Back the Streets takes over the church basement one Wednesday evening a month.

There aren't enough chairs for all the people crowding into the basement area, so Mom "suggests" I stand to let some older person sit. I know most of the adults here: neighbors, some of my teachers who live in the area, even the school janitor, who gets up from his chair to let a pregnant woman sit. I'm surprised to see so many kids here. I expected Dontae. The church building is almost his second home, and his father helped start the group along with Sergeant Rhodes, Carmela's dad. She and her mother have probably been coming to meetings from the beginning. Linda and her older sister are here too, both standing near the front beside their aunt's wheelchair.

I sort of hoped Mr. Owens would be here, but he's not around. He's back from the hospital, but people say he's scared to go outside his home. Mom and some of the other church ladies take food over and help him with his cleaning.

I move close to a refreshment table, beside Dontae. The meeting agenda is on a sign on the wall above us.

```
Collection for Mr. Owens

Neighborhood beautification project

Increasing the playground patrols

Street cleaning

What to do about Lamont?
```

Okay, that last item isn't actually written down, but I wish I could add it. Maybe someone here will talk to Mom and tell her she is wrong to let him invade all our lives.

Linda moves from her spot in the front to stand next to me.

"Why did you come?" I ask, and offer her a cookie from the refreshment table.

"Because I want to be part of something important," she says. "This is how you change the world."

No, this is how I find myself volunteering to join the neighborhood beautification project to plant flowers around the school and playground. Mom smiles and nods when I add my name to the clipboard circulating the room. She looks even more pleased when I empty my pockets and add my change to the collection basket to help Mr. Owens.

So many people in the room make the air hot. Dontae takes a long drink from his water bottle.

Everyone is upset about Mr. Owens. Raised voices grumble at Sergeant Rhodes, as if they want to make him responsible for everything the police do wrong.

"The police don't listen. We live in the forgotten zone. The last to get protection but the first to be harassed or blamed!" someone in the crowd shouts.

I've known that for a long time. Our streets take forever to be plowed after blizzards. We know we have to take care of ourselves because no one else will. The more I listen to the adults around me talk, the more I worry.

"I know there have been a few incidents." Sergeant Rhodes shakes a head covered by a short, salt-and-pepper Afro.

"A few?" That comment is followed by harsh laughter.

"He better not blame my dad," Carmela says grimly to Dontae and me.

"I wish your dad worked here. Maybe then cops would talk to us."

"No offense, Rhodes, but a lot of the men in blue get scared the second they enter our streets. Scared people with guns and a license to kill are a bad combination," a man says.

"We deserve to be heard." The speaker is an older man with a heavy accent. He's from Mexico, I think. "No disrespect, Sergeant, but I fear for my son's life every time he walks out the door. I taught him to look both ways when he crosses the street. But how do I protect him from the people who are supposed to be the good guys?"

Linda's aunt rolls her wheelchair forward. "We can start by cleaning our own houses. I heard a new gang-banger will be coming to live in our neighborhood with Mrs. Rodgers."

Mumbling voices grow loud, and heads turn to Mom. Dontae pats my arm. I think, I wonder . . . maybe they will tell her he can't come.

My mom stands slowly and her voice is measured when she says, "My son is going to be released on parole." Her arms cross over her chest. "His parole officer said being with his family offers him the best chance of success. I agree."

She looks at me. I know she expects me to jump up and tell everyone Lamont is a good guy. I'm supposed to be glad.

I can't. I'm not glad, and I won't lie.

"I want to meet your brother," Dontae whispers as the discussion goes on.

"No," I assure him. "You don't."

"I'm glad you came," Mom says as we walk home after the meeting. The streetlights are on, the moon high in the sky. "I'm dedicated to making things better for you and Rochelle. And for Lamont when he gets here. Things will be different."

Neither her smile nor her confidence fools me. "What if he hasn't changed?" I ask, thinking back to what Linda's aunt said.

"I promise you, he has," she insists. "I see a new maturity every time I visit him."

That sounds good, but mothers sometimes see what they want to see. Doesn't she even worry Lamont might change me? Or maybe she expects me to fix him.

I'm good, but I'm not that good.

CHAPTER
SIX

TWO DAYS LATER, I COME home from school to find Mom and a stranger sitting at our kitchen table. He's an older Asian dude wearing a white collared shirt, khakis, a crooked tie, and a tired expression.

"T!" Rochelle jumps into my arms and kisses my cheek. "Momma has a boyfriend," she whispers.

"I don't think so," I answer, returning her to the floor.

"Who is this?" The man removes a pair of wire-rimmed glasses and uses them to gesture my way. I smell coffee from the half-filled cup in front of him.

"This is my younger son, T'Shawn," Mom says. "Sweetie, this is Mr. Arthur Cho. He's Lamont's parole officer. He wanted to come by to talk with me before your brother comes home."

I wish he was boyfriend material. That I could handle without this sinking feeling in my stomach.

"Actually, I want to talk to the entire family, Mrs. Rodgers," he corrects Mom. "I've come for a prerelease visit with all of you. I find it beneficial to check on the living arrangements before a prisoner is released. No one wants him finding his way back to prison." He smiles at Rochelle, but she backs away, pressing tightly against my leg. "Little Missy here seems a bit shy," he says with a sad sigh.

He puts his glasses back on and studies me for a few seconds. "I'm glad you're letting him stay with you, Mrs. Rodgers. Not every family does."

"Why are you letting him go so early?" I ask, staring at Mr. Cho.

"I don't make the rules," Mr. Cho says.

Adults always say things like that. But if they don't make the rules, who does?

"Do you want your brother to come home?" Mr. Cho asks.

"Of course he does," Mom says quickly.

Does not.

Mr. Cho leans back in the chair. "Support from the family is often a deciding factor on whether a parolee returns to a life of crime or makes a successful transition to the outside world."

"Lamont will have support," Mom assures him, looking at me pointedly. "I won't put any pressure on him."

"Put enough on him to make him understand he doesn't get to decide which rules he wants to obey. He can't go near his victims"—he looks down at a file folder with papers in it—"Pietr Frank or the Murhasselt family. Most important, he has to steer clear of his former associates. That's often the rule that trips these gang members up. They find it nearly impossible to break ties."

"What if he does go back to them?" I ask.

"I will revoke his parole." He sounds reluctant. I feel excited and sit down to hide my joy. Lamont loved gang life and the guys he called his real family. He won't be here long.

"That won't happen," Mom insists. "My son was sucked in when he was young and vulnerable, but he's matured. He was just a boy, not a hardened gang member."

Oh, please, Mom. Lamont thought he was a king. He was never cool with rules. Dad was the only person who could keep him in line. Lamont and Dad would argue. My brother would get angry at our father, and then he would do what Dad said anyway.

I lean closer to Mr. Cho. If he is serious about the rules

thing, then I don't have to worry anymore.

Mr. Cho clears his throat. "I don't want to argue, ma'am, but he never denied his involvement with the Enforcers gang."

"He promised me those days are over," Mom said. "He wouldn't lie to me."

Mr. Cho's knees crack as he climbs to his feet and gathers his files. "I hope so." He pulls a card from his pocket and hands it to Mom. "Program my number into your phone. If you need me, call."

"Thank you," Mom says. "T, walk our guest out, please."

I follow him to the door. He pauses in the hall.

"How old are you, T'Shawn?" he asks.

"Almost thirteen."

"Then you're old enough to understand. I'm afraid your mother might be a little soft with him."

"She's not soft." Only, she does cry about him sometimes. Like on the day he left us. And when he was arrested. And every time she packs him a care package or returns from visiting him in prison.

Mr. Cho steps closer to me. "Your mom looks like she blames herself for your brother's bad choices. None of what happened was her fault. Or yours. Some people are born bad."

"He *wasn't* born bad." I can't believe I feel the urge to defend Lamont. But he wasn't always that way. Once, he was the best brother ever. That only changed after Dad died.

Cho looks unconvinced. "People promise anything to get out of prison. Sometimes they even intend to follow through. But the recidivism rate is still above fifty percent. Do you know what recidivism means?"

I shake my head no.

"It means more than half the people who get out of prison walk through a revolving door and end up back inside."

Recidivism. The word won't be on any of my school vocabulary quizzes, but I don't think I will ever forget it.

He pulls out another card and hands it to me. "This one is for you. If your brother does anything that could hurt any of you, let me know. Okay?"

"You mean be your spy?"

"I mean keep your eyes open. Don't be afraid to tell me if anything goes wrong."

"I'm not afraid," I insist as he starts down the stairs. Then I shut the door and return to the kitchen, struggling to make myself believe my own words.

CHAPTER
SEVEN

MY BIRTHDAY COMES AND GOES. The thirteenth of March is no longer the most important date circled on the calendar. I have to explain to Dontae that I'll be having a brother instead of a birthday celebration. I wait as long as I can, until Dontae shows up at my apartment. Party or not, he intends to give me a present. He whistles when he sees how my room has changed. Mom traded with a coworker my bed for a set of bunk beds her friend no longer needed.

"I still can't believe you have a secret brother," Dontae says. "You told me he was dead."

"I never said dead. I said gone."

"What did he do?" Dontae asks.

I tell myself to lie, but this is my best friend, and I'm too tired to think up a story. I drop down on the bottom bed and close my eyes.

When I remain silent, he pulls out his phone and thumbs through the internet, doing a search for my brother. I've never searched, never looked online to see what information exists. The details of his arrest and conviction for robbery and assault must be there.

"This says your brother almost killed Mr. Frank," Dontae says in a low voice.

"I don't want to talk about this," I say, because the rest of the story goes from bad to really awful. Lamont and other gang members broke into Frank's Place, a local restaurant a few blocks from our apartment, and held Mr. Frank and a waitress, Linda's older sister, hostage. They were there partly for money and partly because Mr. Frank continually defied the gang's attempt at neighborhood domination. There is one thing that won't be in any internet file because I never told and neither did my brother. I would have been with him that night if Malik hadn't found me first and taken me away from my brother and his friends.

"When will your brother be here?" Dontae asks.

"Three days." Crappy birthday to me.

"Is this why your mom had to cancel your party?"

I shrug, unwilling to admit the cancellation was my idea. A bus rumbles by on the street outside my open window.

"You'll have to sleep with your eyes open, you know," Dontae adds, his face as solemn as a teacher giving instructions before a test.

"I won't be able to sleep at all. Worst of all, I'll have to do my not sleeping up here." I climb the shaky ladder to the top bunk. When I sit, I have to hunch my shoulders to keep from hitting my head on the ceiling. I reach up and rub my fingers along the rough, painted surface. "I hate this."

"Claim the bottom, if that's what you want. It was your room first. He has to respect dibs."

"Lamont only respects Lamont. He'll take the bottom bunk just because he can, once he knows I want it."

"Is he smart?" Dontae asks.

I nod. "Real smart. He taught me to fight and stand up to bullies. And how to swim. He's school smart too. He used to help me with my homework. But he was fascinated with the gang life. My dad told him he needed to stay in school and graduate. He used to say, 'If you join,

I'll come back from my grave and go after you.'" Then he died. My brother joined the gang, and Dad never returned.

"I know how to work smart bullies. You know I have to deal with people who think I'm weak all the time. Whenever someone comes after me, I always have something I can pretend I want to protect. They tear into that first, and the rest of my stuff is safe. Survival skills, man." He pretend punches me in the arm. "Fake him out. Tell him you want the top, that you're dying to be up high."

"But I don't want the top."

"Let him *think* you do. Then he'll take what he thinks you want." He rubs his hands together, grinning.

"I could try, I guess."

Dontae frowns for a moment, thinking. Then he adds, "If things get really bad, come to my place. You could live with me. That's what buds are about, man."

That's why friends are better than brothers. And I picked me a good one. We do our special handshake: knuckle fist bump and two snaps.

Mom enters the room, bringing cups of hot chocolate. From up here, I look down at the wrinkles running deep in her forehead. Rochelle follows her and starts up the ladder. I reach down, take her arms, and pull her up. She settles into my lap and giggles.

"You look better," Mom says. "Happier."

I shrug.

"This is going to work. You'll see," Mom continues, handing one cup to me and one to Dontae. "I'm thinking about inviting a few people over once your brother arrives."

"I told you, Mom, no party."

"Not a party, more like a housewarming. Just a little get-together, to help him feel welcome."

I blink back angry tears and finger the parole officer's card in my pocket as my mom leaves, taking Rochelle with her.

Maybe we should have that housewarming bash. We can invite Lamont's old friends, the ones who have escaped arrest, anyway. The sooner he reconnects with his gang, the sooner his parole officer can send him back where he belongs.

"It's still your birthday, and even without a party, you deserve a present." Dontae pulls an envelope from his jacket pocket. "It's no bomb, man," he adds when I don't take it right away. "Are you going to open it or what?"

Inside is an iTunes gift certificate and a birthday card with a picture of a beach. I open the card, read the handwritten inscription, and laugh. "'So you can buy some of that funky music that only you love,'" I read aloud. "Your grandparents sent you this from Florida, didn't they?"

He looks startled for a moment before shrugging. "How did you know?"

"I've seen your grandmother's handwriting before."

He slaps his forehead. "I should have gotten a new card. Anyway, don't you believe in regifting? They sent it last year, but I never used it. If it was supposed to be good enough for me, it has to be good enough for you."

I fall back on the mattress, laughing. "Thanks, man."

"Happy birthday, bud."

He doesn't even realize his friendship is the best present he could ever give me.

CHAPTER
EIGHT

OVER THE NEXT FEW DAYS I keep trying to pretend things are normal. I almost succeed, right up until L day.

Mom puts a vase of fresh flowers in the living room before leaving to go to the prison a couple hours away in Pontiac, Illinois. It's early morning, and the sun is barely visible through a dark haze of clouds. Rochelle and I are supposed to dress nice. Rochelle is wearing a purple dress with lace on the collar. Mom told me to make sure I put on a fresh shirt and the blue pants I wear for church.

I have just finished feeding my sister lunch when I hear Mom's key in the lock. The door opens, and my big brother, Lamont, steps inside the apartment door, holding a gray duffel bag. He crosses the room to stand towering over me and drops the bag with a thump at my feet.

Come on, God. How about a bolt of lightning right between my eyes? Maybe eight feet of snow centered over my head.

Nothing happens.

"You grew, Short Stack," Lamont says, and part of my brain wiggles at the sound of the nickname I haven't heard in forever. He uses his first words to remind me that I'm little, unimportant, someone he can order around.

"My name is T'Shawn," I remind him. It's not old times, and I no longer do hero worship. My heart thumps painfully as I tilt my head to look up into his nearly black eyes. The top of my head almost reaches his shoulder. I had forgotten how much he looks like Dad. He's grown an ugly tuft of hair under his lip and above his chin, a soul patch that doesn't work on his face. Standing in the middle of the living room, he looks sharp wearing the new jacket, shirt, and slacks Mom bought for him. New dress shoes too, not the high-top sneakers he always insisted on wearing. He's put on more muscle. His broader-than-ever shoulders leave him looking huge and menacing in an "I can think of all sorts of creative ways to make you sorry" kind of way. There is a scar over his left eye that wasn't there when he left. But his lips widen in the same sunshine grin that attracted almost everyone, even his enemies.

"I missed you," he continues.

Yeah, sure you did. I barely keep from rolling my eyes. I won't believe anything that comes out of his mouth. I know how easily his expression can change to the sneer that made people back away. Maybe he missed being out, doing whatever he wanted when he wanted. But he didn't miss me enough to put my name on his list of allowed visitors.

Mom pats her hair, a sign she's nervous. She dressed up too and put on jewelry. A bracelet jangles when she moves, and her golden butterfly brooch shines on one shoulder of her pink blouse.

"Let T show you around. I'll be back soon," Mom says before starting out the door.

"But we just got here. Where are you going?" he asks, sounding confused.

"I need to return the car," she says, and hurries out the door.

Lamont turns back to me. "What does she mean 'return'?" He and I walk to the front window, where we watch Mom climb behind the wheel of the metallic blue Chevrolet and drive off.

"It's a rental," I explain.

"Pretty fancy car for a rental." Lamont frowns, apparently finding it hard to believe. It is a neat car, one I never got to ride in. We've never had a car, even when Dad was alive. He always said a car in the city was a crazy expense. A lot of people in Chicago do not own cars. The rental fee for one day would have paid for a week at swimming camp.

"Mom's gotta return it quick or pay a late penalty. You'll have to learn to walk again now that you're back."

He gives me a slit-eyed stare so intense my stomach ties itself into a hangman's noose. "Good thing I've done a lot of walking in the prison yard and on the prison laundry job I had. If you need shirts washed and pressed, I'm your guy." He turns away from the window and rubs a hand over his head. Lamont used to be an imitation Pitbull, Mr. Worldwide, keeping his head shaved completely bald. His hair has grown several inches, dark and thick, hiding the skull tattoos that branded him as a bad guy. He must be aching to get to a barbershop.

"Mom spent a lot of money for the care packages she sent you," I say.

That makes him grin. I was hoping he would feel guilt. "It was nice to get mail and treats. The cigs came in handy too."

"When did you start smoking?"

"I don't. But they were currency on the inside. And even the guards loved her cookies."

"I love cookies," Rochelle says from behind him.

Lamont jumps and turns, crouching slightly. Rochelle stands in a corner with her mouth open. He slowly stands, unclenching his fist. After several deep breaths, he takes a step toward her.

"Hey," I say, moving quickly to try to get between them. But all he does is kneel in front of our sister.

"Do you remember me?" he asks.

She shakes her head. A finger slips into her mouth. He's a stranger, and she's worried.

"I'm your brother."

"Nuh-uh. T is my brother." She runs around him and comes to me. I pick her up and hold her against my chest.

"You can have more than one brother," Lamont says, still on one knee.

"Not you. I don't like you," Rochelle says, because my sister is a smart girl.

"How is she supposed to know who you are?" I ask. "She was barely a year old when you decided to leave our family."

"I didn't decide. The Wiggins Witch kicked me out of the shelter. And Mom let her."

The fury and hate in his voice makes me take a step

backward. Constance Wiggins is the director of the homeless shelter we moved into after we lost our home. Lamont disobeyed rules and scared other residents and staff. That's why he had to leave. I think he enjoys scaring people. Especially me.

He laughs, his voice a little raw, as if he's no longer used to making that sound. He stands and removes his jacket, letting it fall over one lean, muscled arm. Beneath is a black T-shirt. "You're all going to have to get used to me now. Lead the way, Short Stack. Show me where I'm bunking."

T. My name is T'Shawn.

I put Rochelle down and let him follow me down the short hallway to my bedroom. Our bedroom now. Nothing is mine anymore. He steps inside and turns slowly, pausing once to look at the bunk beds, then a second time to gaze at the wall. I tacked up an orange-and-blue Fighting Illini pennant on that wall. It's the emblem of the athletic teams of the University of Illinois at Urbana–Champaign. That's where Malik plays basketball.

Lamont grunts, opens the closet door, and tosses his duffel bag on the floor. An autographed jersey from Malik hangs on the closet door. It's one he wore his freshman year and signed for me as a Christmas present.

"Leaky's shirt," Lamont says, fingering the jersey, a note of annoyance in his voice.

"His name is Malik." I back over to the dresser and grab the picture of Malik I keep there. I shove the picture inside a drawer before my brother turns around. I should have moved it and the jersey before Lamont arrived. Malik is black, like us, but his family is wealthy, not like us. He volunteered to be my imitation big brother after Lamont was banished from the shelter, until his father gave Mom her job. When I was little, the words "Lamont says" fell off my lips a dozen times a day. Lamont acted annoyed until I started saying "Malik says" instead. I forgot how much he hates Malik.

"Are you two still tight?" Lamont asks, clenching his fists.

"We text every week. I follow him on Twitter."

He rolls his eyes. "Your hero isn't that different from me. Just because his father can pay for college and cars and for him to play basketball. I used to play a little ball."

Malik is the opposite of you, I think. Aloud, I say, "You never cared about schools or teams or anything except being in charge."

"Oh, please, Short Stack. People are ready to do anything to be on top, including your special friend."

"Malik is a champion. He doesn't cheat or lie, he's not like—"

I stop too late. The twitching muscle in my brother's jaw tells me he knows what I was about to say.

In a low voice he says, "No, I guess your pal Leaky is nothing like me."

We stand there, tense and in silence, until Rochelle runs into the room and heads for the beds. Thin and wiry, with no fear of heights, she scrambles up the ladder. She bounces around on the top bunk in the middle of the things I scattered on the blanket to stake my phony claim. But I've changed my mind. I won't start out by pretending. No fake-outs. I will just be myself and tell him my rules.

I have dibs on the bottom bed. Live with that, Mr. King of the World.

"You'll be up top. I sleep below," I say. I want to sound firm, only my voice choses this time to crack into a nervous whisper. I begin throwing my stuff from the top bed to the floor.

"But we like being up high!" Rochelle wails.

Lamont bends to pick up some of the papers I tossed down.

"What's this?" He begins reading the swim-team papers.

"That . . . Those are mine." I try to snatch them from his hands.

"The Racing Rays?" The team's name rolls off his tongue as if he's said it before. "Did someone put you up to this?"

"No one put me up to anything. I like to swim and dive. Now give them back!" I try jumping to get the papers, but he steps back, holding them out of reach above his head.

"What makes you want to join a swim team?" Lamont asks, his voice unemotional. I almost confess how being in the water brings back good memories of days when I totally trusted him.

"Seriously, why not try boxing or football?" he continues. "Go where the money flows. Do something with a big-time paycheck." He doesn't mention basketball and never even glances again at the pennant on the wall.

"T wants to dive," Rochelle explains with exaggerated patience. My sister hears all, knows all. Then she adds, "What's dive?"

Lamont keeps looking at me. "You want to be a diver? God, the world really is crazy. My brother wants to be a Racing Ray."

"Why shouldn't I want to be part of something good? Something that would maybe get me a scholarship to college."

"No reason, I guess. If it's *really* what you want."

I'm shaking because I'm mad at Lamont and at myself. Why didn't I toss those forms the minute Mom said no?

Because I still had hope. I believed in miracles.

"T, come back up here," Rochelle calls. "I want you to play with me."

"We can play down below," I mumble.

"No! You come up here with me," she insists, her little hands fisting. She used to have crying meltdowns. Now that's she's older, she just pouts like crazy to get what she wants. And she wants me up there. We only played together up on the top bunk one time since the beds were delivered. Now she's acting like it's our special place. I reach up to lift her down, but she struggles to pull free.

"You come here with me," she says. "This is where you belong."

"Do you want the top bunk?" Lamont asks, looking at me.

"Yeah!" Rochelle yells. "T likes it here, and I like it here too."

I hesitate a second too long.

"You want the high ground, you've got it, Short

Stack." Lamont drops my papers back on the bunk beside Rochelle and then throws himself on the bottom bed. The springs squeak from his weight when he hits the mattress. *My* mattress.

"Get up!" I yell. "That's not what I want."

He lifts an eyebrow. "You know, that tone would make half the guys in the cellblock salute you. The other half would go after you."

I wonder which half he would have belonged to.

"Stay up there," he continues. "It's safer." He places his hands behind his head. I step back, away from my brother and that threat. I should have known I would never win against him.

Even Mom is quiet during dinner. Lamont grabs a second piece of the steak she cooked and bites down hard, caveman style. I move my fork through my food, not very hungry and feeling no need to swallow. Rochelle is the only one who doesn't seem to feel the thick, ropy tension swirling around the table.

"Your parole officer called," Mom says. "He wants you to come to his office at one o'clock tomorrow."

Lamont shrugs, clearly not surprised. "The harassment begins," he says gruffly.

"He has to do his job," Mom says, her voice still calm.

"Just follow the rules. That's your ticket to staying out of prison," she says.

Lamont suddenly looks as uninterested in food as I am. "All that man does is hand me a cup to fill."

My sister, Miss Curiosity, looks up. "What did you put in his cup?"

"Juice," I say quickly, biting back a laugh at the thought of Lamont peeing in a cup for a drug test. He throws me a shaky smile of gratitude. Mom covers her mouth, but I hear the laughter.

"Orange juice or apple juice?" Rochelle asks next.

"Orange," I say, knowing she hates orange juice.

"Apple," my inexperienced brother answers at the same time. If she asks another question, he's on his own. I don't intend to explain drug tests to a four-year-old.

Rochelle blinks and looks from my face to his. Then she holds her empty cup out to him. "I'm thirsty. Please fill mine too."

I laugh, but I'm surprised and a little disappointed Rochelle accepts him so easily. She even giggles when Lamont goes to the fridge and returns with her juice.

I don't forgive like that. She may be too little to remember stuff, but I can't forget.

Ever.

• • •

Just before bedtime, I take my phone to the bathroom. There I slide down the wall and sit on the cold floor. I have to wait until my fingers stop shaking before I can manage to type.

Me: *Lamont is here.*

I send that message to Malik and wait.

Mom says I can't bother Malik too much. College and basketball take up a lot of his time.

Before he left for college, though, he told me I could contact him anytime, for anything.

It only takes a few minutes for him to respond.

Malik: *Hey T. How'd that happen?*

I can't fit the full answer to his question in a text. I take a deep breath before typing,

Me: *Early release, good behavior or something, I guess.*

Malik: *Are you holding up? Do you need anything?*

I'm scared, I type in a rush. Then I pause and stare at the send button. The truth is I'm not scared or apprehensive or nervous, anxious, petrified, or any of the vocabulary words I've learned. I open my pictures file and pull up one of the two of us, taken just before he left for the University of Illinois. Malik is smiling, confident, a black man who is going places. He's a big-time, important basketball player, and the Fighting Illini are on the hunt for a play-off berth. I know he'd come if I asked. But I can't ask. This is not important enough.

I erase those words and type out a new message.

Me: *I'll hang tough.*

Then I hit Send and turn off my phone.

Dressed in the oversize Black Lives Matter shirt and a pair of shorts I use for pajamas, I return to the bedroom. Lamont's chest is bare, revealing an updated version of his iron-hard custom body.

"You've been working out," I say while rubbing my flat stomach. He's got a six-pack; I'm running on empty.

"I had plenty of time for that. You can sit and think for only so long. Of course, I also had to attend anger management sessions."

"Did those work for you?" My heart jumps. What if he really changed? Maybe I have a real brother again.

He looks me over, eyes narrowing. "What do you think?" He flicks a towel at me, snapping me hard in the back before padding down the hall in bare feet for his turn in the bathroom.

I think I'm in trouble.

I grip the ladder, take a deep breath, and force myself to climb to the top. I sink bonelessly on the mattress and pull the blanket over my chest. I lie on my back and stare at the too-close ceiling. Resolute. I remember the word from my vocabulary lesson. I'm not scared; I am resolute. He's not the only one who is older and stronger. He may live here now, only a few feet away from me, but he doesn't get to suck me down his dark hole again.

CHAPTER
NINE

MY ALARM GOES OFF THE next morning at six thirty. I sit up and bump my head on the ceiling. The pain reminds me where I am, so I don't leap out into the darkness the way I normally do.

Mom is already gone, headed for the CTA Red Line train to take her to work downtown. Her commute to the Loop takes almost an hour.

My job is taking care of Rochelle in the mornings. Mom trusts me, and I feel proud. I get my little sister dressed and fed and then take her across the courtyard to Mrs. Kanady in building number four. She does day care in her garden apartment. Rochelle stays there until Mom returns from work and picks her up.

"What are you doing up so early?" Lamont mumbles as I climb down the bunk ladder.

"I have work to do. Do you think life happens by magic?"

He merely grunts. I dress and leave him in the dim light from the rising sun.

Rochelle loves fancy clothes, with lots of bows and lace. Some days she gets picky, but today she agrees to the pale gray sweater trimmed in black lace and beaded jeans Mom chose for her last night. She brings a doll to the table and pretends to feed her from the pancakes I make.

Lamont wanders in mid-breakfast and leans against the wall with arms folded across his chest. His shirt-sleeves are so tight they barely contain his biceps. He rubs the small scar on his forehead, his eyes flickering from me to Rochelle and the doll.

"I have pancakes shaped like bunnies," Rochelle says with her mouth full of pancake and pieces of the banana I used to make ears and nose.

"I see," Lamont says, smiling.

The landline rings. I jump—I've almost forgotten what the home phone sounds like. It hardly ever rings and never in the morning. I lift the receiver and hear an impatient male voice say, "Lamont, you there?"

"Who are you?" I ask. There is something oddly familiar about the voice.

"Get Lamont," the unknown voice insists. "I know he's there."

"You can't call here." I turn to glare at my brother as I speak.

Lamont lifts the phone from my hand and says, "Yeah?" His voice is cautious but firm. "I just got here. Give me a break." A pause while he listens and nods. "Yeah, I got it. Don't worry, that was only my brother."

Only!

"Who was that?" I ask as he hangs up the phone and heads back to the bedroom.

"Nobody," he answers without looking back. I guess that means it was one of his gang friends checking up on him. I glance at Rochelle, who continues eating. She can remain unconcerned by our family drama. I can't.

"Was that Darnell, maybe, or Cisco or . . ." I can't remember all the names of the guys who hung with him two years ago. "You have to stay away from gang members—all of them. That's part of the rules. You can't go back to the old days." *I* can't go back.

He turns around and walks back into the kitchen, shaking his head. "Darnell is still inside."

"Oh. I thought, since they let you out, he'd be out too."

I shake with relief. Darnell is older than Lamont, nastier, and really seemed to hate the whole world. He especially hated taking orders from Lamont.

"It doesn't work like that. I got out because . . ." He pauses. "Doesn't matter."

"How did this guy know you were here?" I ask.

"Someone always knows things. For the right price, you can get them to tell you." He stares at me as he speaks. I'm not sure if that is a warning or some kind of threat.

I turn back to Rochelle. "Come on," I say, pulling her away from the table.

"I'm not finished yet," she complains. I wait while she stuffs the last two bites from her plate into chipmunk cheeks, then lift her from her chair to her feet.

After wiping syrup from her mouth, I point her toward her room. "Get your backpack. It's time for school."

"Hurray!" she squeals, instantly obedient at the thought of getting back to one of her favorite places. I start cleaning the dishes.

"Why does she go to school? She's only three," Lamont says as she disappears down the hall.

"She's four, but I guess that's easy for you to forget. Rochelle likes it when I call her day care school. It makes her feel more grown-up."

"What about you?" he asks. "I used to think school was all boring and bogus, phony stuff. They never taught anything important. Do you like all those lectures and homework and the stuff teachers keep trying to cram down your throat?"

"I love school."

"Love? You have changed," he says softly.

"You bet I have," I say as Rochelle returns dressed in a denim jacket, with one strap of her bunny backpack on her shoulder.

"I'm ready," she says, jumping up and down. "Hurry, T. Let's go!"

"Just a minute," I say. "I have to finish cleaning the dishes."

"I can do that." Lamont steps forward.

"This is *my* job." I don't trust him to help. I don't trust him at all. I stare at my brother until he backs off. He thrusts his hands in his pockets and heads back to the bedroom.

I really do need only another minute or two before I am done. Then I straighten Rochelle's pack on her shoulders, grab my own stuff, and lead her out the door. After leaving her at Mrs. Kanady's, I start for school. Lamont is also leaving, trudging down the street with his head bent, hands deep in his pockets. Heading off to meet his phone friend, I guess. "Keep it up," I murmur at his retreating back. If he spends his time hanging with his gang buddies, Mr. Cho will have him back in prison real soon.

My school is five blocks from my building. I pass a construction site on the way. Several new houses are being erected on a once-vacant lot, and a bunch of construction workers mill around. More houses will mean more families, and that's a good thing. Another construction project is under way a few blocks in the opposite direction, near a park where I sometimes go to play. A sign at that spot identifies the place as the future home of a new grocery store from a major chain. Mom and I will finally have a place to buy food close to home. No more taking a bus to shop in one of the big grocery stores in another neighborhood, then slugging with the bags back home on the bus. Even in good weather, it's hard. In winter, shopping is miserable.

There is another open lot between me and school. No construction here, and no junk or debris litter the ground. Rocks have been moved away, and grass grows in thick, green clumps. More than a dozen old men and women—and Dontae—are on the grass performing morning tai chi. Nothing stops this group from performing their daily ritual. Today, one old man even wears a short-sleeved shirt along with a look of steely concentration. Members of the group move slowly, all at the same time, like some gentle flash mob without music.

Dontae waves when he sees me. He finishes a few more moves, waves goodbye to the others, and grabs his backpack from the ground before rushing to me.

"Take a drink," I remind him as we resume our walk to school. He groans but pulls a water bottle from his pack and drinks deep.

"I didn't expect to like tai chi so much," he says as we walk. "But it's better than all those experimental meds the doc wants me to take. Better than the yoga mess my mom tried pushing me into."

"You just like being with old people." I grin.

"Well, yeah. I mean, they're nice. Not one of them is a bully, and some are interesting. Speaking of bullies, how was your first night with your brother?"

I shrug. "I'm still alive."

Dontae nods. "Well, that's good."

"And I'm sleeping on the top bunk." My voice hitches when I admit that. Lamont pushed and I caved, a memory that makes me angrier every time it whirls through my brain.

"Ouch." Dontae shakes his head sadly. "I guess he's not as smart as we thought."

"No. He's way smarter." I'm not worried about my brother trying to hurt me while I sleep—that was never my real concern about his return. The feeling that tugs at my heart is fear that he's going down a destructive path again. Fear that I'll be sucked down with him all over again if I don't keep pushing him away.

CHAPTER
TEN

WE CONTINUE OUR WALK TO school through the heart of our neighborhood. This part of Chicago is not a stop on any tourist excursion. We have parks and shops and a few small museums, like the Bronzeville Children's Museum on 93rd Street. Rochelle loves visiting that place the way I like going to the Pullman Porter Museum. They both reveal a history experience different from the stuff the Hun hands out in class. I guess tourists to Chicago don't want to see them or anything else in our neighborhood. We have some great block festivals in the summer, but not even the scent of food and sound of music filling the air are enough to coax people into dropping their fears and coming by to see what we have to offer.

We arrive at school, and Dontae and I take our seats in class as the Hun walks in. "Morning, everybody," he says. I try to concentrate on the lesson, but Lamont won't stop popping around inside my head. That makes it hard to think and concentrate on my schoolwork. The day drags until the bell rings announcing the lunch period. Dontae walks next to me as we head down to the cafeteria. Linda walks a little in front of us.

I first met Linda two years ago, but I didn't know much about her until we ended up in the same seventh-grade classroom. I just knew what everyone does. She was eight when her parents divorced. Her mother took out an Order of Protection against her father, but he was so angry, no piece of paper could stop him. Barnetta, Linda's older sister, found their mother dead on the kitchen floor. At least I had time to tell Dad goodbye. As bad as it felt watching the cancer eat at him as he slowly grew weaker and fainter and finally faded away, I'm glad I had those last weeks. Linda woke one morning to find her mother already dead and her father arrested by Carmela's dad.

Linda and I were both in the courtroom with our families the day Lamont was sentenced. Barnetta had been working at Frank's Place when the gang tried to rob the place. She made a short victim statement. Then it was Mr. Frank's turn. The restaurant's owner stood with his arm in a sling and fresh stitches on his face. His victim statement went on forever, cold, angry words that made Mom cry. Linda never looked at me that day.

She stops, waiting for me to catch her near the cafeteria entrance. "Hey, T, Carmela asked me to ask you why you haven't joined the Racing Rays yet." I'm surprised. Carmela usually picks Fantasia to carry her messages.

"I, uh, I changed my mind," I say.

"I don't believe you. Did you know Mr. Hundle is in charge of the swim team?"

"Seriously?" Our Mr. Hundle? Whoa!

"Carmela says he's listed as a managing partner. I think his father started it or something. Yesterday, when I went to practice to watch her, I heard him say he wished more students from the school where he teaches would join. Carmela's the only one."

"Linda," Carmela calls from the lunchroom door, her voice sharp. I realize Linda and I have stopped moving, and everyone else is inside.

"Do you like Carmela?" Linda asks me, making no move to go join her friend.

"Everyone likes her."

"But why do you like her?" Linda insists.

"Because." I like Carmela because . . . There must be dozens, maybe even hundreds of reasons. But with Linda staring at me through brown, knowing eyes, nothing comes into my head right now except, "I like her name."

"Yeah." Linda nods like she expected that. "It's not ordinary, that's for sure."

"Nothing about her is ordinary. And she's a good swimmer too."

"She's not the only good swimmer," Linda says, her voice suddenly harsh.

"You swim too?" I ask another dumb question. "Then why don't you join?"

Linda shakes her head. "You should know."

I look down. How many dumb questions is a guy allowed in one day? She and I have the same problem: money. Her aunt lives on Social Security disability payments. They have less than my family does. "If Mr. Hundle wants kids from our neighborhood to join his team," I say, "why make things cost so much?" Managing partner sounds like he runs things. That means he could let anyone in if he wanted to. Linda and even me.

"Linda!" Carmela calls again, and stomps her foot.

"I have to go," Linda says, but she doesn't move or even turn to look at her friend.

"Why are *you* friends with her?" I ask. Carmela and Linda are so different. I don't understand why they hang together. "You're smarter than she is. Nicer too."

Linda gives me a long, silent stare. "I know she's bossy and controlling and determined and lots of other things. After my mom was killed . . . Well, I wanted to die too. Carmela's dad helped me get help. And she became like a sister, staying with me, talking to me, helping me get over things. I could talk to Carmela. We may not always be best friends, but that doesn't change the ties between us."

We could be friends, I almost say.

"Maybe part of our friendship is because she likes being around people who make her shine. I'm happy to do that."

"You shine pretty good yourself."

She blinks and seems unable to speak for a moment. When she does talk again, her voice breaks a little. "Mr. Hundle really likes you. Maybe if you talk to him, he could show you a way to get in. Just ask. Anything is possible." With those words, she turns and runs after Carmela.

I remain in the hall. Maybe she's right.

I take a deep breath and reverse directions, heading upstairs to the teachers' offices on the second floor.

CHAPTER
ELEVEN

I'VE BEEN IN MR. HUNDLE'S office before, but this is the first time I notice the swimming trophies on one shelf. He doesn't seem to notice me at first. His big shoulders are hunched as he sits bent over a computer keyboard.

I am not sure how to start. I take a breath, clear my throat, and begin. "Excuse—"

"I'm not changing your grade," he says without lifting his head.

"Um, I got a ninety-eight on the last history quiz."

That makes him look up. "Oh, yes, T'Shawn. You were tied for the highest grade. Congratulations."

"*Tied?* Who else got a ninety-eight?"

He leans back in his chair and chuckles. "I don't share student grades. But I like your competitive spirit."

Linda, I think. She and I are always fighting for the top spot. "Actually, I'm here because of the Racing Rays. The swim team that practices at the community college. I heard you were in charge." I point to a trophy on the shelf.

"Yes," he says, crossing his arms. "It was my father's passion. He started the club six years ago. Then I took over when he retired last year. I competed in both freestyle and butterfly when I was younger. Now I'm part of the board." He sounds a little sad. No, wistful: that was the vocabulary word from last month.

"Did you make it to the Olympics?" I ask, voicing my secret dream.

He chuckles again. "Not even close, although these arms set a few records and earned a full ride to college. My father worked in an athletic supply store. I'd never have been able to afford college without a scholarship."

He gestures for me to come closer. "It sounds like you might be interested in becoming a competitive swimmer. What's your stroke?"

"Actually, I want to be a diver."

He nods. "Even better. Mr. Mung, our diving coach, needs more kids your age for his program."

"I hear you don't have many students from here on your team," I say, watching his face carefully.

"Only one. I'd hoped for more. The location makes for an easy commute."

"But the costs don't make anything easy." It's time to ask the big question. He has to know there isn't much money around here. I take a deep breath and continue. "I could be number two from this school if there is maybe some kind of scholarship to pay the fees or something."

"Oh." His face goes blank like a door slamming shut. "I'm afraid not. The Racing Rays are a private club, and we have significant costs. Our goal is to create swimmers and divers prepared to compete at the highest levels, and that takes money. We hire top coaches and have expenses associated with participating in invitational- and championship-style meets. We don't receive any funding from the state, so every member has to pay their own way."

"But you could squeeze one kid in, right?" I lean close and do my best sad-puppy imitation.

"I'm sorry, T'Shawn. I don't have the authority." His voice is kind and sympathetic but full of no.

"Aren't you in charge?"

"It's a family business. I'm part of the governing board, along with my uncles and my sister. Every penny is important. They would never agree to a team member who doesn't pay his way. The club is barely breaking even now; I've put a ton of my own money into things to keep my father's dream going. You have no idea how much we pay to rent the facility, for good coaches, for . . . Sorry." He takes a deep breath. "You don't need to have the details dumped on you. I apologize. This isn't an economics lesson."

No, it's a reality check. It sounds like he and the club have the same money issues as my family. Hope melts and runs down to my shoes. "I get it. Only rich people should apply."

The Hun smiles wanly and remains silent as I walk out.

When I arrive home after school, I head for my room, which is empty. There's no sign of Lamont. Good.

I pull out a set of geometry work sheets and settle down at my study desk. I like school, even math, but we're starting to work on geometry. Geometry is— Well, I call it a challenge. For challenges, my brain needs the special help only the right music brings. I have set my own iTunes playlists with my favorite artists, each playlist designed for a different mood or task. I choose songs from Florida Georgia Line. Dontae laughs at me, but I love the two guys in that country duo. For me, they make music to calculate by. Maybe it's the chords and patterns in the music or the voices and the way country weaves spoken and melodic verse together. Whatever. I have put together the perfect playlist for geometry. I don't think I could find the surfaces and areas of the crazy shapes on my work sheets without the help of these sounds.

An hour goes by, and I'm deep into studying circles and calculating with pi when Lamont walks in. His feet drag.

"Where have you been?" I ask.

"Job hunting. Isn't that all people want from me?"

"How did things go?"

Lamont grips his throat and sticks out his tongue like a cartoon character choking himself.

"That good, huh?" I have to laugh. He should try changing clothes next time. Wearing old jeans and a stained T-shirt, he might be accepted as one of the guys. But hired . . . no way. I did a school report on jobs last year. The research taught me that the unemployment rate here in Illinois is higher than the national average. Chicago unemployment is higher still. And down here, on Chicago's South Side, the unemployment rate is astronomical. People line up outside hardware stores hoping someone with a do-it-yourself project might not want to do it all by himself.

"Once you have a past, hiring managers stare through you, leaving you with no good job choices." My brother kicks off his shoes and throws himself on the bed, one arm behind his head, the other covering his eyes.

"If you can't find a good choice, then take a bad one," I suggest.

"You sound like Cho."

"Just because I sound like your parole officer doesn't mean I'm wrong."

"Do you know how many guys around here are like me? Nothing to do and nowhere to go." He jumps back to his feet, staring at me through tight lips, as if I were an enemy. "I'm not the only guy who's been in trouble, made a few wrong choices. But here's what happens." He steps in the middle of the room, shoulders back, chin up like a stage performer in front of an audience. "No sir, I've never been to college, but I do have a GED. No, it's not a high school diploma, it's a certificate, and it's supposed to be just as good. From where? Oh, I finished my education in prison. Yes, I said prison. . . . Of course, I understand. I won't call you, and you definitely will never call me." He slumps, the performance over. He no longer looks like the self-named King of the World. But something about him remains strong and powerful. Scary, even. Maybe that's part of the reason he can't get a chance.

He moves to the window, hands on his hips, staring out at the world, apparently lost inside his thoughts. There's just him and me and music from Florida Georgia Line streaming from my phone. They are singing about a man surveying the countryside searching for a chance at something better. Change the countryside to a Chicago building courtyard, and the words could be about my brother.

Lamont turns away from the window, frowning and pointing at my phone. "That's country music. Why are you listening to some guy wailing about his dog or his truck or whatever?"

"It's not some guy. They're famous. Florida Georgia Line have lots of country music awards."

"Like I said, country music."

"I don't care. They're great. And I like trucks."

"Look in the mirror, Short Stack. This is not *our* music."

"Music is music. It belongs to everyone. Plus, if white people can listen to J-pop or reggaetón or rap, I can listen to country when it helps me. I get to choose what I like and who I like. You don't know me. You don't care. This is my room. You're just squatting in it. I can play what I want." I try to sound strong, but my voice squeaks a little.

His eyes flicker and my heart jumps. Is he going to hit me? "Not tonight." He grabs the phone and closes the iTunes app. In the silence, his words loom large. "You have no business listening to that, and I'm too tired to keep arguing, Short Stack. You don't know what a bad time I'm having right now."

"What about the bad time I'm having?"

"Why are we arguing about this? Just play something good. It doesn't have to be rap. I'd even take some jazz or blues."

"I can't do math to a blues playlist." Between my anger and the growing silence, I can't even think right now.

He picks up my unfinished work sheet and shakes his head. "Geometry, eh? No one ever cares about a hypotenuse or Pythagoras in real life. I only remembered any of this long enough to pass a test, and then poof, it was gone."

Poof is right. The word explains why he's still stuck on stupid. Bet he wouldn't even remember what a hypotenuse was if the word wasn't written on the page.

"Do you know where I should be right this second?" I ask. "Not here, hurting your poor, precious eardrums with music. I need to study and keep my grades up and actually become something. But right now, I should be at the pool, on the swim team. Only I can't, because you get everything. Your food, your clothes, even these stupid beds cost money, and I have to sleep on top because of you, and I hate being up there."

He flinches. His eyes narrow, his jaw clenches, making him appear less than two steps away from a monster explosion. I'm inside the blast radius, but I don't care! I want to hurt him.

He turns and walks to the window, where he stands, his back toward me, staring out at the world. "If you wanted the lower bed, why didn't you say so?"

Because you said it wasn't safe.

I blink, trying to force back tears I feel pooling in my eyes. It's like we are two enemies in this room instead of two brothers.

Maybe we're both.

"We'll talk about this another day," he mutters after a few moments, his voice so low I almost miss hearing the words. I know the truth. We won't talk, not tomorrow or the next day or ever. He'll order me around and expect me to obey. I'll fight again and then end up being overwhelmed again. I push away from the desk and run from the room because dumb tears are racing down my face.

Rochelle is in the hall, standing in front of me.

"Are you hurt, T?" she asks, gazing into my eyes like

Mom does when I am sick. I wish she wasn't here to see me like this. Next time I need to cry, I'll use a closet.

"No, I'm fine," I say, wiping my cheeks. "There's just something I wish I could have, only no matter how hard I try to get it, I can't."

"If at first you don't succeed, you just have to try real hard." Rochelle repeats Mom's favorite saying with an earnest expression that makes her look just like our mother.

"You don't understand," I say.

"Try!" she insists, flapping her hands in the air. I kneel, pull her close, hug her tight, and wonder if I ever believed the way she does, that wishing my hardest could make miracles happen.

She looks around me at the door and suddenly says, "You better go away! You made my real brother cry."

Turning, I see Lamont staring at both of us. He swallows but doesn't move.

"I don't like you." Rochelle pulls free and stamps her feet. I grab her again to keep her from throwing herself at him. "Go away. Leave my T alone."

He looks at us hard, shakes his head, and turns to go. "Stay here," I tell Rochelle before I follow him back to our room. He grabs a jacket from the closet. Then he pushes past me and Rochelle on his way to the front door.

Mom steps out of the kitchen to ask, "Lamont, where are you going?"

"I need some air," he says.

"But it's almost dinnertime," she pleads to his back. He's already out the door and racing down the staircase so he can't see the worry in her eyes.

"Did I make him go?" Rochelle asks.

"No, I did that," I say. I won't let her blame herself for any of this. I grab her and swing her through the air until she dissolves into giggles. The truth is I don't know what's going on inside my brother's head. I don't understand him.

I barely understand myself.

CHAPTER
TWELVE

WHEN I WAKE UP, THE world is quiet. Sunlight fills the room, and a glance at the clock shows it's after seven. I bolt upright, throw off the blankets, and jump to the floor. What happened to my alarm?

Lamont's bed is empty. A quick glance out the window shows a dusting of snow fell last night. Chicago weather is as undependable as he is.

I rush for Rochelle's room, still in my pajamas, expecting to hear her complaining because I'm late and she's hungry. Her room is empty too.

I follow the smell of bacon and eggs into the kitchen. Lamont is up and dressed in a white T-shirt and black jeans. Rochelle is there too, sitting at the table pretending to feed her doll. Today's fashion choice includes a pink sweater over orange-and-blue polka-dot pants.

"What are you doing?"

"Breaking my fast," he says while shoveling food into his mouth. His shirt makes the muscles under his dark skin look even more intimidating. Watching him makes me sick, and the feeling worsens when I see what he put on the plate in front of my chair. Two big yellow, runny, sunny-side up eggs. His favorite food.

"How could you give her something like this?" I yell. "She doesn't eat runny eggs."

"Eggs don't usually get people this upset," Lamont says, his voice so calm, hearing him only makes me madder.

"You turned off my alarm."

"I thought you needed a little more sleep. Are you that mad because I tried to give you a break?" He winks, grinning like I'm supposed to be grateful or something.

I'm mad for so many reasons I don't know how to reply. Things like, "You stole my job taking care of Rochelle," seem too petty to say out loud. I tell myself I don't want to argue where Rochelle will overhear and get hurt. Maybe I do feel better for the extra half hour, but this is totally *my* job. He had no right to take it from me.

"Note to self," he mutters. "Short Stack no longer likes sleep."

I glance at Rochelle. She continues nibbling on bacon and toast and isn't paying us any attention. "Are you planning to disappear, go away, and leave us again?" I whisper. "Do you have another place to live? Do you still want to run away to Memphis?"

He jerks. "You remember that?"

"How'm I supposed to forget? You talked me into running away and told me I needed to man up when I didn't want to go with you."

"I suppose something like that would burn itself into your memory." He pauses. "Memphis is still an option," he says finally. "I know people there."

"By people you mean gang members, don't you? That's a bad option. Leaving the city means breaking parole."

"Yeah, well, I won't always be on parole," he says.

"When will I be free?"

"I?" He swings around and stares at me.

"You. I meant you," I try correcting. I have to stop saying my thoughts out loud.

He stares at me. "No, I think you said exactly what you meant. Soon, little brother. I'll get you your freedom real soon."

It's a promise that sounds a lot like a threat.

• • •

At school, my day goes from bad to really bad. Someone must have shoved peanut butter in the clock, but eventually the bell sounds and it's time for lunch. I grab my things and rush for the door. I'm only one step away from the hall when I hear the Hun say, "Can I have a word with you, T?"

"Uh, I'm hungry. It's lunchtime, and I have to get to the cafeteria if I'm gonna find a seat."

"I only need a few minutes."

This is going to be bad. Teachers aren't supposed to interfere with a student's lunch period. I think it's some kind of law or something. So this must be really, really super bad. I arrived unprepared and zoning out a few times while he talked. I could blame the stranger in my room, but really, it's all on me. My mind is everywhere except on my work. Dontae throws me a look of sympathy as I reverse direction and walk to the teacher's desk.

"Am I in trouble or something?" I ask once the room empties out.

"You seem to be losing focus lately," the Hun says. "The other teachers have said the same thing. Are you okay? Are there problems at home?"

"I'm fine," I say, and he nods acceptance. The truth is sometimes when I claim to be fine, I want someone to look me in the eyes and say, "Tell the truth." But it never happens.

The Hun drums his fingers on his desk. "You have real potential, T'Shawn. In more ways than one. But you need to keep yourself focused."

"I'm sorry. I'll do better. Can I go now? I mean, I'm really hungry." I rub my stomach to show how empty I feel. I'm glad I'm standing so my feet won't tap. I don't need to hear him lay the "work up to your potential" speech on me. Teachers say that all the time and never explain what it means except do more work.

"Actually, I have an offer for you." The Hun clears his throat and begins pulling papers from his briefcase. "The Racing Rays organization is dedicated to the nurturing and growth of future competitors. We practice four times a week: Monday, Wednesday, and Friday afternoons, and Saturday mornings. If you can handle that, then give these to your mother to sign, and you become a Racing Ray."

"What?" A band tightens around my chest. I think I might stop breathing in a minute. I grab the papers. They are the same swim-club forms I saw before, but the payment amount fields are all marked zero dollars. "I don't understand. You said there weren't any scholarships."

"Yes, well, I decided that desire and drive should

count for something, and I went to the board," he says without looking me in the eye. "We came up with some discretionary funding."

"I don't know what that is," I admit.

"Money for special projects. Congratulations, T. You're a special project."

I'm in.

I'm a Racing Ray.

"I—I don't know what to say. Thanks, I guess." My tongue stumbles over the words.

The Hun smiles. "Now, I don't want you spreading news about this scholarship to other team members, and that includes Carmela Rhodes. They won't understand. The other coaches know, and your mother will need to know, but let's leave it at that."

I can't even tell Dontae. He'd tell everyone.

"You should get your lunch now," he says. I start out the door. "Oh, and one last thing."

I turn and look at him. "Yes?"

"I'll expect another ninety-eight on your next assignment."

I grin. "You'll see a hundred, I swear."

I love this man.

CHAPTER
THIRTEEN

A WEEK LATER, I ONCE again step into the boys'
locker room at the community college. This time things
are different. During Family Time, the place swarms with
lots of people like me. I hear familiar sounds now: the
clang of metal doors opening and closing, bodies bumping into one another, burping, and fart jokes. Instead of
laughing fathers and joking sons, this afternoon brings a
whiff of over a dozen muscled bodies. The few pine air
fresheners hanging from the ceiling don't have a chance
against the odor.

The guys I see joking as they undress are all older
than me. None seem like ordinary people—you know,

guys with clothes from Walmart or Goodwill, wearing old discolored sneakers or carrying patched gym bags like the one I cradle against my chest. This is one of those trendy, Abercrombie & Fitch–type crowds. Something creepy scrambles around my insides. These guys all know some secret password that grants them entry to a different world, one where I'm a forever outsider.

I take a deep breath. I am T. I deserve to be here.

One guy looks up, sees me, and taps another on the shoulder. Soon all of them are staring at me.

"What are you looking at?" the first guy barks as he pulls royal-blue trunks over his pale white legs. He has an accent. New York, I think, or maybe Boston.

"Nothing," I say in a voice that squeaks.

"Oh, man, he got you," another voice declares. He is tall and blond, much older than me, with the name Bishop embroidered on the side of his warm-up jacket.

"No, no, that's not what I meant." Another step backward, and I slam into the wall. I feel cold. These guys are all big, all wearing the same royal-blue swim trunks with matching warm-up jackets across their shoulders. The glossy material reflects the overhead lights. I know this is a club, not a gang, but right now it feels like I'm surrounded by gang members trying to decide if I deserve to become one of them. I look at the only other black guy in the group. He shrugs as if telling me I'm on my own.

"What's your stroke?" Bishop asks.

"He's too puny for butterfly," the Ray beside him says.

"Uh . . . I'm not a swimmer. I'm a diver. I mean, I'm going to be a diver."

"Mung meat," Bishop says, and several others chortle.

"I'm T'Shawn Rodgers," I add. "But people call me T."

An excited voice booms, "You made it!"

I turn and find Sammy running across the locker room in high-top sneakers, pushing his way through the much bigger guys to get to me. I almost jump up and down in relief, knowing I'm not alone anymore.

He grabs my arm and begins pulling me away. "Come on, take a locker near me." With a wave, he indicates a different section of the locker room. There are only a few boys in that corner, all younger and smaller than the ones in the main group.

As I strip down to my trunks, he says, "It's been weeks since you talked about joining. I thought you changed your mind."

"No way. I just, um, had to work out some details with my mom."

"Yeah, moms can be strange," he says with a weird grimace.

A new voice orders people to finish dressing and leave the locker room. I pull my faded jacket back on over my bare chest, slam my locker shut, and start following the others.

Sammy grabs my arm. "You're gonna need your shoes." He's still wearing his sneakers. So are the other guys around us.

"Why? Aren't we going in the water?" I ask. Dontae promised to come and watch me today. He has to see me in the water.

"Yeah, but we have conditioning first. The coaches have this place reserved for us for the first half hour." Sammy leads the way to a glass door marked Fitness Room. The air smells of sweat and rubber and more sweat. The girls are here too—more girls than boys are on the team.

We have a fitness center at school. There are no gleaming treadmills inside that tiny room. We have to run outside on the sidewalk, circling the school building. The center does have some free weights that the bigger guys use to show off with, some mats, and a stationary bike. I knew college would be different from grade school, but the gadgets in this place are, like, wow! I don't like exercise, but looking at the equipment here makes the idea inviting. Especially since this must be where Sammy gets his muscles. I rub the fleece sleeves of my jacket wondering how long before the magic of this place works on me.

Team members form a semicircle. Sammy leads me to a spot on the outer rim of the circle. I glance around, looking for Carmela, and see her standing across the way. We are the only black faces on the team: Carmela, the one black guy from the boys' locker room, and me. Except for Sammy, the rest are all white. I wonder if Carmela gets this all-alone-in-a-crowd feeling too. She stands straight, eyes wide, staring in the direction of the coaches. Probably not.

Mr. Hundle stands in the center of the circle, dressed in another of the gleaming team jackets. Two men and two women stand beside him, all white. Since I am supposed to be Mung meat, I want to know which one is Coach Mung, my guy. The man who will help me achieve my dreams.

The Hun looks around the room, using only his eyes to get, and hold, everyone's attention. "Good afternoon, Rays," he begins. "Since we have a new person starting today, I'll begin with introductions. T'Shawn Rodgers is a brand-new member of the diving group."

I reluctantly step forward and wave. Several guys snicker; most girls look uninterested. Carmela seems surprised. I step back beside Sammy quickly.

The Hun continues, "These are our coaches: Mr. James, Mrs. Henderson, Ms. Watson, and Mr. Mung."

I stare at the man I have to impress. Mr. Mung is at least six feet tall, with blond, almost white hair; blue eyes; and thin, tight lips that look like they forgot how to smile. He wears a white, short-sleeved shirt tucked into pants the same royal-blue shade as the Rays warm-up jackets. The other coaches all nodded at me when their names were called. Mung seems to stare right through me.

"What kind of coach is Mr. Hundle?" I ask Sammy.

"He's not really a coach; he's the guy in charge of everything, including dealing with the college and the boosters."

"What's a booster?"

"A super fan. You know, adults who raise funds, come to our meets and yell. Sometimes they throw cool parties. But mostly they get in the way. Mom's one of the worst. I mean, she's a really big fan. Anyway, Mung is our guy. He really knows his stuff." Sammy's voice shakes with the kind of hero worship I once felt for my brother. "Mom says Mung is one of the best coaches in the city. They both swam at Stanford together and competed in the NCAA. She has a load of trophies. She made my dad build a new trophy case for me. I've already begun filling it for her. They both come to every meet."

"Meet? What's that?"

Sammy rolls his big dark eyes, suddenly looking even younger than twelve. "You have a million questions."

I realize I've missed most of Mr. Hundle's speech when he claps his hands and says, "Okay, Rays, you know the drill. It's cardio time."

I don't know the drill, not until I see the other Rays scampering for different machines.

"Here, T'Shawn," Sammy calls. He rushes to a treadmill and points at an empty machine next to him. I climb on and begin walking. He laughs. "You can do better than that."

A few minutes later, my legs are shaky with fatigue. I have to struggle to keep going and not let anyone see how out of breath I am. Sweat skates down my back, my chest burns, and I wonder if this pain in my ankles is what Dontae feels during a sickle cell crisis.

Coaches walk around the room, talking, sometimes

nodding or patting team members on the back. The Hun acts differently here. There's no fun in his eyes, and he constantly types things into his tablet.

He stops in front of me. "I need your heart rate," he says.

"Must be about a thousand," I say between heavy breaths.

That makes him smile. "Not quite." He takes a reading from the instruments on the treadmill, including my heart rate, speed, and incline.

"I know I'm slower than anyone else."

"Don't worry: it's a baseline. This will track your development over time. That's what we look for—not where you begin but how you change. Improve." He updates his tablet, then asks, "How are you doing?"

"Fine." It's all I can manage. I'm not supposed to stop running. Actually, fast walking.

At least I am moving.

The coaches announce we can begin the cooldown before I collapse, but it's a close thing. So much sweat drips from my skin, I could have already been in the pool.

"Do we always start this way?" I ask Sammy as we file from the room. The coaches can't really expect us to actually have the strength to keep our heads above water after all this.

"There's no cardio at the next practice," he replies. Then, when I begin to relax, he points at different machines around the room and numerous weights racked up against one wall. "We alternate cardio with weight training."

Sammy walks over to the mats with a bounce, as if he could do another mile. "Come on, time for stretches." I take a shaky breath as he and I take adjacent mats, and we start doing stretches. These hurt almost as bad as the cardio. I'm supposed to contort my body into impossible positions that Sammy makes look easy.

Maybe I need to join Dontae in his morning tai chi.

"You're Rodgers, aren't you?" a male voice asks. I look up and see Coach Mung standing over me. There is a deep cleft in his chin, and his eyes, deep set under thick brows, are pulled tight as he looks me over.

"That's right," I say. "But you can call me T."

"Open up your abs, Rodgers," he barks, a big Adam's apple pulsing in his throat.

"Uh, how?" I have no idea what he means.

He sighs heavily. "You are supposed to have the basics down before you become a Ray. If you need beginner treatment, may I suggest you try playing around in a park-district pool in the summer? We are not a developmental club. Our goals are superior performance and competition, against the city's best. Our alumni dive for colleges across the country."

That's what I'm here for too.

He shakes his head before grabbing one of my arms and pulling it straight over my head and then backward.

"Ouch!" I feel like a burning knife is skewering my shoulder.

He releases me and steps back, a frown of contempt on his face. "You'll never be a diver without flexibility."

I rub my arm and remain silent. Talking too much can get a guy in trouble, and Coach Mung already seems unhappy with me.

It's not my imagination. I watch him with the others. He smiles when he helps them. Still no charisma, but he is totally friendly with Sammy and the other divers. Meaning it's just me he has a problem with. Maybe it's because I'm new. He has to get to know me first.

After the cooldown ends, we finally head for the pool. A cloud of humidity and chlorine blasts me in the face. The swimmers move to the left side of the pool, near the bleachers and the now-closed concessions area. Signs in front of four lanes read, Reserved for Racing Rays. Coach Mung calls for the divers to follow him. Sammy and six other Rays hurry after him toward the diving well, a separate pool near the rear of the aquatic facility.

I start to join them, but then I spot Carmela. I change directions and rush after her.

"Hey, I made it. I'm here," I say, stopping in front of her.

"That's . . . good." She barely looks up, busy stuffing her hair into a swimming cap. "What made you decide to join us?"

"You told me you wanted me to come. You said I had to join." How could she forget? She even sent Linda to check on me.

"Oh. And here you are. That's great," she says before turning her back on me. She jumps into the pool, joining one of the lanes where other Rays are already churning the water with quick strokes.

"No, wait." She can't just leave like I don't count.

"T, you have to go with your group!" the Hun yells. I see him up on the balcony with a bunch of other people, spectators. Mostly adults. But Dontae is there, and I see Linda sitting in the front row at the railing.

"Uh, okay," I mumble, nodding as I rush after the

group of divers gathered around Coach Mung beneath the three-meter board.

"You're late, Rodgers," he says, scowling, when I reach the group.

"I was trying to talk to—"

"You're new, so I'll give you one chance. I expect three things from my divers: desire, dedication, and discipline.

"Don't forget flexibility." *Ka-ching*. He'll be impressed because I remembered his words.

Mung's eyes narrow. He stares at me, long and hard, before turning his back on me and going back to the other divers.

"All right, people," he says. "What do you do before every dive?"

"PITA," Sammy and the others recite, all sounding equally bored.

Pita? Like the bread?

"And what does that stand for?" our coach continues.

Another unison chant: "Plan. Imagine. Think. Act."

The coach nods and points to the side of the pool. The divers head for the spot indicated.

Instead of following them, I ask, "What should I imagine?"

He stops and turns back to me, his mouth falling open as if he'd forgotten I was around. "Success," he says after a moment. "You make a plan and then visualize the successful completion of that plan in your mind's eye. Think and then act to make success happen."

"Uh, if I'm supposed to visualize, then shouldn't it be PVTA?"

"It's whatever I say it is, understand?" His eyes rake over me.

"Uh, yeah. So, are we going to dive now?" I point at the boards, eager to get to the main event and show off to Dontae and Linda.

"We'll begin with lineups. I want five good ones from you," Mung says.

"What's a lineup?"

The other divers look at me in surprise. But I really want to learn. All my teachers say ask questions—that if we don't know, we should never assume.

"Did you read the member handbook?" Coach Mung's face grows almost as pink as my sister's favorite pillow.

"Yeah." Some of it, anyway, so that's almost the truth. Okay, the first few pages, and I read that during the bus trip over here today, but that counts.

He shakes his head. "Did *he* put you up to coming here?"

"He? Do you mean the Hun?"

His brow wrinkles. "What are you talking about?"

"Mr. Hundle. He's my teacher."

"The Hun?" Mung's half-smothered laugh makes him seem younger and almost friendly. But the sound quickly grows into a growl. "Don't play dumb. You know who I mean, T'Shawn Rodgers." His voice lingers over my last name. "Your brother."

I freeze. He knows Lamont?

Why am I surprised? I should expect Lamont to cause me trouble. Chicago is a big city with millions of people, yet I can't escape my brother's shadow. Even when he's not around, Lamont messes things up for me. I wonder what he did to Coach Mung?

I say, "No one put me up to anything, and I wouldn't listen to Lamont if he tried. I want to learn to dive, that's all. Sammy said you were the best coach, and I believe him," I quickly add, because Mom always says you can catch flies with honey. Not that I want any flies, but I need this guy.

Mr. Mung grunts, but his face softens slightly. "Only hard workers survive here. If you have a problem doing

133

exactly what I say, you should go now. This isn't play-time."

"I'm here to learn, not play. I've been on the board before," I say.

"How strong is your core?"

"My core?"

Coach Mung pokes me in the stomach. One finger, but it hurts and makes me stumble backward. "You'll dive when you can handle that and prove you've mastered the fundamentals." His eyes bore into me like I'm suspect number one on a TV cop show.

"Yes, sir," I say, and feel myself shrink down to Rochelle's size.

"Now get to the side of the pool."

He walks away.

I turn to Sammy. "Is he like this with everyone new?"

Sammy shakes his head slowly. "He must be having a hard day. Just watch me, and do what I do."

Turns out a lineup means I stand on the side of the pool, clasp my hands together over my head, lean over, and fall in. "It's how we practice the entry," Sammy says after he does the first one.

One by one, my teammates assume the position, arms over their heads, bending over the water, and then falling in headfirst. Mung stands behind each of them as they go in, acting like a real coach. He nods at them after they complete a first lineup, even one who enters the water with his legs making a huge V shape. "Concentrate on keeping your legs together," he tells that diver. "Reach for the water," he says to another. Sammy gets an "Excellent job, son."

Then it's my turn. I lean over the side and let myself fall in. Everything happens fast. There's no time to think, just an instant in midair and then I'm under water. When I climb out of the pool, Mung shakes his head. "Pitiful."

No directions or comments. I turn to Sammy, who shrugs and looks embarrassed for me. Coach Mung turns his back and walks to stand with the next diver.

That's it?

I step back to the side to begin again. This time I'm going to get it right.

I try three more lineups. Each attempt brings another complaint from the coach but no assistance. For my fifth, and thankfully last, try, I work my brain, remembering everything I've heard him say to the others. Body straight, eyes on the water, legs together, toes pointed. But it's too much. I'm lost the instant my feet leave the deck. A second of confusion in the air, then smack! Belly flop. My chest really smarts, and my mouth fills with water when I hit.

"What was that supposed to be?" the coach asks when I surface, sputtering and choking. I look at his face, hoping for a sign of sympathy. I find only a twitch in his cheek that comes from fighting down laughter.

"I think I tried a little too hard," I admit. But I've finished the last one, at least for today.

Mung points at the side of the pool. "Go again."

I glance at Sammy and the other divers who have finished their lineups. They are gathering by the boards. "I finished five like you said."

"Not one of them was acceptable. Show me five more."

"Aw, come on, Coach," I whine. "I'll do better once I get on the board." This whole fall-off-the-side-of-the-pool thing feels phony. Maybe this is a wake-up exercise but not a real dive. I'm here for the good stuff, to do the fancy stuff. Real dives, not learning how to fall.

Coach Mung steps closer and lowers his voice. "Is everyone in your family this disobedient?"

I feel my face heat and lower my head. "I'm not my brother." Water drips from my hair onto the deck. I don't know why I feel so ashamed. I want him to like me. His approval, that's all. Instead, Lamont-size problems follow me everywhere.

"Get back to the side of the pool, and do as you're told." His voice is ice-pick sharp. I glance up at Dontae. He mimes falling asleep.

I trudge back to the edge and continue doing lineups for the next half hour. Climb out of the water. Fall into the water. Climb out again, without ever hearing a single "good job" from my coach. Sometimes he says things like "proper posture" or "core weakness" without explaining what I should do to change. Mostly he barely looks at me, spending his time guiding the other divers through moves that take my breath away. Especially Sammy, who really knows how to fly. I watch, openmouthed, as he glides down the board, hurdles high, and twists himself into a pretzel in midair before entering the water straight up and down. If I ever learn to twist and curl like he does, the rest of this will be worth it. That's why I don't chuck everything and leave. The hope that one day the twisty, flippy guy others stare at will be *me*.

I get no feedback from the coach. I can't even tell if I'm doing better or worse by the time practice ends and the Rays are dismissed. I could quit. Then I wouldn't have to see Mung's angry glare aimed at me ever again. No more cardio until I drop and no dealing with those weights. All I have to do is give up. . . .

No. Giving up is easy. I won't do that, not ever. I'm going to stick this out. No one makes me quit, and I won't hand Coach Mung an excuse to kick me off the team. I'll get past the boring exercises and the coach who yells at me for having bad form. I've started this. I'll finish it.

"He never even explained what I'm doing wrong," I say as Sammy and I head for the locker room. I ache; two hours of weight training and lineups have drained me. Meanwhile, my friend still seems to bounce.

"He's usually real good about breaking things down." Sammy shakes his head, looking bewildered by his hero.

"Did you ever have to do a whole day of lineups?"

"No way, I'd have gone crazy," Sammy admits. "But I have done about a thousand since I first started. Coach should have explained more."

"Look on YouTube. There are some good beginning diving videos posted," one of the girl divers says before entering her locker room.

I add checking YouTube to my other tasks. Those include my math that takes longer now that I can't listen to my music when Lamont is around. I'll finally have to listen to Mom and figure out how to get organized.

How is it fair that I have to learn diving online because my coach dislikes my brother? Coaches should be like teachers and not hate students, no matter who they are related to.

Sammy showers and dresses quickly, claiming he can't keep his mother waiting. I think he's really worried that I will keep asking questions about his hero Mung.

Dontae is waiting for me outside the locker room when I exit, so I'm not alone. "That was totally boring. I've watched more exciting chess matches," he says.

We leave the building together and head off campus to the bus stop. My new teammates are gone. Yet the campus is alive—students, mostly adults, arrive for evening classes. Mom took some business courses here to help her prepare to go back to work after Dad died.

A bus pulls away seconds before we arrive. I just couldn't make myself run. At least Dontae doesn't get angry at me for being so slow.

"Are you sure you really want to be part of this?" he asks while we wait. "I told you they were stuck-up. The people on the team look down on poor people. I bet that's the real reason for all those fees— to keep poor people out. Especially poor, black people."

"I'm not the only black kid on the team."

"Carmela and who else?"

"There's one boy, one of the high school guys. I don't know his name."

"Two other kids. Look, T, *we* don't do water sports."

"*I* do." And I'm going to prove him wrong, him and anyone else who thinks that way.

CHAPTER
FOURTEEN

MY SECOND PRACTICE IS TWO days later. This time I feel prepared. I read every page of the Racing Rays club handbook, from the concussion protocol to the pages on team etiquette. Plus, practice agendas, including the reasons for all the cardio and weight training and dry-land training, and details of other standard activities. There's so much stuff. I didn't know being in a swim team would be like taking another class.

Dontae decided he had better things to do than sit and be bored, so he isn't around. While Sammy has his parents to smile and wave at him, I have no one. At least not until I see Linda sitting at the top of the stands again. She waves at Carmela, then at me. I wave back and walk across the pool deck smiling.

"Is that your girlfriend?" Sammy asks.

"Nah, I don't need a girlfriend." If I did, it would be Carmela. Linda is okay, but quiet and way too smart.

"Keep your minds on long-term goals," Coach Mung tells us after weight training. "Unless you work hard, you won't become champions today, tomorrow, next week, or next month." He looks at me, and I can see he wants to add "or ever."

After the lecture, we start off our practice with more lineups. Thanks to the videos I watched on the computers in the school library during lunch period, I now understand a lot more about them. A dive has five components: approach, takeoff, elevation, execution, and entry. Lineups are about learning how to make a good entry. I got to study Jennifer Abel, a black, Olympic medal–winning, Canadian diver. I want to be just like her. Only not a girl. And not Canadian, since I'm an all-American boy. I'll be a black Chicago hero. Maybe someday kids will study my life and want to be just like me.

Each of the other divers perform their five lineups. I have to do ten before Coach Mung lets me move to board work and a new exercise, this one about elevation. According to the handbook, riding the board is a balance and control exercise that will "help you gain the height you need for success."

"Ten seconds," Mung tells us. "That's the maximum amount of time you'll have from the moment you begin your approach until you enter the water. Ten seconds— less if you don't achieve proper elevation." He bounces on the end of one of the one-meter springboards, facing us with his back to the water, jumping in the air and coming back down as he speaks. I watch him go higher and higher in the air. He owns the air space around the board. His eyes remain on us, and he never once glances at his feet or the board. Yet he never hesitates or misses a word.

"Elevation is your friend," he continues. "Height equals air time and translates into more time to do your tricks and still align yourself for entry."

Air time. Now that's what I'm talking about!

The first time I try the exercise, I barely leave my feet, hopping more than bouncing. But after a few turns on the board my confidence grows. Pretty soon I'm pushing down as hard as I can and getting real height when the springboard pushes back and propels me in the air. I circle my arms for lift and then land safely back on the board, pushing it down to begin the cycle again. This beats playing on a trampoline. I feel awesome getting so high and watching the room move around me.

When my time on the board ends, I bend my knees

and successfully dampen the springboard's movements so that it stops moving without me falling into the water. I feel a little dizzy, but I congratulate myself. Mung shakes his head at me when I climb down the ladder.

"I did it," I say, grinning and waiting for some sign of approval. Come on, Coach. Smile, nod, do something.

"You have no feel for the board." His lips remain tight, eyes narrow.

"What do you mean? I was getting good height." Why can't he give me a little praise? I felt right on the board. It spoke to me, through the soles of my feet all the way into my brain. The more I bounced, rode it, controlled it, the more I knew this was what I wanted to do.

"I don't understand why you even want to be part of this team." Mung's brows pinch together, like he expects me to say something more. "Wait for summer and go to one of the park-district pools and have fun. I'm sure you'll be happier playing around."

"I don't want to play," I tell him again. "I'm not pretending. I want to learn."

I walk to the side where the team keeps a cooler filled with bottled water. The place feels muggier than ever today, like the tropical house at Brookfield Zoo. I fish out a bottle and drink with my back turned to Mung. He's my coach. His opinion matters to me. But I won't let him bring me down.

As I drink, I turn around, facing the pool. Coach Mung and Mr. Hundle are talking. The Hun points at me. Mung shakes his head at first but eventually shrugs and slowly nods. After tossing the empty bottle in the recycling bin—I believe in saving the world from plastic—I turn to see Coach Mung standing behind me.

"What did I do now?" I ask.

"Get on the board. I want a forward dive in the layout position. If you're ready."

"Yes, sir! I am *soooo* ready." I will perform the most perfect forward dive in the history of anything. Carmela is in the water, churning up waves. My family is at home, and there's no Dontae. I should have made him come back today. He could have recorded this event on his phone. I'm finally going to get to do a real dive, and no one will see me. I climb on the board and stare at the spectators. Linda is still here. Someone will see my perfect dive.

"I want a complete dive, beginning with the approach!" Coach Mung yells. "You do know what that means?"

"I know," I mutter. I've watched the others and seen videos. The approach involves three long strides across the length of the board and a hurdle to the tip. It's math.

There's an equation for all this, but my mind doesn't need to know the exact formula right now. Not as long as my body knows how to solve it. I can't help looking at Mr. Hundle. My teacher lifts an encouraging hand from across the pool.

Closing my eyes, I plan my moves, from takeoff to entry. I visualize myself arching high in the air, my body under perfect control. Legs together, arms up, knees stiff, toes pointed, head back, eyes open, and then—wham! Clasped hands knife into the water, nice and clean, and, most important, painless.

Afterward, I'll bob to the surface, where my ears will ring from the applause of my teammates after my perfectly executed plan.

"We're waiting." Mung stands, arms akimbo, voice echoing over the water.

I shake my arms to loosen my muscles, look out at the water, and take the first step of my approach. The rough surface of the board scratches the soles of my feet.

Second step. As I build up speed I see a blur from the corner of my eye. It's Linda, out of her seat and running for the exit. Why?

Third step. The board bends under my weight. I refocus and concentrate on lifting my leg for the hurdle to the end of the board.

"You go, Short Stack!" an unwelcome voice booms.

Lamont?

My stomach performs a triple somersault with a twist.

My body does not. I miss the edge and go flying off, slamming into water that punishes me the way a concrete sidewalk punishes a falling skateboarder.

"Did it hurt? Are you dead?" Sammy asks, running to the side.

"Worst joke ever," I say, and climb from the water.

"Yeah, I know." Sammy nods, looking proud. "That dive was a total fail. Awesome. Any time your feet and butt hit the water at the same time you earn zero points."

"That didn't look too good, Short Stack." Lamont approaches the pool, holding out a hand like a concerned father. Sammy starts and stares at him, and I could almost swear some secret message seems to pass between them. It's almost like they know each other.

I climb out of the water and sputter, "You can't be here. Parents have to stay in the stands during practice."

"I'm not a parent."

"That makes it worse!" I try using my hard stare, but water falls from my wet hair into my face, ruining the effect. "What are you doing here?"

"I wanted to see what was going on."

"You wanted to make things worse. Congrats. What

do you imagine Coach Mung is thinking right now?" I'm wet and cold, and my teeth are chattering. I push him away. "You need to leave before you get me kicked out."

"I have a right to be here. And no one will kick you out, not over me," Lamont says.

"True. I'm more likely to kick you, Lamont," a female voice says.

The voice belongs to one of the older female Rays. I turn around and see an older teen girl with light skin. With her full lips, she could be African American or Latina or maybe mixed. She walks like a model and looks like she should be too smart to come near Lamont. Of course, even Rochelle should be too smart for that, yet she giggles every time he calls her Shelly.

"Who knew you'd find the nerve to show up near me?" she says, ripping off her blue swim cap as she approaches, revealing short, tightly curled brown hair. I haven't paid much attention to the swimmers on the team, but now that I look, this girl seems a little familiar.

Lamont's deep sigh sounds like a tired warrior about to make the ultimate sacrifice. "Oh, I'm deathly afraid of you, Harmony."

"You should be. I heard you were out, but you never contacted me." She moves closer to him, brown eyes flashing. "I sent you letters. All returned unopened. You never put my name on the visitor list, so I couldn't come to see you."

"I knew how your uncle would react if you tried to visit me."

"Uncle Bill doesn't control me," she says, but her voice now shakes.

"Uncle Bill?" I ask.

Sammy leans close to my ear. "Coach Mung is Harmony's uncle."

My coach is her uncle? That answers the question my brother wouldn't. Does he know everyone? I glance at Mung, whose back is turned as he talks to another diver.

"I did a lot of stupid things back then, didn't I?" Lamont says. "No wonder you don't trust me."

Suddenly I remember where I've seen this girl before. Years ago, the day Lamont taught me to swim. Harmony was at the beach, although I didn't know her then. Rocks and seashells scraped the bottoms of my feet as she talked with Lamont and tried to get him to leave the water. She got all in his face, smiling, giggling, and touching his chest; eyeing him like he was a rib slathered with barbecue sauce. I thought he would go off with her. Instead, he put his arm around me.

"This is your day, Short Stack," he told me, leaving her alone on the sand while he walked into the water with me.

"Get back to practice, Harmony," one of the swim coaches calls out.

Harmony turns and walks back to the swimming pool.

"That was harder than I expected," Lamont mumbles, rubbing the back of his neck and staring after her. "I thought she'd forget me."

I could have told him girls never forget. Even Rochelle remembers old dirt when she gets mad at me.

"Do you like her?" I ask.

"No way," he says, the words tumbling off his lips much too quickly.

"*Did* you like her?"

This time he waits for almost a minute before answering, "It's not that simple."

I hear Sammy yell my name.

"You better go," I say. "I don't want you around my friends."

My brother's eyes narrow into dangerous slits. He shoves his hands in his jean pockets and walks away. I am left to wonder, in the past two years, did he ever want to see Harmony? Did he want to see me? Ever? Even once?

I return to the other divers. Mung keeps his back to me, ignoring me. I go to him anyway.

"Did you and your brother have fun?" Mung growls when he sees me.

"I didn't ask him to come," I say.

Mung's eyes run over me like a body scanner, piercing and questioning. The silence goes on and on, with only the sound of splashing in the air.

"I'm not like him," I finally say. "We may look alike, but it's unfair to blame me for anything he did." Sometimes the whole world seems unfair.

Mung's lips twitch. The twitch grows into a smile, as if we have suddenly become buddies. "I may have misjudged a few things," he says. He starts to walk away, then returns, rubbing his chin. "Stand straight, arms stretched out in a T position."

I obey, moving my arms until I am shaped like my name. My mind races, struggling to realize he is actually coaching me for real.

"Rotate your hips forward, tighten your stomach and rear. Concentrate on keeping your head level." He walks around me, studying my position, pulling my shoulders back. "If you want to perform a good layout, you learn this posture. Let your mind remember how this feels. Practice getting into this position often. Repetition is the key."

"Yes, sir."

He pats me on the shoulder for the first time ever. "Now go get with the others, T'Shawn."

No, Coach Mung is not suddenly my best bud or anything, but things are different for the rest of practice. We are united in our dislike of my brother.

CHAPTER
FIFTEEN

THE SHOWER WATER IS HOT, so hot I want to stay in a long time after practice ends. So long I don't hear the voices talking in the locker room until I leave the shower. As I wrap a towel around me, I hear the snort and giggle coming from the boys' bathroom, more laughter than usual from there. It's a typical bully kind of laugh, and I wonder who's being pranked.

"Call for Crapper," one of the older swimmers yells. He and two other guys, one white and one black, are almost falling over one another laughing.

"Crapper?" I ask Sammy, whose locker is next to mine.

"That's what those brain-deficient high school kids call the janitor," he says. "Watch where you step. They stopped up a toilet. Guess there's not enough water in the pool for these dorks."

A too-deep breath brings the stench from a clogged and overflowing toilet. Water spreads rapidly over the tile floor, carrying soggy toilet paper.

The door opens, and an older man walks in wearing a gray shirt and pants and carrying a pail and mop. He looks at the group of boys and snorts as if he's seen the same thing too many times before. His brown skin is wrinkled, and there's almost no hair on his head. Even with the long mop handle, he has to get so close to the smell his nose must be hurting. And the guys who deliberately caused the mess just laugh harder.

"The older, the stupider," one bully snorts.

"Go, Crapper, go," his friends chant.

"He's taking care of your crap, so what does that make you?" I say.

"Who were you talking to?" one of the bullies asks me, his blue eyes shining with menace.

Sammy tugs at my sleeve, whispering, "I think we should leave."

"I'm talking to you," I say. I'm not good at fighting. Awful, really. Lamont tried to teach me, but it never took.

He switched to the next-best thing and instructed me on bluffing. If you look tough, act tough, you can sometimes head off a fight before it begins. These are phony tough guys, anyway—not one would dare to walk down my street at night. I give these guys a hard stare, my meanest expression, copied from Lamont.

Only there are three of them and just one of me. Sammy squeaks and backs away. The older guys move closer, surrounding me. I hear the bathroom door open behind me but keep my eyes on the three faces.

"What's going on here? T, you need help?" There he is, Lamont himself. The man who doesn't need to bluff has entered the bathroom and stands behind me.

"Yes. No. I mean . . ." I thought he'd left. My heart beats a little easier. I'm glad he's still around because the situation could have become a problem. I'm also mad because he's supposed to be gone. I see the original hard stare filling Lamont's face. This will end up getting me the rep of needing my brother to take care of me.

"We're just having a little fun." The speaker stares into Lamont's eyes for a few seconds, then lowers his head.

One shrugs and mumbles, "Come on. Not worth the effort."

"Let's go. My dad's waiting to drive us home," another

says, and all three leave, still chuckling.

"You can thank me later," Lamont tells me.

I whirl on him. "I can take care of myself. Why didn't you leave when I asked you to? Why stay and keep embarrassing me?" I ask, furious at my brother and at the flash of relief I felt when I saw him at my back.

"You used to be proud of me," Lamont muses.

"Used to be. Like that's ever going to happen again."

He nods, looking hurt and disappointed. "I'm trying, T." He shakes his head. "And now I'm gone."

In seconds, I am alone there with the old man and his mop. He looks at me and nods his thanks.

"I actually thought my transfer from the night shift was a promotion," he says, cleaning up. "Maybe I should tell the boss to give me my old shift back. Working nights meant I only dealt with faculty and staff, never with spoiled rich kids."

"I'm not spoiled. Or rich."

"You're new, aren't you?" he says.

"I guess that's pretty obvious."

"You'll change soon enough. You'll get infected and become another club brat, thinking only of yourself."

No way. I will not let them change me. I want my new teammates to accept me as one of them. But there is only so much I can change myself.

Sammy and the other team members dress quickly and scatter. Today I don't ache as much and manage to get out fast too. I run for the CTA bus stop, where I see Linda among the crowd waiting. She is wearing a bright blue coat. Looks like she's trying to ignore the cold and cheer up the world.

I look around, expecting to see Carmela too, but there's no sign of her.

"Where's Carmela?" I ask, trying to sound uncaring as I approach Linda.

She shrugs, staring down the street so all I see is the back of her hair. "Her mother has already driven her home."

"You two live on the same block. Why didn't they take you home too?"

"I always take the bus."

"You come here just to watch her and then go home alone?" That's not the way friends work. "Where're the other two, Fantasia and Marianne?" I ask.

"They don't come to practice."

"But you do?"

Linda sighs. "Carmela likes an audience. She'd be mad if I didn't come."

"She gives orders and you follow them," I mumble. "What if she told you to do something you didn't want to?"

Linda stands so still and calm, I get the feeling that's already happened at least once.

The bus chugs up then, bouncing like a gentle dinosaur. It stops to release some people while swallowing us. Linda is the first to board. She finds an empty seat near the front and sits down, staring out the window. I move to stand beside her, holding the metal top of her seat to stay upright as the bus shakes going down the street. This time of day, Chicago traffic inches along like an overstuffed caterpillar. We are in the middle of the crush of weary commuters on their way home.

"I know how the world works," she says, still staring out the window. "You don't understand because everyone likes you, but I'm invisible."

"I see you just fine." I see everything about her. Her smarts and the way her mouth almost always droops in sadness. Her black hair parted into small squares and twisted into Bantu knots that make her look like she's wearing a crown. Her brown skin, a shade darker than my own. I see *everything* about Linda.

She turns and looks me in the eye. Hers are light brown. "T, you didn't even know I was alive back when we were both in Mrs. Fischer's class for sixth grade."

"I always knew. I was trying to hide from you at first. I thought you probably didn't want to be around me."

"Because of what your brother did?" She shakes her head. "You are not your brother. You may look like him, but that's only the outside. You're a different person, a very funny guy."

"Really?" I brighten from the inside out. "Because that's what I'm trying for, you know, to be funny and cool and . . . likable."

She giggles. "Everyone likes you, T."

I pause. "You know, I didn't know my brother would show up," I say, remembering the moment when she jumped from her seat and ran from the balcony. "I guess he scared you."

"I was just . . . surprised to see him walk in like that. Like he owned the place."

"He was always like that, especially after he joined the gang," I admit. "I think that's what made guys follow him: he knows how to act like a boss."

"He knows how to be mean. Barnetta may not be worried about him, but I am."

"He won't go after her again. I know it." It's not a promise I can actually keep. Who knows what my brother may decide to do once he is settled? The rules say he is not supposed to have contact with his former victims, including the entire Murhasselt family. But he's not really good with rules. The only thing keeping him in check is Mr. Cho. And maybe Mom.

"How do you know? Can you read his mind? My sister helped stop him when he tried robbing Frank's Place. She called the police on him. What if he wants revenge?" Linda's voice grows husky. "I already lost my mother. I don't know what I'd do if I lost my sister too."

The bus slows and turns a corner, pushing me against her shoulder. My stomach jumps. Now that we're no longer talking about Carmela, I'm not sure what to say. We both fall silent, not moving or speaking until the bus enters our neighborhood. It's dark, but the streets are crowded with people. Dog walkers and joggers, baby carriages and bicycles. Some people on their phones, some actually talking to each other. Every inch of our neighborhood is alive. I decide to get off when she does.

She looks confused when the bus pulls away, leaving us on the corner together. "This isn't your stop."

"I know, but it's getting dark, and I thought . . ." I don't know what I thought. Sometimes my brain makes decisions without telling me why. It just want to walk her to her door, make sure she stays safe. I only live three blocks away from her.

We start walking toward the small house her aunt rents. I want to hear her talk again. This is pretty much the longest time I've spent alone with a girl. My heart pounds louder than it did the first time I climbed on a diving board.

Linda hiccups and rubs her eyes. "I'm sorry. Sometimes the bad memories kind of leak out, you know."

"I know. You don't need to be sorry." My chest feels hollow. I want to do something for her. But all I can think of is to dig a tissue from my pocket and hand it to her.

"Thanks," she says, smiling at me while wiping her cheeks. "Do you know . . . did your brother see my father while he was in prison? They were both at Pontiac."

"Lamont was in the medium-security area. Murderers would be in the maximum-security area." Maybe I never went, but that doesn't mean I didn't learn everything I could about the place where Lamont was sent. There are almost two thousand men inside those walls, and more than half are black. The medium-security unit is located on the same grounds but kept separate.

"Oh, yeah. Probably not, then." She rubs her nose again. "Sometimes I hate my father and want to rip him apart. But sometimes I hope he's changed. I hope it's possible for people to change."

Her father, my brother. Both picked up guns, aimed, fired. I don't think you can change back from that. I could never touch a real gun.

But then, I never thought I would dive off a board until the day I did.

I pause at the door of Linda's aunt's house. I have one last question I need answered. "Does Carmela even remember that she asked me to join the club?"

Linda remains silent. That's answer enough.

CHAPTER
SIXTEEN

"NATURALLY THINGS GET INTERESTING THE minute I'm not around," Dontae grumbles the next morning at school. I told him everything that happened at practice. Everything except the ride home with Linda. He leans against his locker, watching me as I try to decide what to do with my geometry book.

"I missed seeing you actually dive and I missed your brother. I still want to meet him," Dontae continues.

"No, you don't."

I plan to dedicate today's lunch *and* study periods to math and science. I can see the Hun revoking my scholarship if any teacher tells him my grades are slumping. I close my locker, and when I turn, I almost bump into

Carmela. She's not alone. She and her friends form a semicircle around me. Linda won't meet my eyes.

"What's up, girls?" Dontae says, smiling all friendly and stuff. He leans one hand against the wall. "I know you're not lost, so if it's me you're after . . ." He pauses and grins.

"Back off. This only concerns T." Carmela holds up a palm like a stop sign in his direction. "You should have told us your brother had been released. How did he get out so early?"

I shrug. "Good behavior, I guess." I've thought about it a lot, but this is the only explanation I can think of.

"That's not how things work. Ten years don't become two just like that."

"So, how do things work?"

She waves my question aside like a leaf in a breeze. "My dad said this sounded shady. He's been a police officer for sixteen years. He knows how the Prisoner Review Board works. They should never have given your brother parole so soon or allowed him to come back here."

"Where should he be?"

"Anywhere. Maybe back in prison."

"My mom wants him here." My voice chooses this moment to crack so I squeak like a mouse.

"You mean you want him. You want a gangbanger

around to show you how it's done." Her glare says Lamont is a slug that deserves to be stepped on, and I'm not much better.

"No, I don't." The words tumble over my tongue. "I want him gone more than anyone. It will happen soon. You'll see. I'm sure he'll get caught doing something wrong, and they'll take him away quick."

"We shouldn't have to wait for that. My dad worked hard to clean up this neighborhood. We don't need another gang leader running around trying to rebuild his reputation." She makes it sound like her father is some kind of superman. He's a police sergeant, a good cop, but he didn't do anything alone. In fact, Dontae's father started Take Back the Streets. They talk about people power and changing the world. And they organize marches and patrols to tell the gangs they are not wanted here. We follow the examples set by other Chicago neighborhoods, other churches. And it's working. No gunfire rings out in the night on our streets anymore. Instead of gang tags, walls are painted with murals of historic events and people. Abandoned buildings are being repaired and occupied.

"Lamont is just one guy," I protest. I don't want him around, in my room, messing things up between me and my friends. I never wanted him released. But now that he is out, I don't want him to have to go back. Going back feels wrong because . . . well, because that would hurt Mom.

"He's a pest, a parasite," Carmela insists. "He's your brother. Do something."

"What do you want me to do?"

"Figure something out! Make him run off and be somewhere else." She gives me that order and then whips around like a junior ROTC cadet performing an about-face. A moment later, she strides away with her head high, her long braids swinging against her back with each step. Her satellites march after her. Only Linda pauses to look back.

"Why does Carmela care so much?" I ask.

"But she's not wrong," Dontae says, moving closer. "My dad had to go across the courtyard to number four late last night to fix a leak. He didn't finish until after midnight and saw your brother leaving your building on his way back."

I keep myself still and quiet, swallowing down an acid taste.

At least he didn't ask me to run the streets with him.

The warning bell rings for first period, so Dontae and I race to class. Things stay quiet for the rest of the day, and I manage to avoid Carmela.

• • •

I go directly to Dontae's apartment after dinner. His father has a second job as the courtyard's superintendent, so he gets free rent for his garden apartment. But that also means he has to spend a lot of time fixing tenant problems. He's out now while Dontae and I study.

"Hey, so I found *The Book of Negroes*—the one the Hun was talking about a few weeks ago." Dontae says.

"Oh, yeah? So, what is it?"

"It has a list of the names of the thousands of slaves, male and female, who helped the British during the Revolutionary War."

I read an explanation about the book over his shoulder. "Even though Britain lost, they kept their word and evacuated thousands of the former slaves who worked with them. Huh. Some white people kept their word. Awesome." I say the word, but I can't keep enthusiasm in my voice.

"What is wrong with you?" Dontae says, turning to me. "You usually love this stuff."

I shrug. "Just a lot of stuff with my brother. I had an argument with him a few days ago. He made me turn off my music. He thinks he owns the place now that he's back."

"I think brothers are destined to fight," Dontae says.

"You once said you wanted a brother," I remind him.

"I want a lot of stuff and most of it ends up being bad for me. Learning about the adventures of T and Lamont cured me. Remember Loki and Thor in the movies. Those dudes tore up the nine realms because they hated each other."

"They were only foster brothers," I say.

"What about Romulus and Remus?" he says, moving on to a Roman myth we studied last year. "They were twins and one still killed the other."

"What do you expect? Those dudes were raised by wolves."

"How is that different from running around with a gang?"

His words stop me. I have no real answer.

He closes the book and turns back to his notebook—the one he uses to draw in. I'm into music. Dontae puts his energy into his drawing. Dontae has his whole future planned. He's a B student now but intends to start getting As once he gets to high school so he can grab a scholarship to college. His father can't get him there on a preacher's salary. He'll become a BIB—a Black Internet Billionaire—by the time he's twenty, and live on the beach surrounded by girls and all the chocolate and chips he can scarf down. And he promises I can be his partner.

Dontae's head is down—he's busy crafting yet another comic panel in his notebook. If he doesn't make it as a billionaire businessman, he'll probably make a fortune creating graphic novels.

"This is real brotherly hatred," he says, holding up the drawing to show off his new creation. The panel shows a battle between the half brothers Shango and Ogun, the deities of storms and of metal from Nigeria. We learned about them from an elderly immigrant from Haiti who sits around the park and shares tales.

In Dontae's picture, both African deities are slugging it out with bulging muscles, angry scowls, and clenched fists. If I stare hard, I can almost see them move, hear their grunts, smell the sweat. Dontae put my face on the figure holding the lightning bolt. Lamont's face is on Ogun's body, pointing an iron sword at my chest. Dontae made only one mistake. Ogun should be holding a gun.

"What will I do if Lamont doesn't leave?" I ask. I couldn't win in any fight between us.

"There's always a way."

Says the preacher's kid.

"They should have sent him somewhere else," Dontae adds.

"You think? His parole officer thinks it's good for him to be accepted back home or something. I really think this was Mom's idea. She arranged for him to be in her home and got Lamont and the parole officer to agree."

"What if you don't accept him?"

"Lamont has to stay with us unless he gets permission to leave."

"That's it." Dontae grabs me by the shoulders and begins dancing. "We'll get him permission. No, wait, he might hang around anyway." Dontae rubs his chin, just like his old man during a sermon. "We have to order him to go."

CHAPTER

SEVENTEEN

INSTEAD OF GOING HOME DIRECTLY after practice on Saturday, I take a detour, stepping off the bus near an old, three-story brownstone building. From the outside, it looks like an ordinary apartment building. You'd never guess how many families are squeezed inside this shelter, the place I called home for over eight months. It's full of people whose lives have been torn up by accidents, job loss, family troubles, or sickness. For us, it was Dad's cancer. He spent almost a year dying of the cancer eating up his pancreas. His hospital bills plus the funeral and Rochelle's birth took all our money. The landlord didn't care about our problems and grief. We were evicted. Two rooms on the second floor of this building became our only shelter.

There are bathrooms at the end of each floor that residents share. The community kitchen is on the first floor. It gets really hot in the summer. Especially for us, crammed into two rooms, right above the kitchen. I hated living here. Lamont hated it more. They try to keep the rest of the world from knowing who lives here, but the kids in school always find out which students have no home.

I stand and stare up at the window with the blue curtains. The curtains were always drawn when that was my room, as if sealing the windows shut could hide the shame. Lamont and I shared that room for the first month, sleeping on the same bed until he was banished.

There's a keypad at the front door, and we had strict orders to keep the code a secret. I walk up three stairs to the front porch and type in the numbers I can never forget. Nothing happens. It's been a year and a half since Mom got a job and we moved out to our own apartment. Of course the code is different now. Besides, I didn't really want to go inside, anyway. I only came here today because . . .

Because . . .

I don't know.

Ever since the last time I walked out these doors, I've wanted to forget the place ever existed.

I start to walk back to the sidewalk when the door opens behind me. "T'Shawn?" I turn to see Constance Wiggins standing there, smiling at me. The last time I saw her, she wore a Bears sweatshirt that was so big it hung down to her knees, covering her blue jeans. Today she's dressed in an oversize White Sox jersey. Her brown face gleams and her long black hair is pulled back in a single braid that hangs down her back.

"What are you doing here?" she continues. "How nice to see you."

"I can't believe you remember me." It's surprising and makes me feel good, even though I used to call her a witch. Actually, wicked old witch, but she doesn't really look that old to me anymore. And definitely not wicked.

"It's been less than two years," she says. "Of course I remember you! Is your mother with you?" She looks around the block behind me.

"She's at home with Rochelle," I say. Mrs. Wiggins smiles when I mention Rochelle. Everyone smiles when they think of my sister. "I was just . . . I was in the neighborhood."

She chuckles. "Traveling down memory lane? Would you like to come in for a bit?"

I shrug. "Maybe for a minute," I mumble. I've confused myself and don't know what to say now that I'm here. I don't know what to say to her, anyway.

I carry my gym bag inside. Dark velvet curtains cover the windows. It's almost like entering a coffin, except the living room holds living people, parents and kids. I even see a kid from my school, a sixth grader and one of the few white kids in school. Redmond, I think his name is, with stringy, dark brown hair. I've seen him in the halls and know he gets in trouble a lot. I didn't know he was homeless.

When I lived in this place, they sent us to school in taxis. We hoped no one would find out we were homeless. It didn't often work. Kids discovered I was a shelter kid. When they did, I was taunted and bullied until I found friends to be on my side.

Redmond walks past me, deliberately bumping my shoulder. His blue eyes hold the set, angry look of people who get pushed around. They also mark him as gang bait, if he hasn't been recruited already.

"Apologize," Mrs. Wiggins says as he continues walking toward the door.

He stops and turns to me. A smirk twists his lips. A thin scar under his lower lip makes the deep cleft look like an upside-down T. "Yeah, apologize for getting in my way."

"I meant you, Redmond." The power in Mrs. Wiggins's voice is much bigger than her body. Redmond's smirk vanishes, and he takes two steps backward.

A white woman holding two struggling kids in her arms says, "You heard her. Do it." Some kids run through the living room, including a boy a little older than Rochelle. He stops and looks at me for a second, then runs to Redmond's mother. He doesn't smile, instead looking wary, as if I am a threat he's trying to assess. The same look I saw in my own mirror back in the days when I lived here.

Redmond shrugs, throws out a word that sort of sounds like, "Sorry," then continues out the door.

I drop into a chair in a corner, glad Mrs. Wiggins doesn't take me to her office in the back. I used to have to spend lots of time there because I was angry and got in a lot of trouble after she forced my brother to leave. Pipes clang as someone somewhere inside the building turns on a faucet.

"Some things don't change," she says with a laugh.

"But some things do. At least, I hope so. I mean . . ." I take a deep breath and then say in a rush, "Lamont is back. He was released early."

"Is he in a halfway house?"

I shake my head. "Mom let him move in with us."

"I see." She sits up straighter. "How are you doing?"

"It's only been a few weeks." It's nice to say just a few words and know someone totally understands everything roiling through my guts. Things I can't say to Mom because she's too happy having number one son back.

She purses her lips. "Do you need anything?"

"No. Right now, he's being quiet." I know what she is really asking me.

"Lamont had a certain charisma that drew in others like quicksand. Unfortunately, he also had something inside compelling him to violate every rule. Even staff members became afraid of him and some of the older girls. He could have hurt some of the other residents, kids like those." She nods toward Redmond's family before adding, "And like you."

I hear the unspoken question in her voice. It's good to have an adult worrying about me as if I come first. I nod but stay quiet for a moment, watching the little boy with his mom. "Maybe I could volunteer around here sometime," I say.

Mrs. Wiggins smiles. "I'd love to have you do just that in a couple of years. Who could understand these kids better than someone who has stood in their shoes?"

"Like Malik, the guy you assigned to babysit me." Malik never stood in my shoes. Both his parents are alive, and his father owns a chain of auto shops. But he was a better brother to me than Lamont.

"Not babysit. You were devastated when I was forced to expel your brother. You needed a friend; Malik needed responsibility. I knew it would be a perfect match."

I nod again. "Thanks, Mrs. Wiggins." I get up to go.

"Anytime, T'Shawn. You can come by whenever you need to."

Redmond is standing on the corner when I leave, smoking. I can't help walking close to him. I can't believe he'd do something like that.

His eyes lower when I come close. "I'm not gonna apologize."

"I never asked you to." I'm still not a fighter. "You know you can't be in a gang and stay here. She won't let you." I set my bag on the sidewalk as I speak.

Something flickers in his eyes. "I'm not in no gang."

"But you want to be." He has some of the same problems with anger I saw in Lamont years ago. And he's heading in the same direction. Standing out here on the corner like this is advertising. He'll meet a recruiter soon enough. He may be younger than Lamont, but if Mrs.

Wiggins decides he is dangerous, she won't let him stay.

"I can't make it alone," he snarls, kicking the ground with his foot.

"We could be friends, then you wouldn't be alone."

He laughs and shakes his head. "We're too different."

"You mean because you're in sixth grade and I'm in seventh?"

He stares like I suddenly grew a second head. "I'm white and you're black."

I keep forgetting that some people think that makes a difference. It's why there are usually only four reasons we see white people this far on the South Side of Chicago. First, they are just passing through (usually driving faster than the speed limit or on the bus with their heads buried in a book or their phone). Second, some might be lost. They don't stay too long either, but sometimes they look around and may even talk to people. The third reason white people come this far on the South Side is to search for drugs. Those people usually come at night in big cars with suburban stickers. They do as much to stain our neighborhood as the gang members.

The fourth reason is because they work around here. People like the Hun and like the police who know even less about us than he does. That's why I don't have any white kids as friends. There are only a few at school and none in my class. I've seen Redmond but just passing in the halls. The guys on the swim team only talk to me if they feel like bullying me around.

"Are you lonely?" I ask Redmond, because I know how that feels.

"I'm alone. It's not the same thing."

Maybe not, but life is easier with friends. "I used to live in that shelter too, after my dad died." I want him to know we have things in common.

"You lost your old man too?" He swallows. "Do you tell people about being in the shelter?"

"Just my friends. Since I told you, you have to be a friend too."

"Maybe. I don't know." He sighs.

"One thing. If you are going to be my friend, you can't join the gang. That's my rule."

He steps back. "I can do what I want."

"Don't join. My brother joined—that's enough. Don't you care about your family?"

He straightens and tosses the cigarette on the sidewalk. "Don't talk about them. You don't know anything about me or my folks." He shoves me.

Before I can shove him back, I hear a siren whoop. A shiny white Chicago police car with a blue stripe and big star on the side comes down the road toward us. The driver slows, gliding to a stop as he reaches us. My feet beg to run, but I know that's the wrong move. I lower my head because I've been warned that police might think I am challenging them if I stare. My heart thumps, boom, boom.

"You okay over there?" the officer calls.

I risk a glance and see him leaning out the car window looking at Redmond.

Redmond grins. "I'm fine. We're just chilling."

"You be careful," the officer says, and drives off.

When I lift my head, Redmond looks amused. "You were scared," he says.

Of course I was. "Why weren't you?"

"I don't get scared of cops. They wouldn't do anything to me, anyway. I'm only twelve."

He sounds like he really believes that. Doesn't he know anything about the world? "Cops killed Tamir Rice, and he was our age."

Redmond scratches his head. "I don't think I know that guy." He sounds like he thinks I'm making something up. As if I could imagine anything as awful as a kid being shot by police while playing in a park. Right after that happened, Mom sat me down for a long lecture. My hands are still shaking. I don't want to be as scared of police as I am of gang members. I just have to be.

Redmond leaves me and goes back inside the house. Maybe he's right and I don't know him, just like he doesn't know the things that scare me. But I bet I know everything about his brothers and sisters. I know their future if he doesn't change. Only there isn't anything I can do with that knowledge. I can't change him. I can't even change my own brother.

Redmond needs his own version of Malik Kaplan, someone who can help him steer his boat through rough waters. But that's not me.

I pull out my phone and tap out a message to Malik.

Me: *I miss you.*

Malik: *Problems? Should I come down there?*

Yes, yes, yes.

And no. He has a real life. He wants to be a lawyer. That means he needs to keep his mind on his studies and on basketball. I wish God had arranged things so he could be my real brother. I can almost see his face, brows arching, white teeth gleaming. Who would want a try-hard loser like Lamont if he could have Malik, the guy who is always good and always succeeds?

Malik: *I know what your brother is going through. I know what the call of the bad feels like. I've been tempted too. I thought my parents didn't understand me and maybe I wanted to be one of the bad guys.*

Me: *But you didn't.*

Malik: *Ready for some truth?*

Am I ready?

Me: *Sure.*

Malik: *I got in trouble after a fight. A judge made me work in the shelter as community service.*

Me: *I was a penalty?*

Malik: *Best penalty ever.*

I can't help feeling proud. It's always nice to be the best at something.

CHAPTER
EIGHTEEN

THAT NIGHT, I LIE IN the darkness, staring at the stars out the window. Moonlight shines through our bedroom window. Funny, I can see much more of the world from on top. We both went to bed at ten. It's amazing that my older brother, who could stay up as long as he wants, goes to bed at the same time I have to.

"Are you asleep?" Lamont's voice rises up in the darkness.

"No."

"Too scared of me to sleep?"

I don't answer. It's not so bad having him below me, not like I thought it would be. It doesn't feel half as strange up here now as it did the first few days.

"I had trouble sleeping in my cell," he says, a strange quiver in his voice. "It was crazy there. People snoring, yelling, or screaming in the middle of the night."

"I don't snore, do I?" I ask, suddenly anxious.

He snorts. The sound is friendly, like old times. "No Short—I mean, T. You're quiet. My first cellmate snored like a sawmill. I almost went crazy trying to sleep with all his noise. Then I got a new guy. He was sneaky quiet." Lamont stops talking, but I hear his ragged breathing grow faster.

"So you had no trouble sleeping around him," I say after a little bit.

"No trouble at all." His words are clipped. I wonder if his jaw muscle is twitching again because that doesn't sound real.

Then he says, "Quiet can be dangerous on the inside. Prison is its own lonely world. If I hadn't had enemies, I wouldn't have had anyone. I had a lot of thinking time. I had a plan for my life. I couldn't let anything take me from that. Sometimes you have to fight hard and prove you're the . . ."

"The worst of the worst," I supply when the silence grows too long.

"Yeah, that too."

"I bet you ruled," I say. He would never lower his

eyes just because a cop rolled by.

"Guess again," he says. "There will always be someone trying to knock you down. We all want to be the best, and we'll tear our opponents down to avoid second place. You get on that diving board because you want to be number one, right? You have to know there is only one first place."

"I won't tear someone else down to get it." When I first wanted to be a diver, I did think about doing anything to become the top guy, the hero. There's more now. I want to impress Mung. I want my friends to feel awed and see Mom cheer for me. And my dad. I sometimes dream Dad's spirit looks down at me from heaven and feels proud. No one will be proud of me if I have to tear someone else down to reach the top. I won't even be proud of me.

"Then we are different, little brother, because I need to feel strong and powerful."

I lean over the side of the bed. In the dim moonlight shining through the curtains, the outline of my brother's body glimmers. His arms are folded under his head and his eyes gleam in the darkness.

"Feeling powerful just because you have a gun in your hands isn't real," I tell him. "I want to do my best. I do good, or I fail; either way it's all up to me. That way, the only weapon I need is me."

"That's why you're the family brains. I was clawing my way to a leadership spot. I didn't stop to realize I'd *always* have to be ready to fight or die, every minute of every day. No matter how high you climb or how bad you are, there's always someone out to knock you down and take your place."

"I couldn't live like that. It can't always be win or die. I want to be like Dad."

"I won't end the way our father did," Lamont announces from out of the darkness. "I won't break my back for years at some sucky job where they throw you out the minute you get sick and can't make more money for them. I had a lot of thinking time on the inside. Being in the general population sucks. Every day is the same. I took a job in the prison laundry because it was something to do. Spent a lot of time in the library too. Books took me out of that hole. Isolation was almost heaven— alone, with only my thoughts and dreams. I was ready to do anything to get out and come back home. But now that I'm here, I'm not so sure."

"Not sure about coming home? Or about staying home?" Why is he breaking rules, running around with gang members, plotting and planning and making sure he will be caught and sent back? I've been hanging upside down too long. I feel blood rushing in my head, so I sit up and stare at the darkness.

After a second I hear the bottom mattress rustle as he turns over.

I drift off to sleep wondering if we had a breakthrough or just a break?

A break. I realize that when a sound wakes me a little later. Lamont is preparing to leave again. I lift myself up on one elbow and see my brother near the closet, dressing. The moon is hidden behind clouds, so only a little light shines outside the curtains.

"Where are you going?" I ask while rubbing sleep from my eyes.

His shadowy form continues to move, stuffing his wallet and phone into his pockets. "Go back to sleep, T."

"Why are you in such a hurry to be sent back to prison? What happens to you happens to us too." I want him to stay here and stay safe. We're blood. I didn't realize how much I missed him until he came home.

"I'm the one who got thrown out of that shelter. *That* didn't happen to you," he growls.

"Are you still mad about having to leave the homeless shelter? You scared people." I swallow, then add, "I went to see Mrs. Wiggins today. She asked about you. I think she's sorry."

"Doubtful. She's probably upset by my release like everyone else." His sigh vibrates off the walls. "I never hurt anyone in the center. Maybe I messed up on a few rules sometimes and said a few things. But the people there were like us. Everyone there had lost a piece of themselves, just like we had. I'd never hurt people like us."

"You scared Linda the day you came to the pool."

"Who is Linda?" he asks, his voice shaking. "Is she your girlfriend?"

"I'm only thirteen. I don't have a girlfriend."

"I had one at your age. You must attend a school full of blind girls if they don't see how special you are."

"Well, there is this one girl," I admit.

"Is she fine?" he asks, and I feel a smile in his voice.

I start to visualize Carmela, but for some reason her face fades away and Linda's floats in my mind. "She is pretty, smart, and . . . and shy. Doesn't talk a lot, but when she does, it's important."

"You should tell her how you feel," Lamont says.

"Maybe you should follow your own advice and give Harmony another try."

"It's different for me," he says. "I'll explain when you're older. For now, it is what it is, Short Stack."

"Yeah, well, I can't say anything to Linda because her sister works at Frank's Place, the restaurant you and your friends tried to rob." That left me so ashamed I never dared go inside the place, even though it's a favorite hangout with some of the kids in my class. When I have to pass it, I look at the street or the sidewalk and go as fast as I can.

His shadowy form raises his hands toward me. "If I could take those days back . . ."

"But you can't. You confessed."

"I took a plea. I had to. My lawyer said it was the only way to escape a Class X felony conviction.

"You're still a felon. Class 1, Class X, what's the difference?"

"Class X could have meant thirty years. Trying to rob that restaurant wasn't my idea. It was small-time and stupid, and I've never been either of those."

"No, you were Mr. Brilliant, who dropped out and went to live in an abandoned building with only rats and other gang members for company. You were supposed to be in charge of Darnell and the others."

"I thought I was," he says softly. "I was wrong."

I don't remember hearing him ever admit to any mistake before. He heads for the door.

"Don't go," I plead.

"I'm not doing anything wrong tonight."

His definition of "wrong" has to be so far off-track

it's in another state. Just tell the truth, I silently beg. *Please*. How twisted am I to wish he'd admit the facts? Get it over with, tell the truth and prove he really has changed. I wish I could see his face, the muscle in the side of his jaw must be dancing from all the lies. My teeth begin to chatter, and I wrap my arms around my chest and shiver. "If you do something that makes the police break in and drag you away, they could go after Mom too—"

"That won't happen," he barks, sounding as if the words alone are enough to kill the threat. But it does happen. I know it, so my big brother must too. She could be arrested if the police think she knows what he does.

I throw back my blanket and jump to the floor.

"If you're not doing anything wrong, then take me with you."

He shakes his head. "I can't. This is . . . It's personal."

"Personal? Are you going to see Harmony?" I wish I could see his face in the dark. His words, his tone, don't let me know anything.

"If that keeps you quiet, yes. Now go back to sleep."

"What did you do to Mr. Mung, my coach?"

"You mean besides hanging with his niece?" Lamont's voice is an Arctic freeze. "It's not important."

I bet his jaw muscle is twitching like crazy.

I *hate* being lied to.

I remain still as he pads silently down the hall and out the front door. No sounds come from Mom's bedroom or from Rochelle's. All I hear is the sound of my own breathing. Sooner or later he will leave and not come back. He will get caught doing something wrong, Mr. Cho will take him away, and life will feel good again.

Or maybe he should stay home where he belongs.

I wish . . .

I wish . . .

I don't know what I wish.

CHAPTER
NINETEEN

SUNDAY MEANS CHURCH. CHURCH IS a special time for connecting with friends, strutting in nice clothes, and listening to moving music. When things get going, half the congregation is on its feet, swinging and swaying and shouting hallelujah and amen. No place on earth is safer or more enjoyable than the inside of our church. This Sunday, for the first time since his return, Lamont decides to come with us.

I eat a huge breakfast: pancakes, eggs, bacon, and juice. Mom makes sure to pack a big snack for Rochelle. Sunday is the go-to-church-and-stay-for-a-long-time day. The service starts at ten thirty exactly. Since Mom is part of the choir, we can't be late. Mom has a solo to sing today. At ten thirty-one exactly, the organ will begin playing, and the choir members will open their lips to sing. After five or six songs, prayers, and announcements, the preacher is just getting into the swing of his sermon around noon. If we are lucky, the benediction ends the service at one.

Mom is as bubbly as one of my classmates when we leave the apartment to walk the three blocks to church. A cool drizzle falls, leaving my cheeks wet. Lamont's decision to come with us has made her too happy to question his motive. I'm not that gullible, though. My brother *never* liked church.

A big sign hangs over the door of the church. It reads, "I love you, signed, God."

Maybe that's what made Lamont unexpectedly decide he needed religion today.

I hold Rochelle's hand as she skips down the block, singing a song she learned from a cartoon. Her braids slap the back of her coat. She loves going to church. She gets to hang with her friends for the children's service in a nursery room with toys and books and caretakers who rock children in their laps while reading bible stories.

I take Rochelle around the building to the entrance closest to the nursery. She walks in with her head held high, strutting across the room like she owns the place. She heads right for the toy chest in the corner. A minute later, she is settled in a beanbag chair with one of her friends. Seeing her happy, I hand over her snack to one of the caretakers and rush to the sanctuary to look for Dontae. Even though he's the preacher's son, he sits in one of the back pews like a lot of kids from our class. Carmela and Linda are here, both dressed in zebra-striped blouses and looking like play sisters. Carmela has a white skirt, Linda a black one. We're much too old to sit with our parents so we all kind of hang together.

"How long is today's sermon?" I ask as I squeeze in beside Dontae. His father is already in the front, wearing a gray robe with wide black bands around wide sleeves. Dontae calls it a wizard robe.

"Long. Marcel is preaching today. You know he loves his own voice. He and Dad have been working on this service for days."

Marcel Johnson is our student intern, a future pastor attending the University of Chicago School of Divinity. He's a large man, young, and packs lots of energy. His voice is like a melody, so I don't care how long he talks.

And he also comes with guests. I'd forgotten one of the other reasons white people come to our neighborhood—because they have black friends and are willing to show up to provide support. Marcel is black, but most of his classmates are white, and five of them—three young men and two women—always show up when he preaches. They sit like an island of white in a back pew, but they always show up to support him. I am always happy to see them show up for Marcel.

I wonder if Redmond would come if I asked him. Or would he be scared to come here? No place is more open and welcoming than our church. I look around for him every day at school. Sometimes I think I see him in the hall, a pale figure walking alone. But only for a second: he always speeds up when I try to get close. Guess he decided he didn't need any friends at school after all.

"My brother came with us today," I tell Dontae.

"Where is he?" Dontae's head turns. He stands and rises to his toes, trying to peer over other heads.

"Don't look," I say, but I turn around too. I finally see his familiar body standing next to someone almost as familiar.

Harmony Mung.

Ah, now it all makes sense. His motive for suddenly deciding he needed church is dressed in tight, decorated jeans and a ruffled purple blouse; not exactly what families around here consider church clothes. She doesn't even have a hat, like most of the women in the church wear. The light streaming through one of the stained-glass windows makes her light brown skin seem almost golden. She is an outsider, straight from the West Side, the part of Chicago where people can pretend the South Side and black people don't exist. Yet she looks as comfortable here as she does at team practice, much more comfortable than the huddled divinity students. It's like being biracial lets her fit in anywhere.

Lamont and Harmony take their seats. At exactly ten thirty, the service begins. The choir rises from their seats behind the altar and begins belting out the opening song. Mom sounds better than any contestant on those TV singing shows.

A woman in the row in front of me jumps to her feet, one arm raised toward the stained-glass windows, her back arched, head lifted. Consumed by the word of God—that's how Mom describes it when people get over-come in church. The man beside the woman bows his head and claps.

My legs tap, not with anxiety but in time with the beat. People around us shout amen as the music grows louder.

"We all know about sin," Marcel begins. "We have people in our lives who have been hurt, or killed, or who have committed crimes. Sometimes even family members. We have to make decisions about ourselves and the future."

Dontae nudges my shoulder. I turn and look at Lamont. He's actually smiling.

Marcel raises his arms to let the wide sleeves of his black robe spread like wings in the air. "The doors of the church are open." That's the call that goes out before the final benediction. It's a call that means anyone in need can come to ask for a prayer, talk about their troubles. Lamont shuffles in his seat, and for a moment, I think he is about to stand and go forward. Then he turns to Harmony and whispers something that makes them both laugh.

Marcel concludes, "Our differences don't matter, only our common humanity counts. Let us pray that we all leave here better men and women than when we entered."

My music teacher sings a soprano that hurts my ears. It may not shatter glass, but the note she holds at the end makes me want to cover my ears.

The word rolls through the congregation. Harmony leans back in the pew, her eyes fixed on the pastor.

People stand, applauding the young preacher. Amens and hallelujahs echo across the sanctuary, accompanied by the sound of frantic claps.

Mom and the choir sing a final song, and the service ends. I start going to the front of the church and see the pastor approach Lamont. "It's always nice to see new people attend," he says, coming up to Lamont and Harmony after the service. Mom has gone to the back to change out of her robe.

"I like your church. It's been a long time since I attended a black church. I've missed the music and joy so much. My father used to attend church with my mother almost every Sunday," Harmony says. "My uncle wouldn't be caught within twenty miles of any church. But I miss this strength, the feeling that comes with those words."

"Any time you are around again, remember what I said. The doors of the church are open." The pastor smiles at Harmony as he speaks.

Lamont pulls her away, and they walk out together. I follow, not quite sure what to think. Maybe she can do what I can't: get close to him and turn him into something new, better.

Maybe she can even help bring back the old Lamont.

CHAPTER
TWENTY

WEEKS PASS, AND I SETTLE into a practice routine with the Rays. March becomes April. Every time the Rays have weight day I stand at the free weights beside Sammy and try outlifting him. And I fail. Lamont has major muscles. Dontae and Sammy do too, and both of them are younger than I am. Every morning I stare at my arms in the mirror and try to make a muscle. Come on, body. Something. Anything.

Nothing.

I am stronger. After almost a month with the club, I can lift more and run farther on the treadmill. My arms and legs remain skinny sticks. I look like a little boy who belongs with the ten- and eleven-year-old group.

"You are a little boy," Harmony says when I complain to her.

"My coach told me divers need muscles." I forget my coach is also her uncle until she frowns.

"He says a lot of stuff," she mutters. She seems to forget herself, sometimes. There are days when she doesn't talk to him or even look in his direction. He ignores her the same way.

"I'm supposed to listen to him."

"You want his approval?" she asks. When I nod, she continues, "Uncle Bill is not a god. Look, T, you have two choices. Keep working out and wait for Mother Nature, or do something to speed things up."

"Like what?" I'd do anything.

"Some people take things to help them build muscle fast."

I've given up candy for protein bars. They taste like yuck, but Coach Mung made the suggestion, so yeah, I'm doing it. But I don't think that's what Harmony is talking about.

"Steroids?" Some kids were tossed from the high school football team last year. We had a big lecture in health class. That stuff does more than grow muscles fast. It can mess up your brain and your whole body. "I'll keep waiting," I say just as Sammy comes to join us. I can see his muscles jump when he lifts. Mine will do the same someday soon.

Meanwhile, I continue with my cardio, weights, and dry-land training.

Dry-land training happens twice a week, when the coach sends half of the diving team to the gymnastics center instead of the pool. I spend a lot of time practicing my pike and tuck positions. A tuck involves grabbing my legs and hugging them close to my body. It looks easy, but I have trouble even when I'm just sitting on the rug. I finally understand what Mung is all about when he yells, "Posture," or sends me to do calisthenics and work on flexibility. Those positions are more difficult than straight dives, so they score higher in competition. Someday I'll make those positions look easy.

In the gym, the coach has a diving board extended over a pit filled with pieces of foam. Sammy takes a harness hanging from the ceiling and fits it around his chest. I work as his partner, grabbing the end of a rope clipped to his harness. When he takes off from the edge of the board, my job is to yank on the rope to provide extra lift so he can practice a two-and-a-half somersault with a twist.

When it's my turn, I try to make my body spin and twist too. There's so much to know and remember. The world spins confusingly around me, and I do a face-plant on the foam. I don't have to worry about my wipeouts hurting, but that doesn't change them into good dives.

Mung appears, taking the end of the rope from Sammy. My next attempt is worse, knowing who is watching me.

"You're late kicking out of the dive," he says as I claw my way out of the foam. "Stop being afraid and really reach for the water."

I try a lay-up next, a plain-vanilla dive, as Sammy would say. I succeed in forgetting who is at the end of the rope and critiquing my every move. This time, when I climb from the pit, Coach Mung takes my upper arm and squeezes tight until I yelp. I can't help it; his fingers are strong. He shakes his head a little and steps back. "You'll also need to build yourself up more. Diving requires muscles."

"Yes, sir." Behind Mung, I see Sammy, face twisted, mimicking those last three words. I can't tell if he's making fun of our coach or me.

"You appear to have skills," Mung says. "And you're getting the timing."

"Yes, sir, I've been trying really hard."

He looks the same as always. On second thought, he looks smug, happier than usual.

"What did my brother do to you?" I ask.

His thin lips draw tight like a stray dog defending a bone. "Not me, my niece. She was only fifteen, still reeling from her parents' death. She needed . . . Well, she didn't need a gang member. I had to force her to stay away from your brother."

"Yeah, but, if they liked each other—"

"He used her. Every time he came around, something valuable disappeared. If you were like your brother—"

"I'm nothing like Lamont."

He pauses, then says, "You live in a dangerous part of the city. The violence rate must make every day horrific for you. Your life must move from one tragedy to another."

"Uh, not really. Life is life. We get by. Besides, my mother is working to make things better. Maybe living in this part of Chicago is dangerous, but it's our home."

I'm not sure he heard me. "Your mother must be working to get you out of there to someplace safe. But why she would add to your danger by allowing Lamont to share space with you is beyond me." He looks at me, at the frown on my face. "It's not about your race. I promise you, I don't see color. That's not how I am. You could be blue or green or purple. I wouldn't care."

But I'm not green or purple.

My skin is brown. I was born this way. And while I want to believe people see me, all of me, I don't want people thinking my color makes me bad or dumb or unable to face the water in a swimming pool.

What makes skin color count for so much to people? Hair color is no big deal, even green or purple hair. Eyes are all different parts of the rainbow. No one thinks brown hair makes someone more violent or brown eyes more stupid. Why does brown skin make them think both? My heart is deep inside me, underneath my skin. My brain, inside my head, is the same as anyone else's.

Coach then says, "Do you think you're ready for a little competition? Some of the Rays are having a meet with a couple of other teams. It might be good for you to attend this meet, just to see what things are like. Everyone has to have a first time."

Including a first time impressing their coach. He thinks I'm ready, and that means something. I nod, jump, and almost fall back into the foam pit.

The aroma of jerk chicken fills our apartment when I return from practice. In my hands is a box holding my newest possessions, including a team jacket. Team picture day is two days away, and no, the picture isn't free. I thought about being a no-show so I wouldn't be the only member who couldn't participate until the Hun told me my picture package was paid for. The scholarship is all-inclusive and even covered team clothes. After a few weeks on the team, my spangled jacket, trunks, and new gym bag arrived today.

"What do you think?" I ask as I enter the kitchen, turning in a circle so they can see me from all sides. Rochelle is sitting at the table playing with her silverware. Mom claps when I lift my arm to show off the shining fabric. Rochelle jumps from her chair to join me. She rubs the side of my jacket and giggles. It is smooth and warm. I will finally look like I belong.

"You look like a champion," Mom gushes.

"Thanks, Mom. I'm not there yet, but I'm getting better with every practice. Mung says I've got potential. I have to work on that." I smile and then take my sister's hands, and soon we're dancing in the middle of the room. She makes her own music by humming.

She finally collapses on the floor and yells, "The end!" Mom applauds. I drop beside my energetic sister. She tired me out. One more minute and I would have had to give up.

Lamont assumes his usual pose, leaning against one wall with his arms crossed and a sneer on his lips. He never joins in when we play around, doesn't act like he really wants to be part of the family. At least he hasn't returned to the pool to embarrass me again. His chin points at my jacket. "Christmas is over. Decorations should be down by now, Short Stack."

My smile disappears.

Rochelle jumps up and runs to him. She squeals when he picks her up and carries her to her chair. He takes a seat beside her and places pieces of chicken from the serving dish onto her plate, even though she can feed herself. I'm no longer her favorite brother. She's becoming too close to Lamont. Something drops in my stomach as I watch them together during dinner.

"Coach says I'm doing great," I tell my mother between bites. "He thinks I'm good enough to compete."

"So, Mung's treating you all right these days?" Lamont asks.

"Better than you are," I mutter, but Mom hears me anyway.

She lifts her head and looks us both over. "What's going on between you two?"

"Nothing," Lamont and I both say. I don't want a Mom moment. When she starts prying, she doesn't stop until she gets to everything.

"I'm attending my first meet soon," I say, trying to change the subject. "It will be Rays against members of the Chicago Park District team and the North—"

"—Side Dolphins," Lamont finishes.

My jaw drops. "How did you know?"

He shrugs. "Harmony used to swim on that team."

After dinner, I watch my brother and sister on the rug, building something with blocks. When the blocks fall, Rochelle laughs and throws herself into his arms.

He and I used to be tight like that. I don't remember much about being four, but I bet he used to do things like that with me. He listened to my stories, bandaged my scrapes, took me to zoos and the circus and ball games, taught me that I should love the White Sox and sneer at the Cubs. I can't remember ever once hearing him say I bothered him. His eyes used to smile. My big brother used to make me feel safe.

"What are you thinking?" Lamont asks me.

I shake my head. "I'm just remembering." I tug one of Rochelle's braids before bending down. "Want a ride?"

"Yeah!" She jumps on my back and I give her a piggy-back ride around the living room. I fall on the sofa and pull her onto my lap. She is soft but solid, real and mine.

Then Lamont comes over, leans close to Rochelle, and asks, "Are you up for spending time with your other brother, Shelly?"

"Will you read me *Ananse the Spider* again?" she asks.

"You bet."

She's a little traitor and likes him better than she likes me.

"Hey, you wanna play outside?" I ask, to win her away from him.

"Come on, T, let's go," Rochelle says, jumping away from Lamont.

I smirk and take her hand, and we head over to the park. Unfortunately, Lamont decides to trail along behind. I can't get away from him, and Rochelle in her bright blue coat runs back and forth between us as we walk.

"He's nice," Rochelle whispers once while she's with me. "Is he really my brother?"

All I have to do is say no. A simple untruth and she will be only mine again.

"Yes, he is our brother," I tell her.

She clasps her hands together. "It's like a story, like the prince coming home."

A prince? Seriously, why does everyone put Lamont first?

A lone cat lifts its head and stares, green eyes bright in its dark fur. We pass an old man sitting on a box at the curb, wearing mismatched shoes and an unbuttoned black coat over a dark blue hoodie. Beside him is a sign propped against a battered shoe box. The sign reads, "Hungry, Need Food, Help."

The shoe box is empty.

Lamont's steps slow. "Toxic, is that you?" he says, coming to a stop.

I look closer at the man, see beyond the black hood covering his hair and ears. This is Toxic, or Howard Jones, one of Lamont's old friends. Lamont began hanging with Toxic after Dad died. He's only about ten years older than Lamont, but right now his hands tremble, and his dry skin makes him seem ancient. Lamont grabs his hand and shakes it. Toxic's voice is calm as he says, "I lost my job, haven't been able to find anything since—not even washing dishes."

"Hey, man, I'm sorry." Lamont now pulls money from his pocket and drops it into the box. "Here. I wish I had more."

"I wish you did too." Toxic coughs when he tries to laugh. "The drugs I used gave me the palsy now. I'm kinda useless. At least I'm outta the gang. We are supposed to be a family, but they don't want me anymore. I never thought I'd consider being worth nothing to them a good thing."

Lamont nods, and we start to walk away. I look at Lamont's face and see a mix of confusion and sadness. "That could've been me," he mumbles.

I guess it could have. The idea that anyone might ever consider him worthless must drive the King of the World crazy.

CHAPTER
TWENTY—ONE

SPRING BREAK IS A WEEK away, but homework is
keeping me from thinking too far ahead. Lamont strolls
into our room. I turn the volume on my music down,
even though I'm only playing Bruno Mars, someone who
doesn't offend my brother's music taste. I keep my head
bent over my book, hoping if I ignore him, he'll do the
same to me. Instead, he stops beside my chair.

"Sorry," I whisper, and this time I stop the iTunes
app. "I was trying to be quiet."

"Try harder," he mutters, and tosses a white box on
the desk in front of me.

"What's this?" I ask, my breath catching.

"I thought you were supposed to be smart. Read the label. You put them over your ears, plug them into the jack of the phone, and I get blessed silence." These are real, blue-tooth-enabled, high-performance, on-ear headphones, electric blue. The tag says, "High-Quality Sound."

The cellophane covering them crinkles in my grip. These are awesome—and expensive. They aren't like my old earbuds that leak and make music sound tinny.

"You may thank me now." My brother adds to his sarcastic voice with a stupid half bow.

I lift the box and look at it. "Where did you get them?"

"I don't suppose you'd believe the box fell off the back of a truck?" He stares at me, and suddenly we're both shaking our heads at that very old and totally impossible joke. "I didn't steal them, if that's what you're thinking. I've never done anything *that* petty."

"Never?"

"How about you let a gift horse lie down and get a little rest, Short Stack?" Lamont says. He walks over to the beds and throws himself on the bottom mattress.

"People let sleeping dogs lie, numbnut. And my name is T! I hate it when you call me Short Stack!"

He stiffens. "Whatever. Just use the headphones!"

I look at the box again. If I wear these, it will be like being at a concert.

Too good to be true, screams a voice inside my head.

I want to believe these are legit, but I know something is off, thanks to the twitch in the side of his jaw.

I toss the box at his chest. "Take them back," I say. "I don't want anything from you."

"I knew you'd feel that way."

"I'm studying," I say, turning so my back faces him.

My brother is nothing but a thief. I look at the headphones lying on his bed. I'm never touching anything he tries to hand me, not ever again.

Finally a week of freedom—Spring Break: no school, just fun. Dontae and I are out enjoying the cool morning under the sun as we head over to the park. The sky is dizzyingly bright. His bike wheels roll on the asphalt street; my feet pound the concrete sidewalk. He actually covers more distance than I do because he is forced to weave his bike around parked cars, sometimes ending up in traffic. Chicago encourages bike riding, supplying Divvy bikes all over the city. But we have no bike lanes painted on our part of the city streets. A river of cars and buses flows down the street. Some roads are so narrow that when cars are parked on both sides it's difficult for two lanes of traffic to proceed.

Dontae has his own bike. I could rent one of the blue Divvy bikes, but instead, I chose to run on the sidewalk while he rides in the street beside me. Cops in our neighborhood give tickets to adults biking on the sidewalk. Technically, he's still twelve, so he's allowed to bike on the sidewalk, but try convincing one of the cops who look at us while we pass. It's like brown skin automatically adds five years to our ages.

The morning rains have left the day cool, and grass stains are all over my gym shoes. The flowers have begun to grow, and some even bloom.

A long-haired dog sits on the sidewalk, scratching behind one ear. The man on the other end of the leash is talking on his cell phone in some unknown language. I know a little Spanish and even some French, thanks to the old Haitian storyteller.

The wind changes, and I get a whiff of the food from a small fish-and-chicken shop. Two women emerge, one holding a bag decorated with a few grease spots. Both have big smiles on their faces. I wish I could follow them. The sauce smells that good.

"Do you think if we beg they might give us a bite?" I ask.

"I don't beg," Dontae says.

"Since when? Does this mean I don't have to give you any more of my fries?"

Five minutes later, we reach a park. I notice Dontae sweating and breathing a little hard. "Time for a pit stop," I call.

"Don't treat me like a baby," he snaps when I insist we sit under a tree to rest. I promised Dontae's mom I'd keep an eye on him—otherwise she wouldn't have let him go out. He knows it. He just doesn't like it.

"I need to chill too." I'm not winded. All those days on the treadmill training for the Rays make this run easy. The gym teacher is even beginning to notice how I can go faster and farther when we run laps.

"You're worse than my mother." He play punches me in the shoulder but dismounts and comes in for a drink.

Dontae bends over the fountain, then stops and points across the street at a basketball court. "Yo, what's that?" He points to a court where Lamont and a skinny white kid are shooting hoops. "I don't know who that guy is, but I know what he is. Did you catch the tombstone drawn on his jacket?"

I know him. It's Redmond. He's here because he's

homeless, I almost say. But that's not my secret to tell. Both Lamont and Redmond look ordinary in the daylight. Just two guys, one white, one black, playing together. Redmond may not want to be my friend, but he and Lamont look like total bros.

"This explains the gang tags that keep appearing on buildings," Dontae adds.

The marks covered the wall of one of the buildings in our courtyard complex. Big ugly spray-painted marks that signal dominance and a call for recruits. Some people wearing red-and-white Take Back the Streets shirts were already painting them over when we passed this morning.

"You don't know they had anything to do with that."

"I have a brain. You should use yours. It's been over a year since anyone tried to tag our building or anyplace on our block. Now your brother is here, and so are they. I bet it's a message, either from him or to him."

"Sometimes where there's smoke, there's just more smoke," I protest.

"And sometimes there's an inferno." Dontae pulls out his phone and begins snapping pictures.

Redmond dribbles his way around Lamont's outstretched hands and scores on a jumper. That must signal a win because he stops and laughs and begins rolling down his sleeves to cover the marks on his arms while Lamont retrieves the ball. They exchange high fives. It's strange to see them act so friendly. Lamont always steamed whenever anyone beat him at anything.

Thunder rumbles in the distance. Dontae takes more pictures. Lamont reaches into his pocket and pulls out a wad of money that he hands over to Redmond, right out in the open where anyone can observe him. "Did you see that?" Dontae asks.

"Uh-huh." A weird taste fills my mouth, like I've been sucking on a penny. Lamont could be paying off a bet because he lost to a new friend, and it's just two guys finishing off a friendly one-on-one game. Or he could be paying for something more.

I should tell Mom.

But I can't. This would kill her.

Miss Wiggins? No, then Redmond would be on the streets. How can I do that to someone else's little sisters and brothers?

"Maybe we should call the police," Dontae says, his voice hesitant.

"No way. You know what they will do. Besides, the guys were just playing ball."

"Are you willing to wait until he brings in even more

new friends? Until he goes after someone else and hurts or maybe kills someone?"

"He would never!"

"Never?"

I don't want my brother hurt or back in jail. I just want him to stop dealing with these bad people. "Maybe Mr. Cho can help. That's Lamont's parole officer." He isn't a cop, not exactly.

"Call him. He could make your brother leave." Dontae is almost jumping.

Mr. Cho's number is programmed into my phone, but my fingers still shake as I press the keys to pull it up from my contact list and call for help.

CHAPTER
TWENTY-TWO

MR. CHO AGREES TO TALK to me, but it has to be now. I don't want to explain things on the phone. He tells me he's having lunch, and Dontae and I head back to the fish-and-chicken place.

While Dontae locks his bike to a post outside the door, I walk inside. Only a few tables are occupied. A family with five kids is sitting in one corner. Mr. Cho is alone at a table near the back. But my eyes spot a bunch of girls from my school, including Carmela, chattering noisily and trying to fit six in a booth meant for four.

I turn to leave and almost bump into Dontae coming in.

"We need to go," I whisper. *"She's* here." I nod to the table where Carmela holds court.

"I don't care about her. We have a mission. Where's the parole officer?"

I point. He is eating a huge burger that looks too big for his mouth.

"Come on." Dontae starts walking. I follow, sliding into the booth opposite Mr. Cho. Dontae squeezes in beside me. "That looks good," he says, licking his lips.

"It's a beef-and-steak burger." Mr. Cho wipes juice from his chin with a napkin. Who comes to a fish-and-chicken place for a burger? There are a couple of dozen items listed on the wall: catfish, shrimp, chicken breasts and wings, even chicken fries. The smells swirl around me. My mouth waters. But I have a mission, even if it means betraying the brother code. Even if Lamont deserves it, this hurts like crazy.

Mr. Cho puts down his napkin and stares at me. "So, what can I help you with? You sounded like you had an emergency."

"Lamont sneaks out at night," I say quickly.

"How do you know? Aren't you supposed to be sleeping at night?" Mr. Cho says.

"*I* know," Dontae says. "My dad saw him walking

through our apartment complex at night. And just a few minutes ago, he was in the park with another gang member. Wasn't that rule number one: He can't associate with other bad guys?"

"Who are you?" Mr. Cho asks sharply.

"T's friend. His *best* friend," Dontae says proudly. "And I have proof. I took pictures." He speaks a little too loudly, and from the corner of my eye, I see Carmela turn to stare at our table.

"Let's see," Mr. Cho says, finally putting down the burger. After wiping his hands on a napkin, he takes the phone Dontae offers. He frowns as he scrolls through the picture gallery and stops at a photo showing the exchange of money.

"Do you know who this boy was?" he finally asks.

"No idea," Dontae says before I have time to decide how to reply. "But look at the insignia on his clothes. He's in the gang, all right." He reaches for Mr. Cho's fries as he speaks. His reward is the kind of glare that would make an alley dog back down. Dontae completes his move, stuffing the fries in his mouth.

"When were these taken?" Mr. Cho asks.

"Just before we called you, in the park at King Drive. Go grab him. Do your job." Dontae's words sound garbled as he chews.

"My job is to help Lamont stay out of prison." Mr. Cho gives Dontae back his phone, then waves a hand, signaling for the waitress to bring his check.

"But aren't you going to do anything?" Dontae asks, his mouth falling open.

"You don't know where he is going at night, and you don't know who this guy is. That isn't much evidence." He looks at me pointedly. "I'll talk to Lamont."

"And?"

"And now I have another appointment."

"That's it?" Dontae asks once Mr. Cho goes to the cashier.

I shrug. "I guess so. He'll talk with Lamont."

"We gave him everything we had and got nada." He begins eating the rest of Cho's fries as he speaks, until Carmela drops into the seat vacated by Mr. Cho.

"What's going on?" she asks. "Wasn't that Lamont's parole officer?"

"Yeah. I asked him to do something about Lamont, but he won't listen to me," I say.

"Or me," Dontae chimes in. "He doesn't listen to any kid."

"He has to listen," Carmela declares. She gets up and runs through the restaurant, out the door after Mr. Cho. I follow her, eager to see what she will do. I stop and blink when the sunlight hits my eyes. She just runs faster and jumps in front of him before he can climb inside his car. "We want Lamont Rodgers out of our neighborhood," she says.

Mr. Cho shakes his head. "Oh, God. Not more of you. Sorry, kids. This isn't a game. This is real life."

"We're not playing," she insists. "You can order him to go away."

Mr. Cho glances at me. "Would you like it if someone ordered *you* to go away?"

"I'm not the bad guy, he is. We all want him gone."

"Maybe you don't want him around, but you're only a few people," Mr. Cho says.

"How many people would it take to make you decide to do something?" Carmela asks. "What if we had hundreds of people from the community who wanted him gone?"

"Then you might have something," Mr. Cho says with a final snort before climbing into the Jeep and driving off. Carmela and I return to the restaurant and our friends.

"That's how adults act. 'You're just kids,' they always say. We're people too," Carmela says. "Mom and Dad have told me about the old days when ordinary people made the big guys back down. War protests and civil rights."

She pauses when Dontae and I stare at her blankly. "Don't either of you know your heritage?"

"We haven't gotten to that part of the history book yet," Dontae says.

Carmela rolls her eyes and gives him a cluck of pity. "Real history isn't in books. My grandparents lived history and fought to make a difference. Now it's my time to do something big and important." She begins pointing at each of us. "Don't you all get tired when people call us thugs because they can't use the N-word without feeling embarrassed? Or they say inner city like we live in a radioactive wasteland where only rats would choose to stay. Even the police. My dad has to hear it all the time. He says the white officers lower their voices when they see him, but he still hears."

She's right. I do hear what people who don't know us, have never spent one day around us, still believe. It's all because we look different on the outside. They don't come close, look close enough to see that we are the same inside.

"T needs our help," Carmela says. "Think about climbing into bed every night with a criminal on the bottom bunk, closing your eyes and wondering if you'll live long enough to open them again."

"Melodrama much?" Linda murmurs. I hadn't

noticed her come after us.

"I don't want him back in prison," I tell Carmela.

"I thought you wanted him gone, T'Shawn."

"I did. I do, but . . ."

"I know he's your blood, but he's also a danger to us all," Carmela says while waving a careless hand. "He pushes you around, bullies you, but I see you feel bound together by blood. Fine. I'm only going to ask that he be moved far away.

"Far away where?" I ask.

"Anywhere."

"My brother hasn't even done anything yet," I protest.

Carmela scowls. "Maybe not, but he will. He pushes you around, bullies you. He took your bed and stole for you." She makes me sound like a total wimp.

"Dontae!" I've never told anyone else about the bed or the headphones. He bends his head, refusing to meet my eyes.

"Walking the streets at night, writing graffiti," Carmela continues

"We don't know that was Lamont," I try again. I wince when some kids snicker.

"Who else could it be?" Dontae asks. "Your mom shouldn't have let him back."

"Don't blame my mom."

"I'll blame you if you don't do something," Carmela says.

Me? I can't win.

Linda looks at me as if I should be stopping her. But Carmela is on her rant, getting everyone riled up, and, well, I guess I see her point.

"What's the plan?" Dontae asks Carmela.

"A petition. We'll get the parole officer a hundred people and even more." She hugs herself, as if embracing her new idea.

Dontae nods. "Like the Olive Branch Petition we studied during American History."

"Not like that. That was colonists begging, 'Please, King, stop treating us so bad.' That won't work, I won't beg. We have to *demand*." Carmela finishes with her arms raised, eyes fiery. Sometimes she makes me think of a thirteen-year-old version of civil rights leader Diane Nash from my grandparents' days. That woman really did help make the world better. I sometimes wonder if the people around her felt as conflicted as I do about this girl.

"You're crazy," someone says.

No, I think she's right. The American Loyalists begged the king of England to treat the people in the colonies like real British citizens. They received nothing but a laugh in response. Nothing changed in America until after the Revolutionary War. Why should we expect begging to work for us here and now?

"We'll go through TBTS," she continues. "They'll help us. We'll get adults to sign, voters, everyone, including our parents."

"No. No way." I can't even picture Mom's face if I asked her to sign something like that.

"You want him gone most of all," Carmela reminds me.

Maybe. But not like this.

Lamont is lying on his bed when I drop down at my desk after dinner and open a book.

"What are you doing?" he asks after a few minutes of silence.

"Are you blind? Homework." I scowl at him.

He walks over to me holding a high-end android phone in his hand.

"Where did you get that?" I ask.

"I'm expanding my horizons," he replies, which isn't really an answer. He messes with the volume control until I hear music. A YouTube music video plays on the screen. The song is a genre-bending blend of country with overtones of rap, pop, and hip-hop, sung by an all-white group. In the video they traipse through woods and fields singing about "rednecks and homies." Some wear hunting caps, others wear camo gear or hoodies—all eventually end up sitting by a river. They are surrounded by cars, cows, horses, shotguns, and one other, all just chillin', like they say.

When the video ends, Lamont says, "I think I get what you see in this stuff. The lyrics are deep and real. They feel about their part of the world the way I do about mine."

I stare at him, fighting disbelief.

He points at the screen. "I mean, that's still not like real music, but, yeah, I feel this. For these dudes, it's take back the river. I could see myself standing on the bank with them and I bet we'd find a lot in common. It's not the truck or the shotgun or even the cows or horses. That song was about living your life your way and owning who you are and where you're from."

"I could show you more." I almost shake I'm so eager to introduce him to more of my world.

"Do it. This stuff makes me think maybe I'd actually like living in Memphis more than I knew."

Which instantly kills the fun feeling. I can't believe he's still thinking of going down there where the only people he knows are gang members.

He slaps me on the back. "We don't want your grades slipping. How about we listen to a few more while I help you with your math?"

"How are *you* going to help me with geometry?"

"I'm not stupid. I have my GED from prison. I think I know enough to help you."

We listen to more videos on YouTube as we work, pausing once when Nelly, complete with tats and chains, appears in a video, joining with Florida Georgia Line to sing "Cruise." The song isn't exactly rap, but it is practically a Southern anthem. This version is a pop remix that I love. I also love watching the outstanding girls riding in cars with the singers.

"Maybe you shouldn't watch this," Lamont declares at one point.

"Why? Because the trucks are too hot?" I say, smirking when he shakes his head.

"Seriously? You're thirteen and only interested in pickup trucks?"

"That big-wheeled blue number is the bomb." Of course I like watching the girls too. But I really would love to cruise down the streets in one of those tricked-out trucks.

Lamont snorts. "If that's your favorite part of this

video, then I've gotta say you're strange, little bro."

I snort and for a moment feel superclose to my brother. He could always make me laugh. Especially when he treated me like an equal. Like now.

"This is bro-country, redneck rap," he continues. "Different package, same feelings. They are like us, stuck in a world that doesn't care about them, but they're still determined to hold onto their place. City street or country lane, a neighborhood should belong to the people who live there, not politicians or cops or fat businessmen who intend to bleed it dry and leave, or . . ."

"Or drug dealers," I throw in when he pauses.

He heaves a sigh filled with regret. "The streets belong to people who care and work to make their blocks better. That was my goal, T—all I ever really wanted."

It doesn't add up to me. "How did pulling a gun in an old man's face help that?"

"I told you, I didn't have the gun. That was one of the other guys."

"But you were the boss, so it was still on you. Did you ever even tell Mr. Frank you were sorry?"

His lips tighten. "You need to be strong to get something in this world."

"Strength isn't always enough," I tell him.

CHAPTER
TWENTY-THREE

THANKS TO SPRING BREAK, MY days are totally free. Mom is at work, Rochelle is at day care, and Lamont is out doing whatever he does when he's not home, which is pretty much all the time now.

Dontae comes over to my apartment on Tuesday, and we sit together at the kitchen table, studying. Our teachers loaded us up with extra homework over the break. Last night Mom made a big bowl of chicken enchilada dip for us to snack on: black beans, corn, chicken, and homemade enchilada sauce. Dontae and I are gorging on chips and dip while we work on our homework. Dontae has an art project. I'm writing a song for music class. I call it, "Second Chance Drive." I guess I could say having Lamont around inspired me. I've written a little, scratched out a lot. I'll type out the final song on the computer, but I use pen and paper for my drafts because I think in music better when I compose by hand. Being creative is a lot of work.

Dontae finishes his art quickly—naturally. He claims he was born to draw. He looks over my shoulder and reads one line aloud. "'Sometimes heroes hide inside the worst disguise.'" He turns to me with a scowl. "Don't pretend your brother is some secret good guy."

"He's not the devil."

"That's not what you said before."

I shrug. "Maybe I was wrong."

Dontae scratches his head and reads a few more of my lines.

> *All the man needs is a chance.*
> *Don't force him to relive*
> *Things he never should have done and things he never*
>   *did."*

He rolls his eyes before tossing my paper on the table. "'Never did?' Don't you know about cause and effect? He arrived, and bad stuff got worse." Dontae sticks his finger in the dip and pulls out one of the black beans. "Did you see your mother fix this?"

"I helped her," I admit, wondering what he's getting

at. He knows I like working in the kitchen with Mom.

"Did you soak the beans?" he asks. When I nod, he continues, "Then you saw the scum that floats to the top."

"Are you calling my brother scum?" My jaw clenches.

"Didn't you?"

A long time ago. Okay, maybe only a few weeks, but it seems to belong in a history lesson now. Lamont is not perfect—he lies and he's up to something at night—but once in a while, I glimpse the brother I used to know and love and trust. I don't know. I'm just confused, I guess.

"Your dad wants us to give people second chances," I say through trembling lips.

"He's a preacher. He has to say that. You need to be smart." He leaves the table and pulls on his jacket. "I need fresh air. Let's go to the park by the school. We can shoot a little basketball." He walks out. I grab my own coat and the basketball from my closet and run to catch up with him.

We walk in silence for a few minutes, pausing to watch an artist painting a mural on a wall near the stores where Mr. Owens was attacked. The elderly figure the artist has placed on the wall is surrounded by a ring of arms in blue sleeves holding guns. His hands are upraised in surrender. "Someday that could be one of us," Dontae says.

We approach a flock of pigeons so bold they barely

lift their tails out of the way until we draw near. I laugh when wings flutter as they rush to lift off and escape the giant human intruders. Then I laugh even harder when the ball slips from Dontae's hands and rolls into King Drive.

"Oh, man." Dontae looks at me.

"You lost it. You have to get it," I say. That's our rule.

Not many cars are on King Drive right now. But still, too many for him to run into the street without checking. I see the approaching car, driving too fast, and yell for him to stop. The silver Audi bucks while the white driver frantically hits the brakes. Dontae jumps back just in time to avoid being hit.

"Sorry, man, I was trying to get my ball." Dontae smiles, the big one that shows all his teeth and keeps him out of trouble with our teachers.

The driver leans out his window and yells, "You almost hit my car, you stupid black punk!"

I stand on the sidewalk, frozen. I've heard words like that shouted out as people drive through our streets. They shock me every time and feel like broken glass pulled through my skin. It's not just the words. It's everything— the whole package burns my insides like crazy. People say a lot just by the way their eyes flicker, lips tighten, heads turn away. His expression, the narrow-eyed glare, said we weren't wanted and didn't count. I feel like an insect skittering across a newly cleaned kitchen table. Tires scream as the man peels away, his front bumper barely missing a Chevy in front of him.

"I didn't do it on purpose," Dontae mumbles, staring after the car and driver.

I take the ball from his trembling hands. "You need to watch out if you want to live long enough to grow up."

"Once again you sound like my mother. Stop it."

I know how I sound. We are buds—that means we look out for each other.

We continue walking, tossing the ball back and forth, the man and the car already forgotten. Dontae returns to his awkward attempts at dribbling until we reach a fenced-off construction site a block away from the park. There we stop in front of the fence to watch the dinosaur-style excavators dig deep into the ground.

"Imagine being in charge of one of those puppies!" Dontae shouts so I can hear him over the sound of the machines.

"Imagine this time next year when the new grocery store opens. Maybe I can work here in a few years. I could bag groceries or maybe stock shelves." Maybe even get Mom an employee discount.

"A hundred people are going to want those jobs."

Maybe two hundred. I can still dream. Dreams keep me going. Dreams of the past, when Dad and Lamont and I were at the beach, splashing and laughing and enjoying being together. And dreams of the future. Me winning diving medals, going to college, making Mom proud. I love those dreams.

A shadow suddenly falls over me. I turn to find Carmela almost on top of me. I didn't hear her approach with all the noise.

"Where did you come from?" Dontae asks.

Carmela rolls her eyes. "I finished writing the petition. I sent you both links. Have you seen it?" she asks, waving her phone at us.

"Not yet," I lie, wishing she would disappear. I saw her message when I was doing homework with Dontae, but I ignored it.

Dontae looks at her and grins. "We're heading to the park to shoot some hoops." He tosses the basketball in the air. "I have skills."

She shrugs, uncaring. "I play better than you."

"I bet you think you're WNBA material."

"I could be, only I'm going to be a police officer and protect people like my dad."

A siren whoops, the high-pitched sound hurting my ears. Carmela jumps in surprise, as if she thinks it might be her father. I wonder too, until I turn and see the two burly white officers in the car stopped a half block away.

"Uh, T . . . ," Dontae says. He stands, jaws open, eyes bugging as the cops get out of their car and walk over to us. One fingers his taser, the other has a hand near his gun. Neither weapon is drawn. They yell something as they approach, sounds my ears cannot process. We're just three seventh graders and one basketball. We're just watching the construction and talking. We will be okay.

"Want to ride the lightning?" the bigger cop yells. He's the one fingering the nightmare-ugly yellow taser.

"No, sir." A froth of fear runs down my back. Not again! my brain screams. I know I shouldn't stare, but I can't take my eyes from his taser. My stomach feels hollow, and my shoulders itch, anticipating the feel of the prongs penetrating my coat. My feet beg me to run. Hands, legs . . . I can't stop shaking. Dontae stands beside me, hands already in the air. He is bigger and darker than I am and looks older than I do, but he's so scared, he's shaking. Only Carmela looks relaxed as we turn to face the approaching officers.

"We didn't do anything," Carmela says, taking a step forward.

"Did I ask you?" the shorter one says. His hand shifts closer to his gun. I grab her coat and pull her back.

These men aren't her family. At least they don't fear for their lives. If they were afraid, they would already be shooting.

"I need names and ID, starting with you," a cop barks. He points at me.

Out of the corner of my eye, I see Carmela tapping on her phone.

"T'Shawn Rodgers," I say, my voice squeaking.

"Shaun?" He lifts an eyebrow as if my name is a joke.

"T'Shawn," I say, pronouncing it correctly. "People call me T."

"ID?"

"I, uh, I don't have any." I usually have my school ID with me anytime I'm out of the house. Mom insists I be prepared, just in case. Today, of all days, I forgot.

The other cop takes a step closer, eyes squinting. "Don't I know you?"

"No-no, sir." It's never good when a cop thinks you look familiar. I wonder if they think I'm Lamont. But he's older and bigger than me, so that can't be it. Maybe the guy in the Audi did more than just hate on us.

The officer shrugs before turning to Dontae. "Who are you?"

"Don—Dontae Morrow, sir." His breathing seems worse, and sweat sprouts all over his forehead.

"Don-Dontae. Cute." The cop barks a laugh. Hasn't he ever been so scared his insides melted? Too scared to think or talk or do anything except panic.

Carmela steps up again. "You're not supposed to treat people this way. I'm Carmela Rhodes, and my father is—"

"I don't care if he's the mayor. I don't need your family history, girl. Stay back." The officer's hand returns to his taser. He looks jittery, as if he is afraid of us. "Don't move or speak unless I say you can."

She squeaks but doesn't say another word.

My terrified feet want to turn and run. Mom's instructions about dealing with the police flood my brain. Number one rule: come home alive. The best way to stay alive is to remain silent and just obey, no matter how badly they treat us. Don't move or give them any excuse. I can only hope that someone, somewhere close, is watching out for us.

Dontae begins wheezing, swaying on his feet, fighting for breath. He drops the ball. It bounces, rolls, and comes to a stop beside my feet.

"Is he on something?" one officer asks, frowning. His expression morphs between fear and confusion. Then he seems to make a decision. He backs up and puts both hands on his weapon. "On the ground, all of you."

I drop so fast I scrape my cheek on the sidewalk. I've heard that the electricity paralyzes people. I don't want to be paralyzed. My face burns. Tears sting my eyes. Carmela crouches down beside me. And Dontae . . .

Dontae is still standing, swaying, his eyes glassy with pain.

"You heard me, punk, get down now. Stop resisting!"

"He's not resisting!" Carmela yells.

"What did they do?" someone yells but not from too close. People know it's dangerous to be near someone stopped by cops. Neither officer answers the question. Only one speaks, telling the person to retreat, threatening them with arrest if they don't move.

A gurgling sound comes from Dontae's throat. He looks like he wants to speak, or scream, but can't find the strength to do either. He grabs for his chest and falls to his knees. "Don't kill me, please."

"He's having an attack!" I scream. I know what is happening. It's a sickle cell crisis, sudden and acute pain. He's described it to me, how every joint burns as his blood clogs his veins.

The cops drop to a fighting crouch, guns extended. In the distance, I hear an approaching siren. More cops. I don't need more cops.

"Hands behind your backs!" one roars.

"Don't move!" the other screams.

The orders beat into my brain. I'm confused, scared, and my heart beats like it's playing chopsticks with my ribs. Even though the orders the cops bark at me contradict each other, I try to obey. So does Carmela. Only Dontae can't. He clutches his chest, moaning with pain. It's Mr. Owens all over again, and I am as helpless now as I was then. Dontae can't stop moving, grabbing at his arms and legs. His body won't let him. His eyes are wide and scared.

"Stop moving or we'll shoot!"

Dontae can't obey that barked order, and I won't do nothing, not this time. I throw myself on my friend, trying to hold him, shield him, and scream, "Please get a doctor. Call nine one one!" Hoping at least one person watching will call for help. I wish I were home. I want Mom. I want Lamont.

Dontae convulses beneath me.

A new cop car arrives, jumping the curb, running from the road onto the sidewalk before the driver, Sergeant Rhodes, positions his vehicle between us and the weapons. Sergeant Rhodes's voice blares over the loudspeaker, "Stand down!"

I manage a quick look at Dontae, his eyes connecting with mine just before he passes out.

• • •

An hour later, Sergeant Rhodes faces the officers who attacked us. Carmela and I are sitting in a back conference room at the police station. An ambulance had raced Dontae north to the University of Chicago children's hospital. Carmela's the reason we are safe, helped things way more than I did by texting her father for help when things escalated. We would probably be in a cell now, or worse, if he hadn't roared to the rescue.

"You were about to use deadly force on three children, including my daughter," Sergeant Rhodes says, the words cold and slow. I'd slink into the ground if anyone ever talked that way to me.

"We were following procedure, doing our jobs," the older officer says, staring back at Sergeant Rhodes defiantly. "They wouldn't cooperate."

"They—they should have followed our orders," his younger partner stammers.

"Dontae couldn't. He was too sick," I say. Both cops look at me. The older one shrugs. The other swallows after a moment and turns away. Carmela stirs on the bench beside me. I take her hand to keep her from jumping to her feet. I know she wants to yell and protest. That won't do any good and might make things worse for us.

"There was no reason to draw your weapons on unarmed children," Sergeant Rhodes says, his voice breaking. I think he and I both feel the same impossible fury.

"When we're on the streets, we do what we have to do," the defiant officer counters. "There was no way to know they were kids. I mean, look at them. You can't trust any of these people." He pauses, face growing a little pale. I think he's remembering whose daughter he's talking about.

"We were following procedures, doing our jobs," his partner says, a defensive note filling his voice. "We acted within the normal parameters of our job."

Against three kids armed with a basketball? They were solving no crime, protecting no lives. Just teaching us to fear them. A chill descends through my body. Will I go to jail, have a record? I'm only thirteen. Will I be marked forever because of this?

"Why did you stop us?" I ask. "We were just talking, laughing, going to play ball. We didn't do anything."

The older cop turns to me, wide-eyed, flushed, and furious. "You acted in a suspicious manner. And you fit the description of a man we've been told to keep an eye out for."

My brother is six years older, six inches taller, with

big shoulders. But both of us have dark-brown skin, so I guess that's enough.

"And you decided my daughter was also a threat?" Sergeant Rhodes says, face grim, jaw muscles quivering.

"We had no idea she was your daughter. Sir," the cop adds, the sir coming a little late.

"And she's black," I add.

The officer turns to me. "Don't bring race into this."

"When is race ever out when you guys deal with us?" I should be quiet. That's the safe way. But I am so angry, and I don't care. I think of other kids shot by police guns. I suppose I should feel lucky because I did not die like Tamir Rice, the twelve-year-old whose name Redmond didn't even know. Or like Jordan Edwards, who was barely fifteen when a policeman shot him; Cameron Tillman, only fourteen. That's why Sergeant Rhodes is still shaking. His daughter could have joined the long, nearly endless list of names of black kids killed by police officers. Names I never had to learn for any class or test, but I cannot forget.

I understand having to fear criminals and gang members: they are the bad guys. But why do I also have to be afraid of the people who are supposed to be on my side and protect me?

I wrap my arms around myself and shiver. "How did

I scare you?" I ask the policemen. They wear armor and hold weapons and yet feared for their lives when they saw us, as if we were the monsters crawling out from under a kid's bed.

Neither officer responds. The younger officer's cheeks grow pink.

Sergeant Rhodes sighs, then takes Carmela and me from the police station.

"We didn't do anything," Carmela says, her voice breaking. "We were just talking when they came after us. I promise, Daddy, that's all."

"Some officers are overly enthusiastic." He speaks slowly. I can tell he is choosing his words carefully. I know a few vocabulary words that fit better than "overly enthusiastic." Words like "aggressive," "hostile," "intimidating," "uncaring."

And "fearful." That one most of all.

We were all afraid out there.

CHAPTER

TWENTY–FOUR

SERGEANT RHODES DRIVES CARMELA AND me to Comer Children's Hospital at the University of Chicago to see Dontae. The astringent scents sting my nose as we walk down the hall to Dontae's third-floor room. He's so full of pain medicine he wears a dopey smile. A bruise on one cheek marks the spot where he fell and hit the sidewalk. There are paintings on the walls with scenes from Disney stories and an alphabet rug on the floor. Rochelle would enjoy being here. I'm just glad to see my friend sitting up. From the window behind Dontae's head, I can see Midway Plaisance, a long, green island between two rivers of city traffic dotted with people walking, biking, or playing ball.

Linda is here, along with several other kids from school. Dontae's mom and dad leave with Sergeant Rhodes to talk in the hallway. Monitor wires snake from a machine next to Dontae's chair down inside the blue hospital gown covering him. He sees me staring at the wires and shrugs. "This stuff tells the nurses everything about me. They even know when I have to pee before I do."

It's funny but not really. Only Carmela laughs.

"It's been a long time since my last attack," Dontae says. "I guess I was due. The pain is so quick, I can't even describe what it feels like. My mind got fuzzy, everything ached, and by the time I realized what was happening, *wham*. I thought I'd wake up dead." He waves his arm, a thin plastic name tag, the one that brands him as a patient, on his wrist. Then he closes his eyes, and I realize his smile is as fake as mine.

"You know why they stopped us," Carmela says. "Cops have an eye out for Lamont. When they saw T, they thought they were looking at his brother." That's one of the things the officers said when we first reached the station, that they felt they had a right to be cautious because Lamont was a dangerous ex-con.

"Are you serious?" Dontae asks, looking from Carmela to me.

She looks around the room before announcing, "I've finished writing the petition. Once we have enough signatures, the petition will go to our ward's alderman, and the mayor, and Lamont's parole officer. To start off, I need everyone in this room to sign. It needs to begin with you, T."

With those words, I feel the walls of a trap snap shut around me.

"I don't want to see my brother back in prison," I say.

She shrugs. "The parole officer said he could send your brother somewhere else, probably to another neighborhood."

"How will that help?"

"He won't be here. That's what matters. He'll be someone else's problem, and we'll be safe. Lamont might even be happier with a brand-new start."

"I have to think." My head hurts. I have to consider what a new start could mean for my brother. Maybe it's like when players get traded on ball teams and play better afterward. She might be right. I could be helping him. Only, if signing is such a good thing, why does the idea of putting my name on her online petition make me feel like I'm stepping on a pond that's supposed to be frozen solid and hear cracks growing beneath my feet?

"Don't think. Act," she says, getting all up in my face. "Sign and then get your mother to sign too." Dontae nods his agreement. Drops fall from the bottle of fluid to his IV line. His face remains ashen. It's not his fault he is here, or Carmela's. Or mine.

But is it really Lamont's?

"No, I won't." I look from Carmela to Linda, hoping to see some acceptance. I can't sign. And I definitely can't ever ask my mom to sign anything designed to kick out her number-one son.

"I'm launching that petition, no matter what," she declares.

I back out of the room while Carmela talks to some of the others. I can't be here anymore.

Dontae's parents are in the corridor by the door, talking with a doctor. I stand hidden behind his father as they talk.

"The tests show that your son suffered a mild stroke," the doctor says, her voice holding the same tone of practiced sympathy I heard from medical people when Dad entered hospice.

"A stroke? Dear God, he's only twelve." Mrs. Morrow whimpers and puts a hand to her mouth.

I almost do the same. Strokes are for old people. Strokes can cause brain damage.

"They are not uncommon in severe sickle cell attacks," the doctor continues. "I want him to stay in the hospital overnight. Fortunately, he's responding to treatment, and so far, tests indicate there are no lasting effects."

His parents clutch each other and nod. The words must make them feel better, but they don't work on me. I didn't protect my friend. I took him into danger, just by being with him.

I have to get away before I begin blubbering. I rush to the elevator. The second the doors open, I push myself inside, merging with the crowd of doctors wearing white coats over their clothes and nurses in multicolored scrubs. Once at the first floor, I rush from the building. I have to get away and don't care where I go. I walk for a couple of blocks, stopping only when I reach congested Cottage Grove Avenue, a four-lane street filled with cars, buses, and trucks. On the west side of Cottage Grove is Washington Park, with trees, grass, and playgrounds stretching west all the way to Martin Luther King Drive and the gray stone of the DuSable Museum of African American History. Here on the east side is the University of Chicago Duchossois Center for Advanced Medicine, where my father received his cancer treatments. This is the last place I want to be. I should grab a bus and head south to get home.

Instead, I move to stand near the circular drive in front of the cancer center. Cars are lined up to enter the parking garage. There are always crowds around this building, and valet parkers stay busy. Patients, family, and people in lab coats. Large bushes in planters attempt to make the area look cheerful. Doesn't work, at least not with me.

Footsteps come hurrying behind me. "Wait up, T." I turn to see Linda rushing toward me. Her hair is pulled back in a lopsided ponytail that waves in the wind as she runs. She stops in front of me and wipes her hands on her jeans while breathing heavily.

"I saw you leave, and I wanted . . . I've been chasing you for blocks. Are you okay?" she asks.

"I'm fine," I say through clenched teeth, and wait for her to leave and return to the others.

"No, you're not," she says immediately, and takes my hand. "Tell me the truth."

The truth is I suddenly feel warm and relieved.

"I hate being here," I mutter. "I haven't come near this part of the city since Dad moved into hospice."

"What is hospice?"

"The place you go after the doctors give up. Dad had

pancreatic cancer and came here nearly every day for his chemoradiotherapy treatments. Lamont came with him because Dad was too weak to travel alone."

I point to a banner flapping in the strong breeze. It reads, "Welcome to the Forefront of Medicine and Science." "They are supposed to make miracles here. Only not for my dad. They removed part of his insides, gave him 'chemo-brain.'"

"What do you mean?"

"That's how my father described what was happening inside his mind. Dontae said his head felt fuzzy, and the doctor said he had a stroke. My dad had strokes too. At times he couldn't talk." I swallow down a hard lump. "In the end, all they could do was reduce the pain, not cure him. And the insurance company wouldn't pay for all those kinds of treatments. My brother was there through it all. He kept the worst news away from me, kept it inside."

Linda stays quiet, then says, "Hey, you want to go for a bike ride?" She points to the Divvy bike stand across the way.

I nod, and we rent a pair of bikes and begin pedaling east, away from the building. Linda stays at my side, not interfering or trying to make me feel better. This is better than being alone.

Linda barely sweats as we ride the nearly two miles between the hospital and the Museum of Science and Industry. We use the pedestrian underpass at 57th Street to cross under Lake Shore Drive, pausing and walking our bikes as we pass the colorful mosaic panels set into the stone walls. Car horns and the rumble of trucks and CTA buses shake the roof. Voices echo off the walls. We emerge into the rocks and sand of the beach. Cooler by the lake is a real thing in Chicago, especially in the spring. I shiver beneath my thin jacket in the too-cold wind. Linda is smarter than me and wears a hooded coat.

In the summer, the 57th Street Beach is always jammed. Now gulls are our only companions.

I pause, just thinking, and Linda stays silent next to me. A squad car goes by on Lake Shore Drive, and I shiver. "I'm scared of a lot of things," I say.

"And here I thought you were supposed to be a top student," she says, smiling.

"Top enough to be duking it out with you for the number-one spot," I say, and elbow her in the side. Gently, so she knows I'm just kidding.

"You don't have a chance of beating me—not in English, anyway, because you messed up your tenses.

Maybe you *used to be* scared of many things, but I don't believe anything scares you anymore. Not even your brother."

"The police scare me."

"Yet you threw yourself on Dontae to protect him."

Yeah, well I'm still a little scared of girls, especially smart ones. I just like being around this girl—something I'll never admit. Not soon, anyway.

I look out over the lake.

"This is where Lamont brought me the day he taught me to swim," I tell her. "He used to say that the prettiest lifeguards were on this beach." I chuckle. "Lake Michigan seemed endless. It looked like all the water in the world stretched out in front of me that day. I was scared and embarrassed to be so afraid, but my big brother never laughed at me. He just walked waist deep into the freezing water and held out his hand to me. 'Do you think I'd let you drown, Short Stack?' he said. 'Trust me.' Those words meant everything to me."

Linda smiles, making her eyes shine.

I step closer. The water is so clear I see the sand and rocks under my shoe. I confirm it's too cold to even think about swimming. I bend down and grab a stone and toss it as far as I can.

"What makes you do that?" Linda asks.

"Nothing. And everything." I needed to let loose some energy. I feel like today will never end. Only a few hours ago, I was doing homework, writing a song as if there was a reason to be happy. I can't believe the sun is still so high in the sky.

"You throw stones just because you can?"

"Yeah." Small stones that fit in your hands exist to be thrown. I pick up another one, feel its smooth, moist surface. Then I pull back my arm and send it soaring far from the beach and watch it go plunk in the water.

"I see." She nods like she's solved some mystery. A moment later, she bends to get a stone of her own. Her throw barely makes it to the water.

"You have to put your whole body into it," I say. "First hold your stone. Let your muscles feel the weight and shape before you throw. Like preparing before a test."

She takes another stone, this one larger, and hefts it for several seconds before throwing again. This one goes almost as far as mine. I clap and congratulate her.

"Feel better?" I ask.

"Actually, yes, that does work," Linda says through teeth that chatter louder than the waves lapping at the rocks. "My father claims he found God in prison." She shudders.

"Do you believe him?"

"I don't care. Maybe he found God, or God found him. It doesn't bring Mom back." She bites her bottom lip and sighs. "My aunt says forgive and forget. She loves him; he's her brother. But that's not always enough." The sadness in her eyes deepens as she looks at me. "I know you want to trust your brother, but trust can be dangerous."

"Don't you think people can change?" A burning sensation grows inside me, flaring from my stomach, up my throat, into my mouth. Sometimes I want Lamont gone, to never see him again. Mostly I want him to change and be my family again.

"I used to think that, before. I wanted to forgive my dad, and now I can't even forgive myself," she says.

"You can't blame yourself. That would be like me blaming me because Lamont's friends attacked Mr. Frank. Your father was the bad man. He messed that up, not you."

Linda rubs her eyes with the back of her hand. "I tried to trust him. I wanted to believe in him. I knew he could get so angry. Enraged is the word. I knew he and Mom fought before she divorced him. But I never thought he would kill her. I thought they were in love, that they would get back together someday."

My months in the shelter taught me not all parents are good or loving like mine. Those ladies talked a lot, and sometimes they were really loud. I know why so many got scared of Lamont when he strutted around the building talking mean. Sometimes I think he wanted to frighten people on purpose.

"Your brother wants a second chance. When he messes that up, who gets the blame?" She hiccups.

I know the answer. Me and Mom and Rochelle. The people closest to him.

"Do you think you'll ever forgive your father?" I ask.

"I can't even forgive myself."

"You aren't to blame for what your parents did."

Linda bites her lower lip before continuing. "I didn't tell you everything about my family and the night my father killed my mother. I didn't tell you what I did." A large tear begins rolling down her cheek. "I was mad at Mom when she divorced him. But I never wanted her dead."

"Of course not, but you couldn't stop your dad."

"That's it. I could have stopped him. Instead . . . I helped him kill my mother." She wipes at the tear and ends up smearing the wet all over her cheek.

"No way. Don't say that about yourself."

"People think Mom caved and let him inside, but it

was me. He begged me, said he only wanted to apologize. I was eight years old, and I wanted my family back together again, so I let him in the house. I never told that to anyone."

Except me. Now I understand too much about Linda Murhasselt.

She hiccups. "Sometimes I want to go to the prison and rip my father to pieces. But I'm the one I really hate. I wasn't strong enough to do what I had to do to protect my mother. Don't be weak like me, T."

Trusting the wrong people only gets you hurt. I know it was the cops who actually hurt us, but blaming them doesn't change anything. Some officer will see me again and decide I might be a threat like my brother. They will come after me again, just as long as he remains around us. This time Dontae and Carmela were hurt. Next time it could be Linda. A cop patrolling this beach right now could see me and . . .

"We have to get back," I say, and grab her arm, leading her back to our bikes.

"What's wrong?"

"You're not safe as long as you're around me." I use my phone to pull up Carmela's petition and read it. "I can't believe she said all this. She did everything except call him a predator."

"I helped with a lot of it," Linda admits. "She wanted to use that word, but I talked her out of it."

"She listened to you?" I say, feeling grateful but confused.

"I know people think she bullies me, but Carmela and I are friends. Besties. We've been close ever since her father arrested mine. After that, we became like sisters." She giggles. "Maybe I am the little sister, but we are friends. And I think her father is a real hero."

CHAPTER
TWENTY—FIVE

AFTER WEDNESDAY'S PRACTICE, I GRAB a quick dinner and rush to the church for the April TBTS meeting. Lamont is home babysitting Rochelle.

Gang issues are on this month's agenda. So is the name Lamont Rodgers. Mom walks in looking like she is a mile past furious. She pauses for a moment, staring at the agenda on the wall, lips pressed tight. Then she lifts her head and makes her way to a seat near the front. She looks like she's daring anyone to say anything to her.

I take a spot against the wall with Carmela and Linda. By the time things begin, the meeting room holds even more people than last month.

"I was out cleaning graffiti again last week," a man says, turning to Mom. "Your son comes home, and now it's twice in the last few weeks."

"Lamont assures me he was not involved," Mom says.

Carmela stands beside me, barely stifling a giggle. "What's he supposed to do, confess?" She steps forward. "Some of you may have heard about the petition on Lamont Rodgers," she begins.

"Someone actually asked me to sign that thing to get my son returned to prison," Mom says.

I slink back against the wall. My face blazes as I wait for Carmela to expose my role in things.

"That's not what it's about," Carmela says.

"It's about my son. I told the guy exactly where he could place that thing," Mom continues, her face a mask of righteous rage.

"The local police have been instructed to let gang members know they aren't wanted around here," Carmela's father says in his official voice.

"My child is wanted," Mom says, her voice still shaking.

"He's not a kid. He's been spotted hanging around the corners with other gangbangers. That's against the rules of his parole. He's not allowed to associate with them, as I'm sure his parole officer informed him," Sergeant Rhodes says.

"Then who does he get to associate with?" Mom asks. "We should all remember these gang members, bangers, whatever we call them—they are still someone's son or daughter."

Several people in the room nod. I hadn't thought much about gang members being kids too. Like I am. Like Lamont used to be.

Carmela begins talking again. She has a tablet full of crime statistics and wants to read them off and lay the blame on Lamont. Robberies in our neighborhood have gone up in the last month. The rise may have begun before his arrival, but it has definitely gotten worse since his return. I wonder if any of those robberies involved headphones.

"I appreciate the numbers." Pastor Morrow steps forward. "But until this young man actually *does* something, he deserves a second chance."

"I knew he would do that," Carmela says, punching me in the arm.

"He has to," I mutter. I rub my shoulder before adding, "It's a God thing, and he really believes all that stuff he preaches."

Our pastor also makes people listen. Throughout the crowd, people nod and begin settling down. They listen when he suggests scheduling a prayer march against gangs.

"Spread the word," he says. "I'll be speaking about the plans for our Unity March every Sunday for the next few weeks. We'll let the world know we may be surrounded by war, but we stand for peace."

"Yeah, that'll help," Carmela mutters.

"Looks like the adults feel there are more important things to worry about than my brother," I say as the discussion moves on to the next agenda item.

Carmela shakes her head. "I won't stop. This is going to happen, with or without them."

"What happens next?" I ask. "How will you get enough people to sign on?"

"We have to go to the next level. Social media. I have followers on Twitter and Instagram. We all do. We'll blast the internet, wage a campaign, and get people lining up to sign."

I just shake my head, knowing I can't stop her.

"The people aren't wrong about your son," Sergeant Rhodes tells Mom after the meeting. I stayed behind to help the pastor clean up. Dontae is still in the hospital.

"You need to think about letting him go."

"Are you trying to order me to send Lamont away?" Mom asks in an icy voice.

"I can't order you to do anything. I'm only asking you to pay attention to your neighbors' welfare and your own. The local police are aware of his presence and his history. They decide what happens if he steps outside the lines. If he even gets too close to whatever line they draw, there could be issues. I'm concerned about you, T, and your daughter. If something happens, don't get caught in the blowback."

I can see why Linda calls him a hero. When he speaks so gently to Mom, he reminds me of my father. A light seems to shine through his dark-brown eyes. He's off duty and out of uniform but still has the quiet air of a protector. I could become a police officer someday if I could be like him, strong and brave and really fight to protect and serve people.

"That's for me to worry about," Mom says.

Dontae has to stay in the hospital a few of days, but he is back in school by Thursday. We go through our classes together and then sit in the cafeteria at lunch. Linda sits with us. After our talk at the lake, things are good between us.

"We have over five hundred names already," Carmela says. "And my friends are asking people to sign, at bus stops, El stations, everywhere."

"My dad's not happy about the idea," Dontae admits. "He keeps talking about people deserving second chances."

"He has to believe in forgiveness. He's a minister," Carmela says with a touch of annoyance.

Linda puts down her plastic fork. Her plate is still half-full. This is burrito day, one of my favorite lunches. Even though she likes it too, she doesn't take another bite. I take her hand; it's trembling.

"You only have to forgive yourself," I tell her, wishing that was as easy to do as it is to say.

CHAPTER
TWENTY–SIX

MEET.

With a million vocabulary words to choose from, why do people use that one to describe this, my first-ever official competition in front of judges and a real audience? Saturday morning, and I wake up at four. The team bus will arrive before six to take me to the suburban pool where the meet will be held. Participants have to be there early. Lamont barely looks up when I leave. He obviously plans to ignore my big moment. I asked him yesterday if he was coming to my meet.

"To some fancy aquatic center in the western suburbs?" He snorted. "I don't belong there, and neither do you."

Mom and Rochelle promise to be there, but they will come later, after breakfast. I choke down a piece of toast because the coach said we should eat before, but that's all. My stomach is too jumpy for anything more. I can't chance embarrassing myself and puking from the board.

Mr. Hundle said we were coming to have fun. The lump jumping around inside my stomach isn't so sure. "It's a chance to get your feet wet," he told me, and then laughed at his unfunny joke.

Only ten other Rays have chosen to compete today. Sammy and I are the only divers attending. The good news: this isn't a real Illinois Swimming–sanctioned competition. I get to do what the Hun said and consider this a day of fun. My entry fee was paid from my scholarship, and I wanted to come to see what a swim meet was like. There will be two other teams: from the Chicago Park District team and from the North Side Dolphins, another private club. Mung says our only real competition is the Dolphins.

"My parents sign me up for every single meet," Sammy tells me during the ride on the team bus down Interstate 55 to the West Side. "I didn't do so good last time, only fourth place. I have to be on top today." I bet he will. His muscles continue to grow. All the calisthenics are working for him. I'm a little jealous. I've been growing stronger but not like him. There will be eight divers in our age group so I would love to finish in fourth place.

I look up at the roof on the bus and pray, "Please God, not last place, okay?"

The team bus carries us west on US 20 past honest-to-God fields, Harmony turns from her seat in front of us. "Calm down. You'll do fine. This is just for fun."

"Maybe for you." Sammy shivers. "I can't have Mom freak out again. My parents think everything is win or die."

"Diving is more his mother's thing than his," Harmony tells me. "She used to be an NCAA champion. His parents sometimes expect too much from him."

"What does your uncle expect from you?"

"Obedience."

The one flat, pain-filled word explains so much. Even the way he seldom talks to her. He ignores her except when she bombs.

"Is he mean to you?" I ask.

"Not according to him. He never wanted his little brother to marry a black woman." Harmony doesn't look angry, just sad, calm, and way older than eighteen.

Our bus glides down the expressway to the West Side of Chicago. I've never been to this area before. Looking out the window, I feel like I'm traveling to a different world, an imaginary place with small buildings instead of apartment houses. Once the bus exits the expressway, we drive down streets lined with trees and big houses that are low and long, instead of tall, compact apartment buildings. Our driver slows down, weaving around to avoid the annual crop of spring potholes just as we have to do in the streets in my neighborhood. Winter makes some things the same all over the city.

Lawns out here are large and surrounded by fences. There are no stoops in front of the houses for people to sit on and talk together or to watch kids play. In fact, the sidewalks are pretty empty, with more trees visible than people. I wonder how many of the people who live on the other side of the fences know one another. Do they feel lonely and need these huge fences because they're scared of something? People around here should just pop over to their neighbors for coffee, cookies, and gossip. That's how we do things on the South Side. It's why Mom has so many friends and everyone knows everyone else.

"People out here mostly have terraces and patios behind their homes, where they relax and forget about the real world," Harmony explains.

"In the alley?" I ask, astounded. We play in the alleys back home.

"Places like these don't have alleys," she says. "These are 'estates.'" She makes air quotes around the word. "Huge yards and fences and a love of privacy."

"How do you know so much about this area?"

"Uncle Bill lives near here. That's how the Rays chose an event at this facility. We do a lot of meets out here."

"Lamont told me you used to be a Dolphin," I say.

She nods. "Back when I lived with my parents in Lincoln Park. But they died when I was fifteen, and I moved in with my uncle and got to know life here on the West Side. He made me switch. Couldn't have someone cavorting with the enemy in his own house."

Our bus pulls into a parking lot and stops in a space not far from the Lexus belonging to Sammy's parents.

"Of course my folks have already arrived," he says, sounding uncomfortable.

Big signs inside the building welcome us and point the way to the registration area. I am once again one of only a handful of nonwhite people around. Then the Chicago Park District team arrives. Twenty people climb off their bus. The CPD team is a diverse group. Some short, some tall, from wiry thin to slightly chunky. White, black, Hispanic, Asian. I wonder which ones are divers.

My teammates don't say much in the crowded locker

room as we change next to the CPD and North Side teams. After, we come together, and Mr. Hundle and Coach Mung give us a pep talk.

"We're after individual scores, but we're still a team. When you are not competing, make sure you're around to cheer on your teammates. Remember to relax. View this as a special practice session featuring friendly rivals."

There is more than just chlorine in the air inside the Y. Voices echo around the pool area and the big table where the judges sit. It all feels so . . . official. So real. I look around at my "friendly rivals" and see one black kid from the CPD team waving at me. I wave back.

"Not too friendly," Carmela whispers to me. "I expect points from you."

Four members of the Chicago Park District team join us at the diving area, including the boy who waved at me. Names come up on the board.

CPD 8: JALEEL WINDSON
RAYS 12: SAMUEL BAKER
RAYS 15: TSHAWN RODGERS

I sigh. Guess they couldn't find an apostrophe to make my name correct.

My schedule calls for me to attempt four simple dives,

all in the layout position. In an official event, divers have to do seven dives from different diving categories, including the dreaded reverse, or gainer. That thing can be a killer unless the hurdle is dead on. Even famous divers like Greg Louganis have hit their heads doing a gainer. Sammy does them in practice and begged the coach to add a reverse somersault to his list of dives. Mung nixed that. He also said no when I asked to add a twist to one of my dives, saying, "It's too soon."

I hate to agree, but the coach is probably right. I wobble more than I twist. Today my dives will all be straight layouts with minimal difficulty. Low difficulty means a low result because the judges' individual scores are multiplied by the difficulty to give the final score.

Members of all three teams take turns doing practice dives from the three-meter board. My first dive in competition will be a back dive. Simple, easy. It's basically a back lineup, and I've probably done dozens of those in the past weeks.

When my name is called for the first round of dives, I mount the ladder and find myself shaking. I feel like I did the first time I stepped on a board and looked over the side at the wall of water so far away.

Be calm, calm, calm.

I can do this. I deserve to be here. PITA—I imagine

myself flying through the air, landing, and scoring a perfect ten.

Mom and Rochelle have arrived, their brown faces are easy to spot among the many paler family members squeezed together on the spectator benches. Mom smiles and waves. She won't stop until I wave back. Linda is here too. There's no sign of Lamont, but then I didn't really expect him.

I walk to the edge of the board on stiff legs, feeling the rough surface bounce under my bare feet. Back dives don't get the three-step approach. At the end of the board, I turn my back on the spectators and stare into the shadows cast by some equipment piled up against a wall. As I watch, I glimpse movement. Two people are in a shadowy downward stairwell. Harmony and Bishop, our team's tall, blond long-distance-swimming, bigmouthed troublemaker. They are almost invisible, and no one else in the stands has my angle. He hands her something that she stuffs in the pocket of her warm-up jacket. Then they kiss. It's one of those big kisses, the kind from movies, a big long, grown-up kind of kiss. I feel a little sorry for Lamont. I don't think he has any chance with her now.

I pull my mind back to my own effort and prepare for flight. With only my toes and the balls of my feet on the board's tip, I circle my arms once for lift while my legs press the board down. The board pushes back, moving me out, up, around, and down. I'm in the air. I'm flying!

My entry feels good; I go deep, always a good sign. When I pull myself out of the pool, I do a victory dance inside my head while waiting for my score. The dance dies when I see the judges' number.

Five point zero.

Mom is on her feet, yelling and clapping. This is going to be so embarrassing.

"Not bad," Jaleel says. "How long have you been diving?"

I stare into his deep-set eyes. He seems to be sincere. "A few weeks."

"And competing already? You must be good. That wasn't bad for a first meet. You kind of forgot to point your toes, and your legs came apart. Just a little bit. Judges notice that kind of thing," he continues, with a wise glint in his eyes.

Fifty percent. That's like getting a D minus or being handed a participation ribbon or something. "It's pitiful."

"No, that's a really cool score," he insists. His voice is low, the words gentle. "I was so nervous on the first dive at my first meet, I made an epic fail, as in zero points. My parents still laugh with me over that one."

He's improved a lot since those days. His first dive is a one-and-a-half somersault in the pike position. There is only the tiniest splash when he enters the water. He looks just like the guys in the videos I've been watching. He gets an eight point five from the judges. He deserves the applause.

"You surprise me," he says when I praise him. "Most of the Rays act like they're the elite and we should be thrilled we're allowed to breathe the same air they do."

Sammy is up next. His face is totally serious as he moves down the board to perform exactly the same dive, only in the tuck position. He gets the same score from the judges. However, the tuck position gives him a lower degree of difficulty than the pike. That makes his total score, the judges' numbers multiplied by the degree of difficulty, lower than Jaleel's.

"Nice going," Jaleel says as Sammy pulls himself out of the pool.

"If I were the judge, I'd give you a perfect ten," I tell my friend.

"I hope the judges listen to you," he sputters. "And why is he here? Go back to your own guys," he says, waving Jaleel toward the rest of the Chicago Park District divers.

Jaleel winces, then turns to go.

"Why did you do that?" I ask. "He was just being friendly."

"Well, I don't want to be friendly. I need to win. He's the enemy—don't you get that?" His words come fast, and he looks ready to separate from his skin.

"Dude, are you okay? Cool it," I say.

"How do I cool down?" he snarls at me, something he's never done before. "I don't have all day. I need to get this done. They need to hurry up."

The men's eight-hundred-meter freestyle begins over in the main pool. Sixteen trips, back and forth, end to end. Boring but somehow hypnotic. People scream out the names of swimmers who can't possibly hear in the middle of the churning water. Harmony comes to stand near us. Bishop is in lane number five.

"Part of me hopes the Dolphins crush us," Harmony murmurs to me as the swimmers continue.

"Aren't you supposed to be rooting for your boy-friend?" I ask. It's supposed to be a joke, but she frowns.

"What boyfriend?" she asks, sounding puzzled.

"Bishop. I saw you kiss him after he handed you a present." Bishop's long arms have him in front of the other racers.

She grabs my arm and jerks me to a corner. "Why were you spying on me?"

"I wasn't spying or anything." I pull free and step back. "I saw you on the stairs while I was up on the board for my first dive, that's all."

She sucks in a deep, shivery breath and calms a little. "Don't say anything, not to my uncle or to anyone. If he finds out, I'll have a huge problem. Uncle Bill considers Bishop the answer to a prayer, the perfect guy for his imperfect niece. He wants to shove us together."

"But if you like him and your uncle likes him, what's the problem?"

"He's not the angel my uncle thinks he is. We're just friends, and I want to keep things that way."

"What are you and Lamont?" I ask.

"We are nothing." The anger in her voice is so thick, my skin itches.

"Coach should have let me do that reverse," Sammy says when he emerges from the pool after his next dive. He receives good scores but remains a few points behind Jaleel. "I could score big and get in front of everyone."

"It's too late now. Your list of dives has already been turned in." Once that happens, we can't change anything.

There's no temptation for me to try to throw in a twist because a change now would have me marked a zero. "You're getting eights and higher. You'll finish near the top."

"I don't want to be near the top, I have to be the top. That Chicago Park District guy is better than I knew. I need a high-difficulty dive." He begins pacing while talking to himself.

"Relax," Harmony tells him.

"Losers relax." His eyes are wide, bright. "Why are there so many people here?"

"I don't know." And I don't know what's wrong with him.

He walks off, scowling and furious, half running. I yell at him to slow down, but he pays no attention. I start after him but stop when he enters the locker room.

"He'll come back when he's ready," Harmony says. "And he'll feel better then." She leaves me staring at the locker room door.

Sammy doesn't want me, but I feel like I should be doing something more. I decide to talk to Coach Mung.

"Sammy's having a problem," I tell him.

Mung shakes his head, tossing my concerns. "No problem. There's nothing wrong with that boy. He's diving well, scoring strong."

"But he's really worked up."

"He's always worked up. He's a competitor, with fire in his blood. You could use a little more of that. I watched you getting a little too close to members of the other team."

"The Hun said we're supposed to have fun."

"That's because he's a businessman, not a real coach. You need to burn with the desire to win." Mung's hands clench into fists as he speaks.

"Is winning that important?" I ask.

His snort echoes across the chamber. "What's the point of being second best?"

He sounds a lot like Sammy's parents. I wonder if Harmony has to listen to that same question.

My score went up on my second dive, although it was still in D territory. Ten is excellent. Nine to seven is good or very good. Five to six is satisfactory, aka a D. Anything less than five is a kind of "at least you tried" score.

I move to a position where I can keep my eyes on Jaleel. Maybe we're not on the same team, but I feel better watching his red-brown legs stride down the board.

Another Park District kid, a Hispanic boy, is up on the board. Jaleel yells up words of encouragement. I cross my fingers. If Harmony is not being a traitor by rooting for the Dolphins, it's okay for me to silently cheer on the Park District kids. The kid does the same back dive I did at the beginning and scores a four point eight. I applaud him but grin inside because I am *not* in last place.

I turn away from the board, happy, and then freeze. Lamont came! My brother is exiting the boys' locker room with Sammy at his side. Lamont is dressed in black pants and a black hoodie, as if the muggy air around the pool is less important than keeping his face hidden.

He nods when he sees me and walks faster, reaching me before Sammy does. It's hard to look at my brother and not think about the petition Carmela keeps urging me to sign.

"How long have you been here?"

He smiles, and my chest does a thump-thump. "Long enough to see you dive twice. Those judges robbed you, Short Stack."

My stomach jumps at the unexpected praise, and I barely notice the hated nickname.

A second later he says, "Sorry, T. I keep forgetting."

"They robbed me too," Sammy says. His eyes gleam. He sounds less hyper than before. I'm glad he found a way to relax and wonder if Lamont said anything to him.

"Yeah, you too," Lamont agrees, but keeps his eyes on me.

Harmony joins us, looking both delighted and surprised. "You actually came."

"You called. Of course I came." Lamont's big grin widens when he sees her. I guess I wasn't the only reason he came. Maybe not even the real reason.

"Some friends are going out to celebrate after the meet," Harmony says. "Want to come along?"

"I can't. Mom's taking me out for lunch," I say.

She frowns, and I realize she hadn't meant me.

"I suppose you'd rather spend time with your mother too," she says to Lamont.

"I'd rather *not* spend time with your uncle."

"That makes two of us." She places a hand on my brother's arm. "That's why he's not invited."

An air horn sounds. The eight-hundred-meter race ends with Bishop taking first place by several seconds. Harmony leaves, saying she has to get back to the other swimmers. Sammy shrugs, then heads for the diving well.

"You should go with her," I say to Lamont. "I know you want to. She's the reason you came."

"I came to be with you," he says, looking at me.

"But you *want* to go with her."

He gives a scornful smile and shakes his head. "I came to see what being on this team has done for you. You've accomplished a lot in a few weeks."

"I couldn't have done it without you," I say. I didn't even expect to—it just slipped out.

"What?" A muscle in his jaw jerks.

"You got me over my fear of water and taught me how to swim."

"Oh, right. I did that." His relief when I explain what I meant seems overdone.

"I, uh . . . I have to get back to diving," I say. "They'll be calling my name soon."

"Go ahead. I'll be watching."

My next dive is a jackknife. By the time I climb the ladder, I feel loose and relaxed. I know my dive is good the moment I hit the water with my hands clasped and toes pointed. Even Coach Mung gives me an approving nod when I climb from the pool. The judges give me seven. That's at least a C. With only one dive left, I am sure I will escape last place.

"Great job," Jaleel says. Of course, he's in first place with only one dive to go, so he gets to be generous. But it still feels like high praise. I look around, searching for Lamont. I find the black-clad form standing in a corner, almost hidden by the stands. He's too far away for me to see his expression.

"Samuel Baker, what are you doing?" a woman yells, jerking my attention up to the stands. Sammy's mother in her Rays jacket stands, pointing at the springboard. People around her begin to rise. An air horn sounds, beginning the next race, the women's two-hundred-meter freestyle. One girl stays in the blocks—Harmony Mung. She stands, stares toward the diving board, her mouth open, and misses the start of her race. Sammy's mother pushes her way through the crowd in her row. I turn to look at the diving board. The three-meter board is empty.

Sammy has climbed up onto the ten-meter board, towering over our heads. We haven't used that during this meet. The board vibrates and rattles under his weight as he jumps around, punching the air like he's boxing with an invisible opponent.

"I'm going to make a ten!" he yells.

"Samuel, get back down here right this second!" his mother screams. She almost falls on her way out of the stands, but people catch her and hold her upright. I don't think Sammy notices what's going on down here. At first, I think he is just being a trickster up on that board. He looks cartoon funny, like he's trying to dance.

Or like a kid high on drugs. My mouth falls open as I realize this is not a performance.

Sammy begins running down the board, arms swinging like wings preparing for lift-off.

He might have managed some kind of dive if his foot didn't slip in the middle of his hurdle. That's practically suicide for almost any dive, double that when attempting a gainer. As soon as I see the misstep, I know what's about to happen. Every diver, coach, and judge in the place knows. Sammy rises in the air, turns like a wounded pigeon, and hits the board solidly with his head on the way back down.

He drops, stone-like, his entire body hitting the water at once.

I jump in the diving well almost before his limp body hits. Three strokes and I grab him, put an arm around him, and struggle to hold his head above water while I sidestroke toward the edge of the pool. He's so muscular, his body doesn't want to stay at the surface. I feel myself being pulled down. Before that happens, a half-dozen adults are in the water, grabbing us both and guiding us to the side of the pool.

Someone wraps a towel around me when I climb out of the water. I watch, shivering, as Mr. Hundle and Coach Mung begin CPR. The Hun does chest compressions; Mr. Mung, mouth-to-mouth. Mom pushes through the crowd to me, towing Rochelle.

"I'm fine," I say through chattering teeth. Rochelle hugs me. She doesn't know what's going on and laughs as she fingers my wet head. Nothing is funny to me. The springboard continues vibrating in the air above us.

Harmony stands nearby, slowly shaking her head.

Members of all three teams hang close, staring. I barely hear the coaches as they count out chest compressions and breaths. The skin on the side of Sammy's head has been torn by his collision with the board. Blood flows sluggishly. His parents stand nearby, hugging each other and sobbing. Lamont . . . I can't see him anywhere. The crowd is too big.

It seems like forever before paramedics rush in. Mr. Hundle and Coach Mung step back to let them take over.

They work on him for several minutes, checking his heart and breathing. My heart barely beats.

"Show's over," Mr. Hundle says. He gestures for us to

leave the area. I can't move, can't jerk my eyes away from the paramedics working on Sammy. I hover as close as I can, hoping to see him wake up. So many people talking, but all I hear is the sound of Sammy's head hitting the board.

"Any idea what drugs he was using?" one paramedic asks his parents.

"Drugs? He's not sick." Sammy's mother shakes her head.

"I think he means illegal drugs," her husband says, wrapping an arm around her.

"Never. He's never taken anything."

"His parents obviously know little about his life," Harmony mutters.

People pat my back and call me a hero. Me, the villain's brother. If Sammy took drugs today, someone gave them to him. I was right not to trust my brother.

"Where's Lamont?" I ask Mom.

She looks puzzled by my question. "He's not here." Shows how little my mother knows.

The paramedics lift Sammy onto a stretcher and take him out. Sammy's arm twitches as the paramedics wheel the stretcher to the exit. His parents clutch each other as they follow. Harmony trails behind them.

A huge hole opens in my heart, and I shiver inside as I drag myself to the locker room. All three teams are heading there. The meet is over. No one wants to race or dive again.

CHAPTER
TWENTY—SEVEN

RUMORS SWIRL INSIDE THE LOCKER room as I struggle to change. My hands fumble with the buttons on my shirt. No one actually knows anything, but many have something to say.

"Had to be drugs. Nothing else makes you that crazy."

"I heard performance enhancers."

"Betcha Sammy put on an act because the Park District kid was creaming him."

"Those guys must have slipped him something," one Ray says. Most of my teammates nod. The Park District kids are huddled in a corner, backs turned, pretending not to hear. I understand. I always wonder what my teammates say about me when I am not around.

The coaches are waiting outside the locker rooms. "Head for the bus," Mr. Hundle says.

"Can we visit Sammy?" Carmela asks. She pauses at the door, blinking rapidly and rubbing her eyes.

"We'll let you know if—I mean, when he can handle visitors," Coach Mung says.

"He meant if," Harmony whispers to me. A tear traces a path down her cheek as we walk out of the building. "His parents worry about brain damage."

"They told you that?" I ask, astonished.

"I overheard them talking with the paramedics." She closes her eyes and wipes her forehead.

"Those who provide drugs to children don't belong around civilized people," Coach Mung says next to me, almost vomiting out the words.

"My brother isn't an animal," I say.

He moves to stand in front of me, breathing heavily. "Apparently we both know who I mean. Where is he now? Don't deny he was around the building. I saw him earlier."

"He didn't do anything. He just came to see me."

Harmony steps up. "Why blame Lamont or members of the Park District team? What about the Dolphins? Or one of the people on our own team? What about me?"

Her voice grows louder and more shrill with each question. "Anyone could be responsible."

"But it wasn't anyone," Carmela says, eyes still on me.

I shake my head, walk out, and ride the bus the rest of the way in silence.

My mother and sister are already home when the bus drops me off. Lamont is nowhere around.

Hours pass, and nothing about the event appears on any official news outlet. An accident involving a solitary boy is too unimportant, I guess. The networks are full of stories of shootings, stories that are repeated again and again, leaving no room for things that are important to us. Only rumors fill social media. Neither Sammy's parents nor our coaches post any information about what happened at the pool.

All I find online are posts and tweets from team members and spectators continuing the rumors I first heard in the locker room. Mom always says you can't trust rumors. But they are all I have. Lamont used to deal drugs when he was in the gang. What if he's begun doing it again? And the thefts that have occurred around W3C and the neighborhood. Maybe he . . .

No. I don't want to think he had anything to do with any of this. But the headphones are still sitting in their box in the closet. He has money but still claims to have no job. That adds up to trouble. That I can't deny.

Rochelle wanders into the room while I sit on the bottom bunk with my head in my hands.

"You're in the wrong bed," she says in a solemn imitation-Mom voice. "Where is my other brother?"

"I don't know, and I don't care," I admit. Then I calm down. She's too young to really understand, so I gently add, "I think Lamont messed up and doesn't want to come home."

Rochelle gives me a long, quiet look and tilts her head to one side. It's another imitation-Mom attitude, used when my mother has difficult choices. Then Rochelle climbs on the mattress beside me and leans close to my ear. "I mess up too. Then I say I'm sorry, and things get all better."

I smile at her. She makes everything sound simple.

I brush a braid aside and kiss her forehead. "You're smarter than me, Shelly." I don't remember when I started using Lamont's nickname for her.

"Yeah, I'm this smart," she says, throwing her arms wide and almost hitting my nose.

My phone buzzes with a text from Carmela asking—practically demanding—I go.

I text her back, saying I'm on my way. I tell my mom I'm only going to Dontae's—otherwise she'll worry.

The Rhodes family lives in a small two-story bunga-low with a tiny lawn and a garage opening onto the alley. Both Dontae and Linda are waiting for me there.

"What's so important?" I ask Carmela, feeling grumpy.

"What happened to Sammy is all Lamont's fault."

"You can't say that. There's no proof," I insist.

"I can say whatever I want."

"Even if it's not true?"

"*I* think it is true," she snarls, which doesn't answer my question. Carmela always thinks everything she believes has to be true. "He was at the meet. I saw him."

"Sammy was worried about his scores. That's all I know." It's all I will say.

"Someone is responsible for what happened to him. Did you see anything unusual at the swim meet?" she asks.

Unusual like Sammy worried and shaky before he entered the locker room and all smiles when he walked out with my brother?

"I didn't see Sammy take anything. Lamont wouldn't hurt him, but he was there, in the locker room, with Sammy."

"I see your loyalty and understand you don't want to believe the worst. You need to accept the truth." She points to her computer. "Sign. Or else whatever he does next is your fault."

Lamont doesn't come home until after dinner.

He appears unconcerned, pulls a can of soda from the fridge, and starts drinking. He says nothing about what happened at the pool this morning, almost like he wasn't there, didn't see what happened. Or maybe he wants to forget. He never asks anything about what happened at the pool. It's like he pushed it all from his brain.

"What did you say to Sammy in the locker room?" I ask.

"What? Nothing. I didn't . . ."

His head snaps around, and he looks directly into my eyes. "You think I had something to do with what happened to that kid? That I'm a dealer? Maybe handing out drugs wholesale?"

"I didn't say anything about drugs."

"Oh, please. Everyone else has. All I did was see what happened to that kid. I recognized the signs—I've seen them often enough. For that, I spent the last few hours being questioned by the police."

"You've done bad things before."

He crushes the can in his hands and tosses it toward the garbage can. It clangs on the floor when he misses.

"The world has done bad things to me."

Like that's supposed to be an excuse. Does he expect me to feel sorry for him? The world has done bad things to me, too.

CHAPTER
TWENTY-EIGHT

THE NEXT DAY, WHEN MOM takes Rochelle for a walk after church and I sit at the kitchen table trying to make my mind concentrate on homework, a sudden buzzing noise jerks me from my funk. It's the intercom, someone is downstairs outside the security door, asking to be buzzed through the lock. I look at Lamont. We aren't expecting any visitors. He gives an anxious shrug.

"Maybe Mom lost her key," I mutter as I push aside the math work sheets and head down the hall.

"Who is it?" I call into the security phone on the wall.

"Arthur Cho," is the surprising answer.

"What does *he* want now?" Lamont grumbles. I

wonder the same thing.

I press the buzzer to unlock the building security door. Then I open our apartment door and stand at the top of the landing to watch Mr. Cho climb up and enter our apartment. Someone in the apartment unit opposite ours opens their door and watches. I quickly close our door; I don't want the neighbors all up in our business. Lamont stands in the middle of the front room, looking strangely unsurprised.

"Are you searching for a reason to bust me?" he snarls as Mr. Cho walks in. "You had me in your office last week." He crosses his arms over his chest, but I don't think he feels as uncaring as he appears. I move closer to my brother, surprised by an urge to defend him.

Mr. Cho walks around the room, stopping to touch the lamp on a table, then sitting on the sofa as if he owned the place. He removes his glasses and pulls a handkerchief from his pocket to wipe them. "I don't have time to harass anyone except idiots dying to go back inside. Is that your goal?"

"What am I supposed to be guilty of now?" Lamont snaps.

Mr. Cho resettles the glasses on his face and opens his briefcase. He pulls out a plastic cup and holds it out to Lamont. "You know what to do with this."

"Again?" Lamont shakes his head. "I gave you one last week."

"And you'll give me another one now. And any time I ask." Mr. Cho seems to be enjoying this.

Lamont snatches the cup and starts for the bathroom. He pauses at the door to ask, "Sure you don't want to come and watch, make sure I do things right?"

"Maybe next time." Mr. Cho chuckles.

Lamont snorts before slamming the door.

Mr. Cho turns to me. "I don't need another drug drop from your brother. I really came here to talk to you. I want to see how you are doing in person. I've dealt with a lot of men and women just like your brother, seen a lot return to their old ways. I'm not allowed to consider his presence at the swimming event a coincidence." He flushes and wipes his forehead. "You need to think long and hard. This petition . . . what do you expect it to accomplish?"

"You know about it?"

"I use the internet too. I have alerts set on all my charges."

What if Mom set some kind of alert on her kids? She's not an online expert, but I bet she knows how to do that much. Sooner or later she'll find the petition page and see my name.

"Once you get the petition, how quickly would he be gone?"

"I could have him back in prison by this evening," Mr. Cho says. "Is that what you want?"

"No! We thought—I mean, I thought you said you had choices. That's what discretion means, right? Just send him somewhere that's not here but not back in a cell."

Lamont returns and tosses the plastic container at him. Luckily the cap is on tight.

"Ooops," Lamont says, grinning as Mr. Cho juggles the cup. My brother doesn't seem to get how close he is to being in major trouble.

The parole office struggles to keep the jar from landing in his lap. His bulging eyes are priceless. Even I have to laugh.

"That was a stupid thing to do," I say after Mr. Cho leaves.

Lamont flops down on the sofa and lets out a long, defeated sigh. "Maybe, but it felt good."

"When I do things just because they feel good, it usually lands me in trouble."

"No matter what I do, I find trouble," he answers. "Dealing with that man and the things he wants me to do for him is exhausting."

I leave him alone in the living room. Inside my bedroom, I climb up to the top bunk and sit with my head brushing the ceiling. Through the window, I see the clear sky and squirrels bouncing along the budding branches. Down in the courtyard, people walk. The snow is gone, the ground clear. My mind is the only thing that's messed up.

CHAPTER
TWENTY–NINE

CARMELA WAS RIGHT. PETITIONS PULL people. Those five hundred names have grown to almost a thousand online signatures. While most of the names are from the neighborhood, people from other parts of Chicago have signed. Some are from other states and even from other countries. People who don't even know Lamont want him banished. I scroll through the comments listing reasons for signing. Some contain brutal words from people who don't even know the man they are happy to condemn. Hearing about a black ex-con is enough for them to believe the worst.

"We're trending," Carmela exclaims, waving her phone. "Hashtag 'Lose Lamont' is officially viral. All my friends posted links to the petition on Facebook, Instagram, Snapchat, and Twitter. And . . ." She pauses for drama. "I got a call from a couple of newspapers asking for me to comment on what we're doing."

"I thought you hated the media," I remind her.

"Not when they actually get things right. But I need Mr. Frank to sign the petition. He's the number one victim; his name will mean a lot."

Meaning the media she can't stand doesn't want to hear from her if she doesn't have him. "Why hasn't he signed already?"

"He's old. I bet he doesn't know what the internet is. We're going to have to go see him."

I protest but let Carmela, Dontae, and Linda lead me away from school at lunchtime. I've never been inside Frank's Place before.

I look around at the dimly lit restaurant, somehow expecting to see an old man with long, gray hair come rushing to chase me out. Mr. Frank is like eighty years old or something and rumored to have secret ninja skills. Kanye is rapping over the speakers. It's a family-friendly remix of one of his early hits. The restaurant is crowded with families and men and women in business suits.

Carmela grabs a booth when a group leaves. A thin-faced waitress arrives to take our order.

"I want a Mondo Burger, please," Dontae says, naming one of Frank's specialties. He licks his lips. "A half pound of pure beef."

"Pure fat," Carmela corrects with a scowl. "Melted cheese plus grilled onions. You just had an attack. You're not doing that to your body." She orders a Coke for herself. Linda gets hot chocolate. Dontae scowls, but instead of complaining about Carmela's mothering ways, he only asks for water. I'm hungry and nervous, so I order fries with my drink. The waitress glares, impatient with our small order.

"I want to see Mr. Frank," Carmela says when the woman returns with our drinks and fries. "He's my uncle. Tell him Carmela's here."

I'm happy to let her do all the talking since she will anyway. Those words earn us an even fiercer scowl before the waitress disappears. The old man arrives a few minutes later. He's just a balding black man I remember from that day in court. The sling I saw him wearing two years ago is gone, but he uses a cane to walk.

"So I've been promoted to uncle?" he asks with a sly grin, and pats Carmela's hand.

"I knew that would work better than saying my father's old friend. Besides, you are practically part of our family."

"I love flattery, but as you see, things are busy today." Mr. Frank looks over the drinks and half-eaten fries on the table. My stomach rumbles, so I dip a fry in ketchup and chew slowly, letting the salty tang fill my throat. Then I push the dish close to Linda so she can take some.

"This won't take long, I promise," Carmela says. "Do you know there is a petition to get rid of Lamont Rodgers?"

"That's not exactly what it's for," I say. I don't like the way she put that or the eager gleam in her eyes.

The old man looks at me while he says, "I know about the petition."

"But you haven't added your name," Carmela says, leaning closer to him.

"I'm not sure if I should."

"He attacked you. Do you want him to walk back in here someday and do it again?"

"Lamont wouldn't do that," I say. Then, "Ow!" as Carmela kicks me under the table.

She pulls out her phone and hands it to Mr. Frank. I move my chair until I see the screen he's looking at. She's showing him the comments from signers explaining how unsafe they feel with Lamont around.

Mr. Frank looks at me more closely. "Aren't you his brother?"

"Uh. Yeah."

"And *you* want me to sign?"

"Sort of," I say. I really want to kick myself for ever adding my name to the thing. Then I think about being stopped by the police again because of something Lamont did. Or of another kid overdosing like Sammy. Maybe next time they will raid our apartment and terrify Rochelle when searching for him. I've heard of people losing everything, homes, money, even their lives, because one family member broke a law. I want Mom safe. I'll take the pain of losing my brother again to keep people safe. "Yes, I want you to sign," I say.

"We have to make sure he goes away," Carmela says. "Imagine him walking in the door ready to hurt you again. This is important to your neighbors. To your customers. To you."

"I understand one of the conditions of his parole is that he stay away from me and my restaurant."

"He's been awful at obeying orders so far," Carmela says. "Don't you think he should be punished for what he did to you?"

"He has been punished," Mr. Frank says.

"He got only two years for almost killing you. That's not real punishment. It's not right."

The old man's fingers tighten around the head of his

cane. Does that mean he's agreeing with her, that he hates my brother too?

"He's here," Linda says, her soft voice breaking into the sudden stillness. I follow her gaze to the front window and see the impossible: my brother standing outside the window, staring in. My stomach does an atomic nosedive to the floor. I jump to my feet, horrified by the sight of Lamont in his hoodie, like some kind of ghost.

"He looks angry," Carmela says with notes of triumph and fear in her voice. I hover over Linda, but she's not in danger. Lamont is staring directly at Mr. Frank. I know that look. It's not about anger. He's thinking, planning, evaluating. Coming to a decision.

"I'll call nine one one," Carmela says, but hesitates. Even the daughter of a police officer is no longer sure whether Lamont or the cops is the bigger threat.

"Don't. I can get him to leave." This is my job, and I'm sure I can handle him. I head for the entrance and arrive at the door just as my brother reaches for the doorknob. I push Lamont, forcing him to step back on the sidewalk. "You know you can't be here." The wind tries to steal my words away.

"I'm taking your advice," he says. "You said things were my fault no matter whose gun it was, and you were right. It's time I faced my past and made amends."

Now he listens to me. Great timing, bro. "Not a good idea." Not when the old man has been reading about how awful he is.

"Frank will listen. I can make him." My too-optimistic-for-words brother refuses to even admit there might be a problem. And then it's too late. The door opens, and Frank limps out into the sunlight. I look into my brother's eyes and silently beg him to stay calm, hoping that will be enough. Mr. Frank is not as tall as Lamont, but his bushy eyebrows draw together, making him look fierce. He takes three steps, stopping only when he and Lamont are just a few feet apart.

"My name is Lamont Rodgers."

"You think I don't remember you?" Mr. Frank shakes his cane. "I'm old, not senile."

"Did I . . ." Lamont begins, his hesitant voice and wide eyes indicating his fear that he caused an injury that left Mr. Frank unable to walk without assistance.

"Arthritis." The old man shakes his head.

Lamont's shoulders slump with relief. "I came to tell you I'm sorry."

"Real convenient, you being sorry now." Carmela steps out to join us, her mouth twisting in an ugly frown. "Your phony apology doesn't fool anyone."

"I'm not trying to fool anyone. I was barely eighteen.

Not an excuse, just a fact. My father was dead, and I felt alone, without options or opportunities. The gang wanted me, my brains, what I had to give. All I had to do was hand over my loyalty. Small price to pay, I thought." He grimaces. "That was my first mistake. They said I was important, and I needed to hear that. But they lied. I thought I could stop, could leave whenever I wanted. I was wrong. I thought they valued me and what I had to say and do. I needed to be respected, to matter to someone the way I used to matter to Dad. Again, not an excuse, just a fact."

"What the gang offers is not real respect," the old man says.

"I know that now, but back then I thought my words and smart ideas made me a leader. The guys I was running with hated the way you stood up to them. Darnell, one of the older men, had a thing for your waitress." That brings an apologetic glance at Linda. "That's why this place became the target. When I called the robbery proposal a stupid idea, Darnell decided he'd had enough of me and let me know who was really in charge. The night of the robbery, I had little more choice about my actions than you did. A big piece of me was glad when the police caught us."

"No one believes any of that," Carmela says.

"If he's truly sorry . . ." Linda begins.

"You don't care," Carmela informs her. "How many people have to disappoint you before you learn? He's as phony as the apologies your father tries to spread. Thanks to our petition, he'll soon be sent away, right, T?" She puts an arm around my shoulders.

I didn't expect her to pull me into this discussion. My jaw drops, and I can't find the strength to say anything when my brother turns to me. Disappointment rolls off him like physical waves that slap me in the face.

"Petition?" he says in a choked voice. "Was that thing your idea?"

"No, but I mean, sort of."

He doesn't look angry, not even hurt. Just resigned. "I thought nothing would ever throw me again, but you managed." He turns and leaves with a swagger in his walk, the special move that's supposed to convince the world he's in total control.

"I know you're going to sign my petition now," Carmela says, turning to Mr. Frank.

"Then you know wrong. We all make mistakes, including that boy," he says. "You don't know half the mess I got into at your age. No one should have his entire life ruined because of a foolish mistake made as a teen. Especially when half the problem is geography. Think of those kids living in Streeterville or Lincoln Park."

He's named two of the more affluent neighborhoods on Chicago's North Side. Streeterville is a land of wealth where people live in high-rise buildings looking out onto Lake Michigan. Lincoln Park, home of the zoo, is almost like a suburb or the countryside. Both neighborhoods are places where most of the people are white and have money. Where cops act like they believe kids should get to be kids and residents are listened to if they contact the authorities about problems.

Mr. Frank continues, "Let a kid from one of those neighborhoods make a mistake, and they get sympathy and a second chance. Kids down here just get condemned."

"But he did try to rob you," Carmela says. "He didn't wave his gun in your face by mistake."

"Two years ago he was only eighteen. Only a few years older than you are now. Think about the many mistakes you make every day. Think about one of them closing doors for you for the rest of your life. You'll see for yourself soon."

Soon? Like now! I'm confused all the time. Scary to

think life could get even rockier.

He continues, "Carmela, all of you, I like you thinking you can control the world. That's what being young is all about. But not by sending a man into exile instead of helping him fix the problems that put him in trouble in the first place."

Even Carmela is silent when we walk back to school. I'm tired of her personal crusade. She likes being important, and she believes she is right. A bad combination. Mr. Frank was right. If only I had never signed that dumb petition.

If only. The two most useless words in English. Because I did sign, and now I have to live with that.

When school ends, I'm not sure I want to go to swim team practice, not after all that drama. But the alternative is going home, and possibly dealing with Lamont, who will probably still be in a rage at me. I rush for the bus and head for W3C. I could use a workout, a way to get all my energy out without exploding. The treadmill, I think. This is a cardio day, and I can run until I can't breathe or think. Then dive and dive until I have nothing left.

The bus is filled, jolting through crowded traffic with people who have their own lives. Babies cry. Older people sit and look worried. I'm surrounded by tired, sad faces of every age and race. Maybe I'm not the only one with a Lamont-size problem in his life.

Carmela grabs me by the arm as I enter the door of the aquatic facility.

"Hurry up, he's waiting." She begins pulling me down the hall, away from the locker rooms.

"Who?" I stop dead, refusing to move another step no matter how hard she tugs.

"Your coach wants to talk to you before he'll sign."

"Sign what? Are you still talking about the petition?" I protest. I stare at her for a long moment, unsure whether I am angry or sad. I glance at the door and think about running out and jumping back on the bus to get away from her. Instead, I let her drag me down the hall to a door labeled, Rays Swim Team. I hear angry voices coming through the closed door.

Carmela pushes the door open without knocking. Coach Mung is inside, along with Harmony. The room is small and stacks of paper lie haphazardly across a narrow metal desk. Even in the dim light of a single bulb hanging from the ceiling, I see that the coach's face is bright red, hers so pale she could be a ghost.

Carmela pushes past Harmony, acting like she doesn't

notice we interrupted some kind of family drama. "I found T for you," she says, almost singing, her voice full of the old Carmela Rhodes charm.

"You're a rude little girl." Harmony scowls. She is one of the few charisma-proof people I know.

"Is this your idea?" Mung asks me, pointing to a tablet open to the website containing Carmela's petition.

"Absolutely," Carmela interjects before I can make my tongue work.

"Your words moved me," Mung says. "If there's any chance I can help, I'm happy to sign."

"But you don't even live near our neighborhood," I say.

"Your brother doesn't limit himself to going after those close to him." He looks at Harmony.

"What makes you so sure Lamont supplied the Adderall Sammy took?" Harmony asks bitterly.

"I don't forget he used to be *your* supplier. Do I need to have you tested as well? Face facts. He was there with the boy. At least pretend your IQ is higher than room temperature."

Harmony goes pale.

"What's Adderall?" I ask, hoping to make them stop arguing.

Both Carmela and Coach Mung look at me like I have two heads, neither one working well.

"It's a med used to help people with ADHD," Harmony says. "It's practically a wonder drug that helps them pay attention and focus."

"Helps athletes cheat," Mung snarls. "I can't believe I harbored that cheater on my squad."

"Be careful, Uncle. Your true colors are showing," she says before strolling from the room.

"I'm sorry you two were exposed to that," Coach Mung says once his niece is gone. He adjusts his jacket. "My niece is . . . well, she's complex."

Not complex. She's sad and almost never smiles. "Do you love her?" I ask.

"That's a foolish question. She's my brother's only child, all that I have left of him. Of course I love her." He takes a deep breath. "I'll sign your petition and get the other coaches to do the same. I'm sure members of the Boosters will join in. Everyone wants him punished. You've done something good here, T'Shawn. Be proud."

"Why did you tell him that was my petition?" I ask Carmela as we head for the locker rooms. It's bad enough that Mr. Cho and my brother know I am a part of the petition. Pretty soon the whole team will know.

Next, Mom will find out. Even the thought makes me shiver.

"I could tell Coach Mung liked thinking this was all your idea," Carmela says, her voice so smug, I want to puke. My coach likes thinking of me as what I am—a Benedict Arnold.

CHAPTER THIRTY

MOM IS BAKING A CAKE when I get home from practice, whipping the batter with fast, furious strokes. Rochelle follows me into the kitchen whispering, "Mom's mad." My too-smart sister has already figured out about our mother and baking.

"Where's Lamont?" I ask. He is usually sitting on the sofa playing with Rochelle when I get home, but she's alone, dragging her floppy pretend puppy behind her.

"He's in your room. Packing." The words come out slowly, as if they are being torn from Mom's throat. "He's leaving."

"He can't go."

"I told him that. But he claims he has no choice."

I rush down the hall to our bedroom, where I see his open bag on the bottom mattress, already half filled with his things. He pulls a blue sweater from the closet, wads it up, and tosses it toward the open bag. He almost scores, but his stiff arms shake, and the sweater falls short, fluttering half in, half out of the opening. I grab handfuls of his things out of the bag and hurl them on the floor. Clothes, papers, anything, everything.

"What are you doing?" I ask. This is too fast, too soon. "You can't go now."

"Says the guy who most wants me gone. I'm not blind, T. You never wanted me here. I saw that on your face the first day."

I wonder what my face says now.

"Turns out your petition had one good effect. Mr. Cho agrees I need a change of venue."

He moves like a tired old man as he bends to pick up the things I threw on the floor and shoves them back in the bag. "I did try to change, but I can't escape the past. So it's best I take my wreck of a life somewhere else."

I search for words, new and better words, something right, anything to make him see how sorry I am. There is a big giant blank where my vocabulary should be.

He opens one of the drawers that holds my things. Realizing his mistake, he starts to close it, then pauses.

He reaches inside and pulls out the picture of Malik I stuffed in there the first day Lamont came home. "The guy who has everything, including my brother. No one can compete against the rich guys."

"Malik wasn't born with money. He told me his father built his business from nothing while his mother waited tables so she could bring home leftovers so they had enough to eat. He and his brother used to thank God for school lunches."

"And he grew up rich, talented, and good-looking, plus he saved you from me and my gun. No wonder you worship him." His shoulders droop. "You had every right to be scared of me that night."

My thoughts race back to the night I ran away to be with my brother and the gang, until cold and fear left me praying to escape. That was the first time I faced a gun.

"When Darnell reached for the gun, I froze. I had to take the gun and point it at you, make a show to hold them off. I'd begun to realize I had no real control over any of them. I had to make Darnell think I agreed with him." The twitching muscle in Lamont's jaw is pulsing hard and heavy. That doesn't just happen when he's lying, I realize now. It's also about guilt.

"All I could do was text your friend Malik. I knew I couldn't get you from there alone. I don't hate him. I thank him for rescuing you out of the mess I caused."

He zips up his bag and starts for the door.

"Wait." I grab the chair from my desk and drag it to the closet. The treasure box is there, still hidden behind my rock collection. I pull it down and place it in the middle of his bed.

"That's the box," he mutters. The mattress squeaks when he sits down. "Are you trying to make me remember? I hate wandering through the past." He continues touching the contents as he speaks, revisiting the time *before*.

With shaking hands, he pulls out the tiny plastic toy soldiers we played with when we were a whole family and cancer was just a word. "My guys can still crush yours," I say with a growl and a grin because I know he used to let me win our play fights. For a few minutes, we tussle, our soldiers battling on the bed. Again he lets me win.

We continue to go through the contents of the box. "Does Jekyll tell Hyde?" he mutters once, touching the old horror movie DVD while wiping the back of his hand across his eyes. The torn card announcing Mom's pregnancy makes him pause. He and I drew that card, using big letters to be sure Dad could read the words, since he was already in hospice by then and had trouble seeing.

"Remember when we spent a whole day terrified, thinking Mom's morning sickness meant she had caught Dad's cancer?" he asks.

I nod. I endured a long, sleepless night before I learned cancer isn't contagious. As scary as it had been hearing Mom throw up, the memory is now a blessing. We kept each other going through all the bad times. We still do. That's why I can't let him leave me, not ever again.

His fingers tremble when he pulls out the belt with the extra holes punched in so Dad could keep using it as he grew thinner and thinner in the months before his death. "I told some of the guys in prison about Dad dying, and they said I was lucky to be rid of him. *Lucky.*" His voice deepens into a growl.

Then he picks up Dad's heavy, silver ring. This time his whole body shudders. "I thought this was lost long ago."

He pulls it over his finger. Perfect fit.

That ring first belonged to our great-great grand-father who fought for the Union in the Civil War. It meant enough to the former slave that he refused to sell it, instead giving it to his son, the first Rodgers born in America as a free man. The ring continued on to his son, who wore it during World War II, and then my dad, who carried it on the battlefields of Iraq. And now, the ring that has seen so many changes in the world and been worn by so many good men, sits on my brother's finger.

"I still miss Dad," I say. "When he died, I put everything on you. I wanted you to be perfect."

"I can't be perfect," he whispers. "I can't even be like him. Every time I look at you, I remember I put you in danger. I know why you want me gone."

That's the thing, I don't anymore. I want things the way they were. Lamont and me, closer than friends.

The ring fits so well, he has to struggle to remove it.

"Keep it," I say, trying to make my voice light. I hope the ring helps him be more like Dad.

He shakes his head. "I can't take this from you. You carried this box through every temporary situation, the shelter, now here. You saved our family history. Everything in here belongs to you."

"You're the oldest. The ring was supposed to go to you." I hold up my right hand. "See, it wouldn't stay on my skinny fingers."

He stops struggling with the ring and climbs to his feet. "When you get bigger, it'll go on your hand, where it really belongs. Until then, I'll keep it safe." He takes my hand and shakes it like we're making a solemn vow. "Now I'd better bounce."

He pauses in the living room. Rochelle looks up from

the picture book in her lap. Mom comes close, puts her hands on Lamont's shoulders, and looks up into his eyes. "Are you too old to hug your mother goodbye?" she asks, her voice wistful.

He bends to kiss her forehead. She presses against his chest. His arms go around her, like he's the parent and she's the child. Then he peers over her head at me. "I don't blame any of you." I believe him the way I do when Rochelle claims that cookies just find their way into her mouth by magic.

He walks out the door with his old King of the World swagger.

I return to my room, climb up to my bed, sit and stare down at my empty room. I guess I'm safe now. Through the window, I see him cross the courtyard and walk down the block.

The swagger is missing.

CHAPTER
THIRTY—ONE

LAMONT HAS BEEN GONE A whole week, and each day feels like forever. No one seemed more surprised by the news of his departure than Carmela.

"Are you sure?" she asked after I told her and the rest of my friends he was gone. "That means we won!" she squealed, threw her arms around me, and kissed me on the cheek.

I stepped back and wiped my face with the back of my hand.

That night, like every other night, Rochelle comes in my room to look for Lamont. She expects me to go out and find him.

"Try, just try," she pleads, her eyes wide and glistening

with tears. I don't know how to explain that life is not that simple. I needed two days before I got up the nerve to try calling him. No answer, and there's no voice mail on his line. He doesn't respond to the texts I send. Mom hasn't heard from him either. I guess only Mr. Cho knows where he's gone.

I see Redmond in school the next day while Dontae and I are on our way to the lunchroom. He doesn't slink back into the crowd when our eyes meet. I can tell the instant Dontae recognizes Redmond: my friend's mouth drops open into a perfect O.

"That—that's the guy," he says, pointing with a shaky finger when Redmond stops in front of me.

"Where's your brother?" Redmond asks.

"He's gone."

"He can't be." A heavy frown draws a big eleven into the pale skin above Redmond's nose. "We were supposed to . . ."

"Go out banging together?"

Blue eyes widen, and he shakes his head. "No, we never did that." He scratches the back of his neck before adding, "Sorry about the way I acted the day we met. I was angry."

"I could tell." Me, I was sad. The words "confused" and "lost" would also describe me, then and now.

"When I first saw Lamont, I thought it was you again," Redmond continues. "Then I realized he was much too big."

See? Even a guy who saw me only one time could tell Lamont and I don't look that much alike. I shouldn't keep blaming my brother for the cops making a totally crazy mistake.

"Your brother is awesome. We see each other sometimes; he talks to me, explains stuff. He boasted on his short-stack brother all the time. He told me I should stop hiding myself," Redmond adds, brushing back wisps of hair from his face.

He begins telling Dontae about himself, explaining about living in the homeless shelter while his father is in jail. "My old man keeps getting out and doing something else so they put him back in again. Your brother told me about himself and prison life. He said it was dangerous. Nights especially."

"He talked to you." I push back jealousy.

"When will he come back?"

"Never," Dontae volunteers. "He's a bad guy. You too. At least I thought you were." He looks at me for confirmation.

"We saw you together and thought he was trying to pull you into his gang," I admit.

"Nah, he said he won't let himself be pulled back into that life. Connie asked him to talk me out of making a 'poor decision.'"

Connie? Lamont didn't even teach him to call Miss Wiggins "the witch"?

"He told me I'd better not join," Redmond continues.

"I told you that," I remind him, feeling indignant.

"Yeah, I know. But your brother made things seem real." As he talks, Redmond digs in his backpack. His hand comes out holding a portable drive. "When I told him I was into music and computers, he paid me to make this for you. It's a mix tape, a custom country-rap mash-up. Are you two country music fans?"

"Not me, no way, never. He is." Dontae points at me.

I take the device in my hands.

"Well, I gotta go." Redmond steps back awkwardly. The hall is almost empty, most students now either in their classes or the lunchroom. I remember how I always see Redmond alone.

"You wanna have lunch with us?" I ask.

Surprise lights up his face. "Yeah, totally."

As we walk into the lunchroom, I ask, "Did my brother ever tell you why the top bunk was supposed to be safer?" I'm sure now his words about the bunk couldn't have been the threat they first seemed.

"He said there's no real safety in prison. If you're on top you can at least attempt to fight back when you're attacked. He said that if they really want to get you, there is no help, but taking the high ground gives an advantage to more than just the army."

He was thinking of me. My brother has always thought of me.

CHAPTER
THIRTY-TWO

IT'S REALLY HARD TO CONCENTRATE in school the next day. I want the clock to run backward, the calendar to reverse, but new seconds and minutes keep flowing, like mud sliding down a hill. I head to practice to escape those thoughts; glad today is a strength-training day. Crunches, lunges, push-ups—it's hard to believe that only a month ago I thought this was impossible. The Hun's charts show how much I've changed. Using my muscles helps me calm down, and I need that big-time. I wish Sammy were here on the mat beside me. We used to push each other to do better. I know he did something wrong, but he is still my friend. I miss him.

I lie on a bench and begin doing presses: ten lifts each set and all getting to be so easy, it's probably time to talk to the coaches about increasing my weight a few pounds. Suddenly I notice voices around the workout room growing still. The clank of moving metal goes silent. I sit up and look at the entrance to find Sammy and his parents standing just inside the door.

My breath catches when I see the bulky bandage wound around my friend's head. He goes right to Harmony and they hug.

"I was so worried. I'm glad you're back," I say when I get close.

He releases her and looks at me. "Just to say goodbye. I'm going into rehab in a place out of state."

Drug rehab. I thrust my hands deep in the pockets of my warm-up jacket and remain silent.

"A jail for kids." Harmony sniffles and touches the bandage around his head.

"Not exactly. And my parents get therapy too." For a second, the old Sammy grin fills his face. "Mom told the therapist to fix me, and he said we all needed to change. He says it's never just about the identified patient. That's what he called me, an identified patient. At least my parents are calmer now." He sounds a little surprised as he says those last words, as if he never expected that to happen.

"Are we still friends?" I ask Sammy.

"Always.

I remain motionless as he and his family leave. The door has barely closed behind them when the Hun makes the announcement I feared. "Sammy is off the team. He has been suspended for drug use. We have rules," he continues when some team members protest. His lips tighten for a moment. "I should have seen things sooner. Apparently he'd been using performance enhancers for months. That accounts for his muscle and weight increase. I charted the changes in him, but"—he sighs, and his eyes roll toward the ceiling—"I chalked things up to early puberty and the success of our program training methods."

Most of the team appear to accept that. The club handbook used the words "zero tolerance." That really means no second chances. Mess up once, make a single mistake, and it's Game Over.

"He wanted to win," Harmony says. Her chin quivers.

"We all want to win. But winning is never worth this."

We're supposed to forget and pretend Sammy was never one of us.

Most team members are already slipping out of the

weight room, along with several coaches. In a few minutes, only the Hun, Mung, Harmony, and I are left.

"You should join the others," the Hun tells me. "Coach Mung and I have to stay here a little longer to deal with one additional matter." Mr. Hundle and Mung stare at each other. Looking at their expressions and seeing the way Harmony eyes me, I know this additional matter is something big and that it involves me.

"What else is wrong?" I ask.

Mung turns to Harmony, ignoring my question. "Go with him. The campus police will be here in a few minutes."

Instead of obeying, Harmony takes a seat on one of the abandoned weight benches. "Some things have been disappearing from around the campus and the locker rooms," she says, her voice smooth and even. "Uncle Bill lost his laptop, and now he's rushing to blame Lamont."

"I didn't *lose* anything." Mung's face flushes a dark, angry scarlet. "Lamont Rodgers broke into my office and stole that laptop."

"Why blame my brother?" I ask. "He doesn't come near this place. There was just that one time, and he only came to see me."

"He's been hanging around campus almost every day," Mung says. "He works here."

"Worked," Harmony corrects him. "Before my uncle persuaded the administration to fire him, Lamont had a part-time position as a night janitor."

"He had a job?" My question is mostly a stall for time to digest the information. I thought he was playing around about the job thing, that his parole officer was letting him get away with ignoring that obligation. Instead, he was here all along, close to me.

"My uncle is eager to accuse Lamont of something because he can't be blamed for selling drugs to Sammy."

"How do you know?" I ask, my mind spinning.

"Sammy's been using for months," the Hun answers for Harmony. Simple math, Sammy had connections before Lamont came home.

"Tell T the real reason you blame his brother for everything. And why you got him fired," Harmony insists.

"Why do you defend him?" Mung waves a hand in the air, swatting at nothing and glaring at his niece. "You wanted him gone too, but you enjoyed seeing the man who dumped you reduced to slinging a mop. You certainly spent enough time watching him."

"Yes, I did." She sighs, looking like someone who

dived into the deep end before realizing the pool was empty. "I thought seeing him in the muck would be fun. No one was supposed to be hurt except you and Lamont, and you both deserved that. But now there's Sammy, and T, and, well, turns out revenge isn't fun after all." Harmony extends her hands, wrists together as if in anticipation of handcuffs. "When the campus police arrive, I'll have to confess."

The color drains from Mung's face, leaving it pasty white. "What are you saying?"

"I'm the thief. You'll find the missing computer in the trunk of my car, along with a few other items that have gone missing over the last few weeks. Wallets and electronics and any equipment your golden boy Bishop thought he could sell."

"Bishop! He can't be part of any of this," Mung insists. "He's a fine young man."

"You bought Bishop's good-boy act. He does anything I ask, even supplies the drugs I need to survive life with you. Why else would I spend five minutes with that jerk?"

"Why did you give drugs to Sammy?" I ask her while Mung paces. She turns her back on her uncle and comes to me. "I never meant to hurt him. I've taken those pills for years myself and never had a reaction like that."

Mung runs a hand over his face and looks like he wishes he wore a mask. "I took you into my home, and this is what you do to my good name?"

"It's *my* name too. Mung has always been my name."

"Why are you confessing?" I ask her.

"Because I'm tired. When I saw Sammy today, I realized what I'd done. I have to tell someone the truth."

Two campus police officers arrive a few minutes later. Both seem confused as she repeats her confession. Her uncle sits, tightlipped and silent. At least they are gentle when they put her in handcuffs. She smiles as the officers march her down the hall.

"Aren't you going with her?" I ask Coach Mung.

"I have—I need . . ." He looks at the retreating figures for a moment, then lifts his head and squares his shoulders. "My team needs me," he says, and heads toward the pool entrance.

I am left alone with Mr. Hundle.

"That was . . . unexpected," the Hun says.

I knew she was unhappy. Unhappy people sometimes do bad things.

He stares at the phone he holds as if expecting it to

grow jaws and bite him.

"What about my brother?" I ask. "Since he didn't do the things Coach Mung accused him of, will he get his job back?"

"I'm sorry he was let go," the Hun says. "With that petition and the adverse publicity, the college board couldn't keep him on in the face of growing community outrage."

"So, no second chances for him, even if he's not guilty?"

More zero tolerance. It's not about what Lamont actually did. It's what people say and think. What I once thought. I tore support from my brother by believing the worst. Maybe I'm more like Mung than I realized in my willingness to believe anything about Lamont as long as it was bad.

"You should get to the pool with the others, give yourself a little time to think," Mr. Hundle tells me.

"No." I head back toward the locker room. "I quit."

"Hold on, T. That's a little extreme. I understand you're upset with Coach Mung, but he's not a bad man at heart."

"Upset?" Is that the best word a teacher can manage? "I can't work with Coach Mung and pretend what he thinks doesn't matter."

"Please understand we don't all share Mung's views."

"But you didn't do anything to change them." Neither did I. I'm disappointed in the Hun. I disappoint myself. "I have to go."

"Your fees are paid for the remainder of the season. You have potential, a future. Don't let that go because of one person."

"Give another kid my scholarship." Maybe then I'll feel better, as if I've done one good thing.

"There was no scholarship," Mr. Hundle says. The confession makes me stop on my way out the door. "There was only your brother. He came to see me weeks ago. We worked out an arrangement: he took the job with the night maintenance squad and his pay went to your club fees. He asked me not to tell you, but I think you need to know."

I shouldn't have needed to know. My brother has been trying to do things right from the start, and I screwed that up for him.

"You've improved tremendously in such a short time, T'Shawn. I hope you will remain on the team."

I shake my head. "I can't be part of this anymore. Find another kid and give them my spot. In fact, there's this girl I know, Linda Murhasselt. She's a good swimmer. Let her have the scholarship."

Mung starts to say something, but I turn and walk out of the locker room.

CHAPTER

THIRTY—THREE

I HAVE TO TALK TO Lamont. Since he's not answering his phone, I decide to ask his parole officer where he sent my brother. I take the bus from W3C to Mr. Cho's office and I find him slumped behind his desk.

"Where is Lamont?" I ask as soon as I see him.

He looks up and scowls. "Good question, one I should ask you. He was supposed to be here an hour ago."

"Ask me? He moved out."

After a long pause, Mr. Cho removes his glasses and sits polishing them with a tissue. "He can't move anywhere without my permission."

"He said you gave him permission, that you found a halfway house for him." My stomach suddenly aches as if I had done a belly flop from the board.

"Not only did I not tell him to go anywhere, I've been trying to reach him. How does anyone live without voice mail these days? We set up a meeting a week ago. I owe him, but he's not allowed to blow me off."

"Owe him what?" I ask.

After a short pause, Mr. Cho asks his own question. "Do you know why your brother only served two years?"

I feel silly having to admit I have no idea.

"My cousin is a guard at Pontiac. Last fall there was a riot at the prison."

"I remember there was a problem," I say. "Mom couldn't make her normal visit in October."

Cho nods. "Staff put things in lockdown for a week after the riot to remind the inmates who was really in charge. The uprising was small and quickly contained. But even a small riot can be dangerous for any guard caught on the wrong side, the way my cousin was. Lamont defended him, held off other prisoners who wanted to use him like a punching bag or worse."

My brother is a hero?

"His actions drew the interest of some law students. They took up his case, filed a motion to get his sentence reduced. When the reduction was granted, I volunteered to be his PO."

"Because you're grateful." Lamont changed from villain to hero. I can't stop thinking about that.

"Gratitude is one thing, my job is another." Mr. Cho laces his hands under his chin and stares at me intently. "He must see me today. I can give him until nine tonight before I'm forced to report him. Then it's out of my hands. An arrest warrant will be issued, and he goes back inside."

It's already after four. I have less than five hours to find him and get him to Cho, and I have no idea where to start looking.

"So your brother did one good thing, what does that change?" Carmela says when I explain what Mr. Cho told me.

I ignore her and look at Dontae, Linda, and Redmond. We're gathered in my bedroom. He's not what we thought. He was helping people. I think all he ever really wanted to do, he just tried the wrong way."

An idea bubbles into my brain. I'm going to find my brother and tell him I forgive him. And then hope he can forgive me. "I need the recording you made of my Second Chance Drive," I tell Redmond. "I'll use it to reach out to people to help me find him."

"Excellent," he says with a big grin. "I've been playing around with it on my music app. If you've got some pictures, I could jazz it up, add a few memes to give it punch."

"A music video," Linda says, and nods. "We can sing and dance. Only cat videos go viral faster."

"You'll help too," I inform Carmela. "You have a zillion online friends who keep liking your stuff. They can help spread the word."

"He's a gang member," she scoffs.

"*Former* gang member. I need you to help me save him."

Her mouth opens, closes, and opens again. I don't think she can believe I'm still arguing instead of giving in to her. I barely believe it myself.

Carmela suddenly shrugs. "Fine. But only for you."

My phone is filled with pictures of Lamont. While we talk, Redmond selects a few of me and of Lamont for his video. He also records me asking for help to add to the message. He posts the package under the hashtag #helpmefindLamont.

The big problem is the clock. I'm just throwing a small bottle into a big ocean. It has four hours to reach the shore.

"Do you really trust your brother?" Linda asks. I understand what she's thinking.

"You don't have to forgive your father, but I have to

give my brother a second chance."

She gives me a long look, then nods and begins tagging her friends.

Within minutes, comments start rolling in:

> Your brother sounds like a good guy—
> #helpmefindLamont

> Much respect, little bro—#helpmefindLamont

There is even a comment from Malik that makes me smile.

> I'm with you in spirit, T. Let me know if I can
> help—#helpmefindLamont

The number of shares, retweets, and comments rise every minute. Not one includes information or a sighting. I only have four hours before Mr. Cho's deadline. How many people will view the video before then? How many of those will also see Lamont?

I slump, knowing the answer is too small to count. Chicago is too big. I need a bigger idea, something better. Someone has to know something. Maybe one of his friends. I turn to the only guy I know who liked Lamont.

"What do my brother's friends say?" I ask Redmond.

"He doesn't have many, at least not that I know. He doesn't deal with his old friends. Except maybe this one guy. He moves slow, shakes a lot, and your brother called him . . . "

"Toxic!" Why didn't I think of him? Another former gang member, the only kind who would still be his friend.

Redmond knows the fast-food place where Toxic now works nights. He's moved up in the world. Cleaned up too.

"Your brother pushed me into this," he says as he offers us free sodas. "It's not much of a job, only pays a few bucks, but it's mine." He seems proud, and his hands don't shake as much.

"I have to find him. It's urgent." I barely taste my Mountain Dew. "He's gonna be in so much trouble if he's not back by nine."

Toxic glances at the clock on the wall. "Then he's gonna be in trouble. He was bunking with me, but he packed up and left this morning. Said he had to get away, go to where he knew people."

That phrase strikes a memory. "Memphis."

Toxic nods. "I told him he was being a fool, but no one could ever change his mind."

If he flew, I'm already too late. He always liked trains,

and planes cost more. Using the Amtrak app, I find that the train that will stop in Memphis leaves just after eight.

I run back home and tell my friends, "He's taking the train." It's almost seven. Expressway traffic is always heavy. Neither a cab nor the CTA can get me from the far South Side to Union Station in an hour. Even a bird would have trouble.

"We could call the station and ask them to page him," Redmond says.

"He wouldn't answer. We couldn't talk them into doing it anyway."

"I need my dad." Carmela goes to leave the apartment and then turns, frowning when she sees that none of us are with her. She waves. "Move it."

Why? She doesn't need me to get to her old man. But something in her expression makes me run after her. When we reach her house, her father is waiting in a squad car.

"Carmela says you need to get to Union Station, stat," he says.

My jaw falls open and I stand motionless, astonished.

"You said I had to help. Go on, get in before he changes his mind," she says, giving me a push toward the car.

"Your brother's not thinking on all cylinders," Sergeant Rhodes says as we enter traffic on the Dan

Ryan. It's supposed to be an expressway, but right now it's a centipede, with cars weaving slowly toward downtown like tiny, useless legs.

"I could try calling ahead to have officers find and hold him for us," he adds.

We eye each other. I ask, "What would you say? 'I promise he's not dangerous, but he might resist because he really wants to be left alone.'" I would rather Lamont get on that train and leave alive than be stopped by someone with a gun and a fear for his life.

Sergeant Rhodes grimaces while fighting the stop-and-go traffic. After two minutes he suddenly shrugs. "Screw it."

A second later we are on an off-ramp up to the city streets. His siren wails and lights flash, signaling other drivers to move aside. "I could get in so much trouble for this," he mutters as we careen down State Street. "But then I'm not supposed to have you in the car anyway. The risk is worth it if we can keep another black life from being wasted."

"Thank you," I say.

We reach the Loop, Chicago's downtown, and head west toward Canal Street and the entrance to Union Station. Just for a second, I close my eyes, take a deep breath, and visualize a future with all of us together:

Mom, me, Rochelle, and Lamont. He will be here. I will find him, and I will make him agree to come home.

Sergeant Rhodes stops the car in front of the station. I race out and through the entrance, ready to make my vision real.

CHAPTER
THIRTY–FOUR

THE INTERIOR OF UNION STATION is like a palace with gilded roads that all lead down. I run down the stairs so fast I almost slip and fall, but that's faster than using the crowded escalator.

"City of New Orleans?" I ask a man in a uniform. He grunts and points at a big sign on the wall listing trains and track numbers. My eyes race over words that blur as I try to read them.

"Track eight," he finally says, and points to a wide door. "Go through and turn right."

People are already in line before the door leading to the waiting train. A man in a uniform is at the front taking tickets before allowing people to pass through to the waiting train. I search through the people waiting patiently, looking for the familiar face, or my brother's big gray bag, or . . .

Or a flash of light shining off the surface of my father's ring.

I run to my brother's side.

"You will be in so much trouble if you get on that train."

He missteps and almost plunges into the back of the man beside him. "What are you doing here, T?"

"I came to bring you home."

"Not happening." He turns away, staring at the front of the line. "You signed the petition. I got the message. You will all be happier without me."

"I can't be happier without you. If you leave, I'll never forgive you."

"Get back to your life, the club. Enjoy yourself."

"I quit that stupid club," I say.

"You what!" he roars, rounding on me, once again the King of the World. "You can't quit, not after I—"

"I know what you did," I say as the silence grows long.

"You can't know," he growls, eyes widening with something like fear.

"I know you played janitor at night to pay for my spot on the Rays. Why didn't you tell me the truth?"

He relaxes as if my information doesn't hit as hard as he expected. "Confess that the only job I could get left me cleaning toilets and mopping up vomit. I have my pride."

"You always had too much pride."

"There's no such thing as too much. Besides, I was afraid you'd refuse to take it if you knew the money came from me."

I deserve that. The headphones I never touched are still in a corner of the closet. But he is wrong; people can have too much pride.

"I . . . I need you."

His Adam's apple jumps. "Don't worry, I'll send money to you and Mom when I can."

"Not your money. You." We're getting closer to the front of the line. Too close.

"Stay," I insist.

"How? I can't get a real job around here. Between my record and that petition and now getting fired, there's no hope. No job, no money. No money and sooner or later I'll end up back inside."

"Sooner if you leave the state without permission. You have only an hour to meet with Mr. Cho."

"They'll have to find me first." He laughs as if he thinks that will never happen.

We've reached the front of the line. He lifts his bag

and slings it on his shoulder and holds his ticket ready in one hand.

"Are you sorry I'm your brother now?" I ask.

Spiderwebs crinkle around his eyes as he says, "There's lots of stuff I regret. Having you as my brother was never one of them." Then he hands over his ticket and walks through a door where I cannot follow.

It's over. I have no more arguments.

This is the end. I lower my head and turn in defeat.

No. I didn't come here to give up. This can't be the end. I have to make one last try.

I lift my head and stare at his retreating back. Then I open my mouth and begin to sing my words. The crazy rap of love I wrote for my brother. I rush back to the door he walked through and begin singing as loud as I can.

My voice cracks horribly. People stare. They laugh.

He stops walking.

My brother stands motionless as I sing about him and how much I love him, need him. Slowly he turns. He comes back through the door to me, ignoring the gate agent's protests. I finish singing, and we simply look into each other's eyes.

"You wrote that?" he asks.

"I wrote it about you. I love you, and it hurt remembering how I lost you. That's what you saw in my face when you first came home."

"Last call!" the ticket taker yells.

Lamont doesn't move. "If I stay, I'm keeping the bottom bed. And I'm calling you Short Stack."

I jump him, grabbing his shoulders, and hoisting myself onto his back. "Deal," I say.

I've learned to enjoy being on top.

EPILOGUE

THREE WEEKS LATER, LAMONT AND I stand outside the church. An annoying drizzle drips from the sky, but it's a warm Saturday afternoon. Our neighbors are around us, all waiting for Pastor Morrow to begin the Unity Prayer and March that was planned at the last TBTS meeting. This will be a peaceful display against violence. A few police officers stand around, just to make sure everything remains safe. I see the young officer who wanted to arrest me. He nods and smiles at me. I wave.

Lamont is wearing a red Take Back the Streets T-shirt with sleeves long enough to hide his tattoos. He's planning to have them removed. He isn't too proud to be a janitor anymore, and Mr. Morrow hired him to do maintenance for the five buildings in our courtyard complex. Mr. Morrow has decided he's too old to have to jump up in the middle of the night because someone's pipe is leaking.

He stops in front of one family, saying Miss Wiggins also offered him a job. She thinks his firsthand experience with the gang and prison makes him the perfect guy to talk to the shelter kids. She's probably right. It helps to have someone who's been where you are tell you the hard truths.

My brother circulates among our neighbors now, using his charisma to build bridges. The more he gets out and meets with people, the more they like him.

"I joined the gang because I knew I couldn't make it through life alone and I forgot how many people like you all were around to help me. What do you think people do in prison?"

"Plot world domination?" Malik asks from the crowd. He came down from Champaign to be here with us for the march. Now he steps in front of my brother.

He and Lamont share a long look. They once fought a tug-of-war over me, literally. My arms tingle at the memory.

"Or maybe revenge on your enemies," Malik continues. He is a little taller than my brother, but both have an air of control.

My brother throws back his head and laughs. "Mostly we'd plot how to make it from one day to the next." He holds out a hand to Malik. "I've changed, thanks to T," Lamont continues. "I like the view of myself through his eyes."

I'm learning a lot from him and from all my new friends. Like the ones I'll be meeting with on Monday after school, the guys on my new team. I'll be part of the Chicago Park District swim team from now on.

For now, the pastor is calling for us to begin. Once the march ends, the church will hold the first of the anger management sessions he will lead. Lamont was the first to sign up. Linda asked to join too. She isn't ready to forgive her father, but she might learn to forgive herself.

I hope she does. Everyone deserves forgiveness.

ACKNOWLEDGMENTS

SO MANY PEOPLE ASSISTED WITH the creation of this story I barely know where to start. I guess I'll do so by thanking my agent, Andrea Somberg. She saw something in this story and sent it to Harper Collins. From there, my editor, Karen Chaplin, took over. She put her faith in me and worked with me over the last year to make T's story a reality.

I also want to send hugs and kisses to Gay Lynn Cronin and Julie Golden, members of my home critique group. (I already gave them chocolate.) These gracious ladies helped provide background about police work and assisted me in smoothing out some of the edges of the early version of the manuscript. That was essential, because good writing is really revising, and they gave critical insight into that arduous process. In fact, a big thanks to all my SCBWI friends for their continued encouragement. To my sister Sharon Binns, a Chicago public school teacher, who generously answered questions about school procedures and student activities.

I am forever grateful to the numerous members of the Chicago Park District Swim Team for their patience and love. Yes, I know they don't have a diving squad in real life, but I gave them one for the benefit of this story. I know that if there was a Park District diving team, the members would be just as gracious and my characters would feel right at home with them.

Last but not in the least least, a special thanks to the people who live in Chicago's Chatham, Pullman, Roseland, Englewood, and Hyde Park neighborhoods. I have lived in most of those areas myself during my early life. The people are wonderful, and many graciously spoke with me about themselves and the beauty of their surroundings. I hope they see a little of themselves in this story.